THE
WELL
TEMPERED
LISTENER

By

Deems Taylor

GREENWOOD PRESS, PUBLISHERS
WESTPORT, CONNECTICUT

The Library of Congress has catalogued this publication as follows:

Library of Congress Cataloging in Publication Data

Taylor, Deems, 1885-1966.
　　The well tempered listener.

　　1.　Music--Analysis, appreciation.　I.　Title.
MT6.T26W3　1972　　　　780'.15　　　70-138190
ISBN 0-8371-5647-5

Originally published in 1940
by Simon and Schuster, New York

Reprinted with the permission
of Joan Taylor Dawson

First Greenwood Reprinting 1972

Library of Congress Catalogue Card Number 70-138190

ISBN 0-8371-5647-5

Printed in the United States of America

Table of Contents

THE MAKERS

v

CONTENTS

vi

CONTENTS

CONTENTS

THE GIVERS

CONTENTS

ix

CONTENTS

CONTENTS

THE HEARERS

CONTENTS

CONTENTS

Introduction

LIKE *its predecessor,* Of Men and Music, *this book is based on a series of radio talks. They were delivered as part of the Columbia Broadcasting System's broadcasts of the Sunday-afternoon concerts of the New York Philharmonic-Symphony Orchestra during the seasons of 1937–1938 and 1938–1939, and have been augmented by various articles and reviews that I wrote for* Stage, Woman's Day, *and the late New York World and* Vanity Fair. *I say "based" because the chapters that follow are the result of considerable editing and rewriting. The radio talks, especially, had to undergo rather drastic revision in order to eliminate the colloquialisms and occasional downright illiteracies that distinguish spoken from written English. Speaking of revisions, I owe a debt of thanks to the brilliant young pianist, Abram Chasins, for making valuable suggestions regarding the facts and conclusions in the chapter entitled "Sir James's Umbrella."*

For convenience I have divided the book into three sections. The first, The Makers, *is devoted to discussions of music in the abstract, and from the point of view of the composer. In the second,* The Givers, *we discuss music with particular reference to its performers and interpreters. The third section,* The Hearers, *is written largely from the point of view of those who listen to it. Naturally, there is no razor-keen line of cleavage among these three*

*divisions, and certain chapters grouped under one cate-
gory might arguably be grouped equally well under
another. Nevertheless this somewhat arbitrary method
of segregation does serve to give the book whatever form
it may possess.*

*You will find, if you read the book, frequent allusions
to my correspondents, together with numerous and often
lengthy quotations from their letters. These are the listeners to the Philharmonic-Symphony broadcasts who
have taken the trouble, during the past two years, to write
down, and post, their agreement or disagreement with
what I had to say. Without the stimulus of their questions
and comments many of the chapters in this book would
never have been written. There have been literally thousands of them—an army of anonymous collaborators to
whom I can never be sufficiently grateful.*

DEEMS TAYLOR

*Beverly Hills, California
September, 1939*

PART ONE

The Makers

The Old Contemporaries

THE program that afternoon—it was a Sunday in November, 1938—included one work, Schumann's Fourth
Symphony, that was 96 years old; another, a Schubert
cello concerto, that was 114 years old; and still another,
the Beethoven Seventh, that had seen the light of day 125
years before. The baby of the list, Debussy's *Berceuse
héroïque,* had at least reached voting age. But this was
not being offered as a concert of ancient music, or a concert of unusual music, or of music seldom heard. It was a
good representative of the average program that is heard,
and heard with pleasure, every week, by symphony subscribers throughout this country.

Just the same, the list set me to wondering: to wondering why it is that we get so much pleasure out of music
that, in point of time at least, is hopelessly out of date.
Materially, outside the fact that they ate, drank, and slept,
three of the composers on that program had led daily
lives that had very little in common with ours. None of
them had ever seen an automobile, a trolley car, an airplane, a movie, or even a telegraph pole. Debussy, the
most nearly contemporary of the four, had never owned
a radio set. Why does their music say something that still
has meaning for us?

There are two reasons, I believe. One is that music has
very little to do with the way men live, or even with what

3

they think. The human mind progresses much more slowly than human ingenuity. I remember once hearing a professor of anthropology from a famous Eastern university say that, so far as he could discover, the intelligence of the average member of the human race is, today, exactly what it was in the days of the Pharaohs. This may or may not be true. Certainly, some of my fellow motorists that I encounter on our highways do leave me with the impression that we would all be better off if they were building pyramids instead of driving motorcars.

But music is not primarily concerned even with thought. It is not a branch of politics, or economics, or sociology. I think of it as the most subtle, because the most intangible, and at the same time the most primitive, of all the arts. It makes its fundamental appeal to something that changes even more slowly than our intelligence. And that is what, roughly, we call emotion. It is a poor word, because it isn't inclusive enough. It sounds as if the sole function of music was to make us laugh or cry—which, of course, is not true. What I mean by emotions are the wordless thoughts, the subterranean impulses and aspirations that we all have, and which no spoken language can convey. Music is a definite language, one that allows the Dutch-descended, German-speaking Beethoven of 125 years ago to say his particular say to us as well—much better, in fact—than if he were speaking contemporary English. In consequence, whatever it was in his music that moved the first hearers of any great composer is likely to find a ready response among his hearers of more than a century later.

But there is yet another reason, I think, why men like Beethoven and Schubert and Schumann and the rest are

4

perennially satisfying. And that is because they are preoccupied with what I'm coming to believe more and more
to be the two essential elements of music: rhythm and
melody. What is the quality of Beethoven's music, or that
of any other master, that makes a fundamental appeal to
you, that sticks in your mind, that makes you willing, and
eager, to hear it over and over again? Analyze your impressions, and I think you'll find that it is his themes—
and what he does with them. In other words, his line.
When he hears the finale of the Beethoven Seventh I
doubt very much whether the average listener is conscious
of the way its themes are harmonized. If the harmoniza-
tion were inappropriate, he might be unpleasantly aware
of that fact; but if it fits perfectly, he is more or less unconscious of it.

Now that seems hardly to be the case with much modern music. I have had a lot to say about the obligation
that lies upon every professed music lover to give a fair
hearing to contemporary music. I have said—and written
—many times that no one has the right to dismiss it
merely because it may not make a favorable first impression. As a result, from time to time I have had to take a
certain amount of scolding from correspondents who seem
to think that I don't like any *other* kind of music. But
wanting to see fair play does not necessarily convict the
umpire of favoring the side for which he is asking justice.
As a matter of fact, I find a great deal wrong with a great
deal of modern music.

What I find most wrong with it is that so much of it
resolves itself, in the last analysis, down to a series of experiments in making novel and hitherto unheard-of combinations of notes—in other words, experiments in har-

mony. So many contemporary composers seem bent on proving that there is no chord so discordant and ugly at first hearing that it cannot eventually be heard without discomfort. That is an argument that I'll concede before they advance it. One of the commonplaces of musical history is that the harmony that annoys the ears of one generation becomes acceptable to the ears of the next. Think of the things that used to be said about Wagner's harmony—poor old Wagner, who is now such a classic that he is never mentioned in advanced musical circles. You may not believe it now, but all this atonality and polytonality that makes you squirm today won't raise the temperature of your grandchildren by a fraction of a degree.

I remember my own experience with Stravinsky's *The Rite of Spring*. I heard it first about a dozen years ago, and though I was tremendously struck by its emotional power, it sounded arbitrarily ugly and discordant to me. I have heard it a good many times since, and by now, those chords that used to sound so dissonant no longer bother me in the least. That being so, I begin to discover why *The Rite of Spring* has survived for twenty-five years, and seems destined to survive indefinitely. And the reason, in my opinion, is not those strange harmonies, but the fact that the work contains some vital themes, which are handled in a masterly manner.

And that is precisely what I do *not* find in the work of most so-called ultramodern composers. Once I've developed an immunity to the poisonous harmonic ingredients of their music, and can listen to it really critically, I find that their themes, and the handling of them, are neither attractive nor significant. They are busy harmonizing tunes that don't exist. After all, if you undertake to cook

6

a Spanish omelet, you're rather a fool if you make the tomato-and-onion sauce first, and then look in the icebox to see if you have any eggs. It is well to be provided with the main ingredient of a dish before you start to make it.

On the other hand, many musicians will tell you that contemporary music isn't concerned with melody in the old sense of the word, that the important element nowadays is rhythm and color; that music has reached the end of what can be said through the medium of the old-style, obvious type of melody. That may be so. If it is so, we are in the midst of an esthetic revolution; because up to now, all the music that has continued to interest audiences has been music based on themes—tunes, if you like—that people could either remember or want to remember.

As for the much-discussed rhythmic distinctiveness of contemporary music—that depends upon what you mean by rhythm. If you mean just the beat in the bar, then any rumba is more complex than all nine of Beethoven's symphonies. But to me it is not just the beat in the bar. It is also the alternation of slow and fast passages, the transitions from one to the other, the relative length or brevity with which given themes are stated and developed—the general balance and proportion, in short, that give a sense of inevitability to the structure of a great composition. Listening to a Beethoven symphony, you have the impression that Beethoven heard it, in his mind, all at once, so to speak, that it couldn't have been anything but the length that it is, and that every part of it grows out of what came before.

I find no such quality in most modern music. A composer doesn't necessarily make a piece rhythmically interesting by changing the time signature every other bar. That may make an interesting-*looking* score, and may be very useful in helping the orchestra players to earn overtime rehearsal money. But looks aren't everything, especially in music, and much of the rhythmic complexity that many present-day innovators talk about is likely to give the impression either of an attempt to give arbitrary variety to an essentially feeble musical structure, or just plain, simple incoherence. Listening to modern chamber music, supposedly the most abstract of all music, I frequently have the uneasy feeling, hearing its rhythmic fits and starts, that the composer has written a setting for a secret and highly complicated pantomime, and that I would be much happier if he would just come clean and tell me the plot beforehand.

I sometimes wonder whether the appalling speed with which our mechanical civilization has advanced during the past thirty years hasn't lured a whole generation of composers into trying to keep up with it. When you consider that a man of fifty, today, makes constant use, as a matter of course, of six devices—the electric light, the telephone, the oil burner, the motion picture, the airplane, and the radio—that were either scientific curiosities or undreamed-of miracles when he was a child,·you begin to realize how fast we are moving. But many other artists, as well as the composers, apparently fail to see that that advancement is *only* physical and mechanical. Our thoughts and emotions haven't moved correspondingly. Nevertheless I sense, among a vast number and variety of composers, an uneasy impulse to keep abreast of their times, a dread of being thought old-fashioned. They must, they will tell you, reflect in their art the increased complexity and speed with which we live today; and in the effort to do so they become self-conscious and experimental. They want very much to say something, but instead of looking within themselves for their particular message, they try to translate the material world around them into terms of music. In the effort to keep up to the musical minute, they change their own style of writing almost from day to day. As if a man could deliberately change his style—if he has one—any more than he can change the color of his eyes.

Apropos, let me quote from a delightful book, *Music, Ho!*, by Constant Lambert. Speaking of Stravinsky, he writes, "As an example of Stravinsky's attitude towards reaction for its own sake, may I quote an instance of his urging young composers to give their tunes to the violins and not to the trumpet, on the grounds that too many people had been writing tunes for the trumpet in the last few years. So might Patou and Poiret forecast the colors for the coming season. It does not seem to have occurred to him that orchestration has any relation to the technical nature or expressive quality of a given theme, that one writes for the English horn because that is the tone color one wants, and not because it happens to be a Tuesday. Similarly, Stravinsky's followers will say with all the withering satisfaction of those who have caught the last seat in a crowded bus, 'It's no use writing that sort of harmony *now*,' and will themselves admittedly falsify their originally conceived harmonies with a view to giving them a more strictly contemporary quality."

People have always lived in troubled times—if they chose to look for trouble. When Schubert was a schoolboy in Vienna, his school was hit by a shell from Napoleon's artillery; when Beethoven was writing the Seventh Symphony, Napoleon was retreating from Moscow. But Schubert, and Beethoven, and all the other great composers, were not keeping abreast of the times, or trying to express the present. They were trying to write music, to find expressive and beautiful themes, and develop them as best they could.

No real artist *deliberately* goes about expressing his time. In the last analysis he looks within himself for the picture he paints or the book that he writes, or the symphony that he composes. And since that self is a product of his times, it is, of course, an expression of his times, an expression over which he has no more control, and of which he is no more conscious, than your hand mirror is conscious of reflecting your face. And if the artist is a reflection of the noblest and best of his times, then his work will be the same; and it will be understood, and loved, long after its creator is dead. It will not grow old-fashioned, because it was never stylish.

Guesswork

G RANTED that an artist is an expression of his times, how would some of the masters of the past fare if they could be transplanted from their times to ours? Specifically, suppose there were living today five American composers whose personalities, characters, and musical gifts were precisely those of Bach, Mozart, Beethoven, Berlioz, and Wagner. What would we think of them, and what would they be doing? As a matter of convenience, let us *call* them Bach, Mozart, Beethoven, Berlioz, and Wagner. Naturally, they would be writing in the idiom of their own time—that is, today; but their music would bear the same stamp of genius as marked that of the men of whom they would be the reincarnations. What would happen?

Suppose we take Bach first. Here we would have a supreme master of contrapuntal writing, a man whose melodic genius was such that, writing in the most restricted and academic forms, he could make those forms produce something overwhelmingly moving and eloquent. He would be one of the few living organists who could truly be called a master of that instrument. Personally, he would be a simple, home-loving, mild-mannered person, and a devout churchgoer. What would he do?

As a matter of fact, I think that his career today would be, in the main, very much what it was two hundred years ago. As a boy, his fine soprano voice would have secured him a position as soloist in a church choir, and by the time his voice had broken his musical gifts would have become so apparent that someone would undoubtedly have arranged to get him a scholarship at the Curtis Institute in Philadelphia. Graduating from Curtis, he would have obtained a position as organist and choirmaster, playing in several smaller churches until he was offered a well-paying position in some wealthy and fashionable New York church. In his leisure time he would be composing, both for the organ and for his own choir. The choral works would find a ready market among the music publishers, and from them he would enjoy a small, but steady income—perhaps a thousand or twelve hundred dollars a year. He would marry early, but I doubt if he would raise a family of nineteen children. He might have three or four, however, and for the childrens' sake he and Mrs. Bach would rent a house in the suburbs.

His organ works would not find so ready a market, because of their extreme difficulty. Nevertheless, many of them would eventually find their way into print. Word would begin to go around that there was an extraordinary musician in the organ loft of Saint Soandso's Church, and his vesper organ recitals would attract large audiences of people who would hardly otherwise be churchgoers. One of the broadcasting networks would offer him a regular fifteen-minute spot, say on Sunday evenings between 11:45 and midnight. It would be a sustaining program, because no commercial sponsor would buy an organ recital, but he would have a comparatively small but faithful radio audience. His fame would spread largely by word of mouth, because music critics have little time for covering church services. But his *Christmas Oratorio,* written for the Schola Cantorum in New York, would get favorable notices, and would make his name known to choral societies throughout the country. He would be offered the chair of counterpoint and organ-playing at some large conservatory or university—the Eastman School of Music, perhaps. This he would accept, eventually giving up his church work. He would be invited to play on various great organs, both in America and Europe. All in all he would lead a busy, rather prosperous, and reasonably happy life, much appreciated by musicians, but hardly more than a name to the average concert- or operagoer. At the time of his death, the papers would print obituaries running to two and three columns, and we would all be a little astonished to discover the number of his compositions and the extent of his influence upon other musicians. Ten or fifteen years after his death, we would finally decide that he was a great man.

Mozart, I think, would have a much happier life than the one he led between 1756 and 1791. He would have begun as a boy prodigy at the piano, and under his father's management would have earned a large fortune from concertizing before his twenty-first year. Most of this his father would have spent. As his creative gifts developed more and more, he would probably have rebelled at so much piano playing, have quarreled with his father, and abruptly quit the concert stage in order to have time to compose. He would have won a two-year fellowship from the American Academy in Rome, and would have returned from Italy with several symphonic works that would be accepted by several American orchestras. Thus encouraged, he would have applied for a Guggenheim

Fellowship, and would undoubtedly have won it. This would have given him another year, and probably two, of freedom to compose without worrying about making a living.

By this time he would be established as one of the most brilliant of the younger American composers. He would be somewhat underrated by the critics, who would be a little suspicious of his inexhaustible supply of melody; but the public, when they got a chance to hear him, would love him. His works, though frequently played, would bring him little income, as there is no market for the sale of orchestral music, and being an American, he would have a hard time getting adequate performance fees out of American symphony orchestras. He would eke out his income by teaching composition and piano at the Juilliard School or the New England Conservatory. This would give him a comfortable, if not an extravagant, living.

Nevertheless, his life would be a short one. What hours of leisure he possessed would be spent in such a fury of incessant composing that his health would inevitably fail. More healthful and comfortable living conditions might prolong his life for a few years, but not many. He would pay the penalty of overwork, as he did previously, and at about the age of forty he would die—as he did previously —of Bright's disease, with the press and public agreeing that we had lost a composer of great promise.

Berlioz, a man with grandiose ideas of composition, with a wonderful feeling for orchestration, and with more technical ingenuity than creative genius, would have had a severe struggle after graduating from the Cincinnati Conservatory. For a time, during these hard years, he would work in the musical library of some broadcasting station, making special arrangements, but would finally revolt at the quality of the music that he was called upon to orchestrate, and would resign. He would have applied for a Rome fellowship, and would probably have won it, as the judges would have been struck by his talent for handling orchestral masses.

He would return from Rome with a work entitled *Harold in Italy,* which would have its first performance at one of the Sunday-afternoon concerts of the New York Philharmonic-Symphony Orchestra, the composer conducting. It would be played widely during the ensuing two seasons, and would then be quietly dropped from the American orchestral repertoire. Meanwhile, the problem of making a living would become increasingly acute. At length, more by luck than management, he would obtain a position as music critic on a New York morning paper. His natural tendency to melancholy and irritability would be aggravated by the nervous strain of covering two concerts a day for eight months out of the year, and after a few seasons he would resign.

An opera of his would be produced by the Metropolitan, but would fail because of its bad libretto. However, he would conduct the opening performance himself, and several critics would remark upon his obvious gifts as a conductor. Consequently, after his retirement from newspaper work, he would be offered the post of conductor of one of the Midwestern orchestras. This post he would retain until his death, continuing to compose, but never quite succeeding in establishing himself among the front-rank American composers. After his death, special memorial performances of some of his more ambitious orchestral works would make us realize that we had greatly underrated him.

Beethoven would have a more comfortable time than

before, although his radical innovations in musical structure would make his music incomprehensible to many
listeners. One or two of the critics would back him to the
limit, but the majority would call him undisciplined and
formless. Some of his simpler piano pieces would bring
him moderate royalties, but the bulk of his music would
return him virtually no income whatsoever. His *"Eroica"*
Symphony would have enjoyed considerable popularity,
but his Seventh, Eighth, and Ninth, while occasionally
performed, would probably remain in manuscript until
after his death, because no publisher would risk the expense of having them engraved.

He would write very little chamber music, because of
the lack of demand for this form of composition. Luckily,
his gifts as a pianist would bring him a large number of
concert offers, and he would have appeared many times,
both in recitals and with orchestras. He would enjoy a
moderate income from the royalties on his recordings of
piano music. This, together with what he had saved from
his concert fees, would be enough to keep him from actual
want when his increasing deafness made further public
appearances impossible. During his latter years he would
enjoy increasing admiration and respect from the critics
and the public, and on his fiftieth birthday Postmaster
Farley would probably issue a two-and-a-half-cent stamp
bearing his portrait.

Wagner would always be in trouble. He would emerge
first as the conductor of a small traveling Italian opera
company. Leaving this, he would spend several years as
conductor of the house orchestras in various broadcasting
stations. Once in a while he would get a commercial program to conduct, but would always end up by quarreling

with the sponsor and resigning. Meanwhile, however, he would be composing, and at length his three-act opera, with a prologue, *The Ring of the Nibelungs,* would be accepted for production by the Metropolitan. It would be an instantaneous success, and Wagner would be established overnight as a coming man.

About this time, a motion-picture producer, impressed by the gorgeous color and dramatic intensity of his music, would offer him ten thousand dollars to compose the music for a feature film. Wagner, dissatisfied with the conventions and limitations of grand opera, and seeing the possibilities of this new medium, would accept eagerly. His stay in Hollywood would not be a long one. He would have ideas about the script, the music, the setting, the direction, and the casting, all of which horrify everyone in the studio. After a few stormy and unhappy weeks, he would request, and receive, a release from his contract.

But this would not stop him. He would have a vision of the motion picture of the future—of a perfect union and blending of sound, color, acting, speech, spectacle, and music—something of which the motion picture of today is only a hint. He would determine to create such a film, writing the screen play as well as the music, realizing perfectly well that its production, if ever it came about, would necessitate the creation of new techniques in photography and sound-recording, a new school of motion-picture actors and directors, and a new kind of motion-picture house. And somewhere, ridiculed and all but forgotten, in a lodge in the Adirondacks, a bungalow in Santa Fe, or a ranch house in Wyoming, he would be busying himself with that epoch-making work today.

More of the Same

So MUCH for the possible careers of the five, their external lives and fortunes if they had happened to live in our times. But what *kind* of music would they be writing? How would the content of their music differ, if at all, from their works of yesterday? Would they be interested in our present-day world struggles, in the rise and threat of the Fascist states, in the bloody events in Europe and Asia? Would these events be reflected in their music?

Speculating in this wise, it occurred to me that it might be helpful, in trying to find the answers to those questions, to cast a backward glance at the world in which they actually did live, and study their reactions to what was going on. So I looked up a few dates, to see just what *was* going on during their lifetimes.

Let us consider first the case of Bach. He was born in 1685 and died in 1750. His world was hardly a quiet one. In 1688 James II abandoned the throne of England and fled to France, leaving William and Mary as his successors. A war, lasting nine years, broke out between France and England and her allies. In 1698 the Spanish empire was divided up among France, Austria, and Bavaria. Three years later came the War of the Spanish Succession, with England getting into it a year after that. In 1706 Italy fell into the hands of the allies. A year later, Charles XII of Sweden appeared in Germany. In 1713 the French were finally beaten, and lost a number of their American possessions, as well as Gibraltar and Minorca. In 1720 war again, between France and Spain. In 1733, a war over the Polish succession. Four years later, war between England and Spain. In 1740, Frederick the Great of Prussia went to war with Austria, settling it five years before Bach's death.

Now, Mozart. He was born in Salzburg, in 1756, the year the Seven Years' War broke out between England and Prussia on one side and France, Austria, Russia, Saxony, and Sweden on the other. He was four years old when the Russians entered Berlin. He was seven when the Seven Years' War ended. When he was twenty-two, war broke out between Bavaria and Austria. When he was thirty-three, two years before his death, the French Revolution exploded.

Beethoven was nineteen at the time of the French Revolution. In 1792 Prussia declared war on France. In '93 France declared war on England. In '95 England declared war on Holland. In '96 Spain declared war on England. In 1803 they all declared war on Napoleon. In 1813, when Beethoven was forty-three, Napoleon entered Berlin. In 1815 came Waterloo.

Berlioz was twelve years old at the time of Waterloo. When he was twenty-seven, the July Revolution drove Charles X from the throne of France and put Louis Philippe in his place. Two years later there were serious socialist uprisings in France. In 1848, when Berlioz was forty-five, Louis Napoleon was elected president of France, and made himself Emperor Napoleon III several years later. Berlioz died a year before the outbreak of the Franco-Prussian War.

Wagner was born in Leipzig the year of the battle of Leipzig. He was a witness of the same world events that Berlioz saw, and in addition, as we all know, had to flee Germany as a result of sympathizing too openly with the revolutionary uprisings of 1849.

In compiling that list of events, I have left out almost as many as I have included—events such as the Crimean War, for one instance—because they were too far out of the orbit of the men we are discussing. On the other hand, I think you will admit that the world between 1685 and 1871 was in a sufficiently upset state to have enlisted the interest of any socially conscious composer.

And did it? I think the answer is, no. I can find nothing in Bach's music that in any way reflects the trouble that was going on literally all around him. And I think the same can be said of Mozart. The fact that he produced a vast quantity of chamber music is, to some extent, a result of the period in which he lived, that is, a period in which wealthy aristocrats maintained private string quartets and chamber orchestras, and wanted music written for them. Otherwise, it seems to me, his music has little direct connection with when and where it was written. Beethoven, considering his aggressively democratic turn of mind, seems amazingly little concerned with the state of his external world. You hear much made of the fact that his *"Eroica"* Symphony was titled originally, "Grand Napoleon Bonaparte Symphony," and that after Napoleon had proclaimed himself emperor, Beethoven tore off the title page and put on a new one, reading, "Heroic Symphony Composed to Celebrate the Memory of a Great Man." But the significant thing about that anecdote is the fact that that is *all* he changed. Beethoven the man may have been angry and disillusioned by Napoleon's betrayal of democratic ideals; but Beethoven the composer did not alter a measure of the music. He knew instinctively that while Napoleon may have been on the title page, he wasn't in the notes.

Berlioz's life is the same story. The titles of his most ambitious works—*Episode in the Life of an Artist, Harold in Italy, Roman Carnival Overture, The Damnation of Faust,* the *Fantastic Symphony*—would hardly give you a clue to the fact that their composer lived through two revolutions and died just before a third.

Wagner is the only one of the five who took any active part in the disturbances of his day; and I have a suspicion that his revolutionary leanings were far more histrionic than they were intellectual or idealistic. During his exile he did write one pamphlet entitled *Art and Revolution,* but he also wrote one entitled *Judaism in Music.* For never forget that Wagner, the great democratic sympathizer, was as hysterically anti-Semitic, at least in the field of art, as Adolf Hitler has ever been. So far as concerns his work's reflecting any profound interest in the world's troubles, I find no evidence of it. *Rienzi* does so, faintly, perhaps, in that it deals with a revolutionary phase of history. Otherwise, *The Ring, Lohengrin, Tannhäuser, The Flying Dutchman* are legendary, and hardly allegorical, *Parsifal* is religious, and *Die Meistersinger* is a medieval love story.

And so, I think, we are justified in saying that the music of these five composers is very little, if at all, preoccupied with the events of their own times. In fairness, it must be said that world events were much less close to the average artist in those days than they are now. Beethoven's *Fidelio* was produced in Vienna just one week after it had been occupied by the French army. It would not have been produced in Prague a week after Hitler had entered. War in those days was almost entirely a professional matter, to say nothing of being infinitely less destructive of life and property. Anyone who wasn't actually a soldier could ignore it without much difficulty. Moreover, while a few of the wars of the eighteenth and nineteenth centuries had religious causes, the majority of them were not, as they are today, wars of conflicting ideas. They were either frank attempts to grab territory, or conflicts designed to exchange one king or emperor for another.

It is, therefore, incontrovertible that if our five were contemporary composers, born, not in America, but in the countries in which they actually *were* born—if you follow me—they would be much more keenly conscious of the world's troubles than they were in the past. As to what extent that consciousness would show in their music—that is another question. About Bach I am positive. He strikes me as being, somewhat like Albert Einstein, an interested and compassionate, but essentially remote, observer of the world around him. As a devout Lutheran and a composer of church music he might be in enforced or voluntary exile from Hitler's Germany. If he were, I think he would shrug his shoulders and go on with his work. Mozart was likewise remote, in a different way, in that there was little of the philosopher in his make-up; but he, too, had little connection with the world, except to try to make a living in it. Had he lived in modern Vienna, he might have mingled with the saluting crowds of the *Anschluss,* listened to the roars of *"Heil, Hitler!"* and noted with interest the swastika decorations. Then, I think, he would have hurried home to finish the scherzo of his latest symphony.

Beethoven would be in exile, here, in England, or in France, as a penalty for not keeping his mouth shut. He wouldn't have liked *anybody*! If anything, he was a democrat, but not a very good one. His chief idea was to be let alone. I suspect him of having been a philosophic anarchist. Certainly his was a nature too fiercely independent and individualistic to have allowed him to entertain the idea of submerging his personality to the greater glory of either a Fascist or a Communist state. As to how far the state of the world would be reflected in his music—I should say, just about as far as it was in the *"Eroica."* His happiness over the so-called "Peace of Munich" might have inspired him to write a symphony, which he would have dedicated to Neville Chamberlain. Later, angered by the disasters that followed Chamberlain's "appeasement" policies, he might have torn off the dedication. But hearing the music, you would not know that the dedication was gone—or that it had ever existed.

Wagner, like Beethoven, would have been thrown out of Germany years ago. He would then have gone to Vienna, would have been driven out by the *Anschluss*, would have gone to Prague, and finally, to Paris. There he would be writing a series of fiery pamphlets, attacking alternately Hitler and the Jews, and meanwhile working on the score of a music drama based on the life of Buddha. Berlioz, whose attitude toward political affairs, if we are to judge from his memoirs, was pretty cynical, would probably be in Paris, working on a new symphony of gigantic proportions.

I say this about these five composers for two reasons.

First, because the emotions aroused by crises such as we are now going through are not conducive to the creation of good works of art. Look around you; look at China, Germany, Spain, Czechoslovakia, Austria, Poland. Does their sight make you feel happy, exalted, admiring? Do they inspire you with a sense of well-being? I doubt it. Your principal emotions are likely to be indignation and despair. So far as the art of music is concerned, both these emotions are destructive. I have yet to hear of a composer's working out an inspired musical idea in a fit of indignation or despair. For these are not creative emotions. They lower the physical and nervous vitality of a man; and creative power *is* vitality. It may happen that the composer, remembering his old anger or his former despair, a year, two years, ten years later, may evolve, out of his now tranquil mind, music that expresses it in a transmuted, exalted form. But at the given moment, when he goes to his music desk you will probably find him trying, *for* that moment, to forget the world.

I say it secondly, because these men were great artists. Great artists are not interested in passing things. They are interested in life as a whole, in man as a race, rather than in the silly or cruel things that he may do on any particular occasion. I venture to say that Beethoven, looking at Spain, would have been moved neither by enthusiasm for Franco nor by sympathy for the loyalists. He would rather, I think, have been saddened by the sight of men of the same birth and blood slaughtering one another— for no matter what cause. These ideas that we are fighting, these horrors through which we are living—it is hard for us to conceive of their not being of terrific importance, of not being a crisis in the history of civilization. But the history of civilization is crowded with dead crises. Ideas come, and pass, whether social, political, or economic. But music is the custodian of ideas that are far different, ideas that no dictatorship—and no democracy, for that matter—can ever alter. A hundred years from now, to-day's barbarities may seem nothing more than a nasty accident. But some composer, somewhere, may today be writing a piece of music that, a hundred years from now, will be as irrelevant, and as beautiful and alive, as it was when the ink was still wet upon the paper.

4

Down, But Hardly Out

SUPPOSE we study, in a little more detail, this question of how specifically a composer's personal problems, and his reactions to the state of the world about him, are reflected in his work. Let us take an all-Wagner program, such as I heard played by the New York Philharmonic-Symphony Orchestra in the fall of 1938, and consider the circumstances surrounding the composition of the various excerpts that the orchestra played.

1. Overture to *Rienzi*

This was Wagner's first successful attempt at opera. Chronologically, it was his fourth try. He made his first two between his eighteenth and twentieth years. He had been rather a problem child to his family, as he had no liking or aptitude for anything but music, but on the other hand could neither sing nor play any instrument well enough to make a living. Finally his brother Albert, who was a fairly successful provincial operatic tenor, got him a job in the opera house at Würzburg as a sort of unofficial accompanist and chorus master. It wasn't a very imposing job—there were fifteen people in the chorus—but it did give young Richard something that he very much wanted, some contact with the musical stage. A short time before, he had written the libretto of a gruesome, romantic opera,

Die Hochzeit—The Wedding—and had composed some of the music; but his sister Rosalie, who was a talented young actress, didn't like it. So he destroyed the manuscript.

In 1833, when he was just twenty, he tried again, and this time finished a work. It was an opera called *Die Feen* —The Fairies—written, as all of his operas were, to his own libretto. There was talk of producing it at Würzburg, but as he left the following season to become musical director of the opera house in Magdeburg, the project fell through. *Die Feen* was never produced during his lifetime. At Magdeburg he tried again, with an opera entitled *Das Liebesverbot,* based in part on Shakespeare's *Measure for Measure,* and actually had it produced. The leading tenor forgot most of his music, and filled in the gaps in his performance with what he could remember of *Fra Diavolo* and *Zampa.* The rest of the company were about as well rehearsed. Under the circumstances, the audience was considerably bewildered, and at the second performance the house was almost empty. Which was providential, in a way, as the husband of the prima donna picked a fight with the second tenor, backstage, and knocked him out, just at the rise of the curtain. The curtain was rung down again, and there *was* no second performance.

Then Wagner went to Riga, in Russia, to be conductor at the opera house. It was there that his money troubles, which were to haunt him all his life, became really serious —so much so that in 1839 he lost his position because his debts had become a public scandal. Nevertheless, he had managed to write the libretto of *Rienzi* and one act of the music. He had also had some correspondence with Meyerbeer, who seemed very cordial, and was sure that Wagner could get his opera produced in Paris if only he could get there. So he and his wife, Minna, and their dog, Robber, slipped across the border—they had to, on account of his creditors—into Prussia, and took ship for London. This was probably one of the worst experiences even in Wagner's life, but it is characteristic of the incredible driving energy of the man that out of a frightful storm they encountered in the North Sea he got the idea for *The Flying Dutchman*. Incidentally, three weeks before leaving Riga, he decided to learn French, and started taking lessons. Realizing that he wouldn't learn much French in three weeks, and also that he needed a French text for *Rienzi*, he used the lessons as a pretext for getting his teacher to write out a complete French translation for him.

From London he went to Paris, where he made a starvation living by writing a few songs, making arrangements for music publishers, and contributing to magazines. Somehow, however, he managed to complete the music and the orchestration of *Rienzi*, and to write the libretto of *The Flying Dutchman*. He finished the overture on October 23, 1840. One can derive some idea of the state of his finances from the fact that he had to borrow a metronome in order to put the correct tempo markings in the score. In order to raise a little money, he sold the French rights of *The Flying Dutchman* libretto to the Paris Opéra, which promptly turned it over to another composer. Meanwhile, despairing of getting a production of *Rienzi* in Paris, he sent the score to Dresden. While waiting for a decision from the opera house there, he wrote the music for *The Flying Dutchman*—in seven weeks.

Rienzi was accepted by Dresden, and was produced there on October 20, 1842. Its sensational success brought its twenty-nine-year-old composer fame and money—most of the latter went to his creditors—and a position as conductor at the Dresden Opera House. It also brought him a production, the following season, of *The Flying Dutchman*. This was not a success, as it lacked the spectacular stage and musical effects that the audience expected from the composer of *Rienzi*. Nevertheless he was a much admired and much discussed young man, and the time he spent in Dresden was one of the happiest periods in his early life. It was there, in the summer of 1845, that he wrote the scenarios both of *Lohengrin* and *Die Meistersinger*, and it was there, too, in October, 1845, that he had *Tannhäuser* produced.

2. Venusberg Music from *Tannhäuser*

As a matter of fact, of course, the Venusberg music was not in the score of *Tannhäuser* as it was produced in Dresden. Wagner wrote it, sixteen years later, for the performance, on March 13, 1861, at the Paris Opéra, where the gentlemen of the Jockey Club successfully whistled the work into failure. A good deal had happened to Wagner in the meantime. In Dresden he had got into financial trouble again by a course of ill-advised spending that began with his having the full orchestral score of *Tannhäuser* printed at his own expense. Then came his embroilment in the revolutionary uprisings of 1849, with the result that for eleven years he was an exile from Germany.

He fled first to Weimar, at Liszt's invitation, but had to leave on the very day of a performance of *Tannhäuser*. He went to Zurich, then back to Paris, where he wrote the poem, *Siegfried's Death*. (This was later to expand into the *Ring* cycle.) Then back to Zurich. He sent the score of *Lohengrin* to Liszt, who produced it in Weimar in 1850.

3. Ride of the Valkyries from *Die Walküre*

For six years, between 1847, when he finished *Lohengrin,* and 1853, when he began *Das Rheingold,* he wrote not a single bar of music. He commenced the *Ring* music in Zurich, finished *Das Rheingold* in May of 1853, and began at once on *Die Walküre.* In 1855 he went over to England to conduct the London Philharmonic. At about the same time he was invited to come to America to conduct some concerts of his own music, and very nearly did come.

4. Prelude and Finale from *Tristan and Isolde*

By 1857 he was halfway through the score of *Siegfried,* when the Emperor of Brazil invited him to write an opera in the Italian style for his opera company. Since he saw no hope of ever getting a production of *The Ring,* he abandoned *Siegfried* in order to write this new, comparatively simple work—which, of course, was never produced by the Emperor's opera company.

In 1857 he went to Paris in the vain hope of seeing something of his produced. Then back to Zurich, and on to Venice. In '59 he finished the last act of *Tristan* in Zurich, then went back to Paris, where he conducted some highly unsuccessful concerts. He was now granted an amnesty, and was no longer a fugitive from Germany, but his professional and financial affairs were as discouraging as ever. The one ray of light was the offer of a performance of *Tristan* in Vienna. He went there in '61, where, among other things, he first saw a performance of *Lohengrin,* fourteen years after he had written it. In the spring of that year he had gone to Paris for the *Tannhäuser* fiasco, and in the winter of '61 and '62 he went back again, to live in poverty and write the libretto of *Die Meistersinger.*

5. Excerpts from *Die Meistersinger*

(*a*) Prelude to Act III
(*b*) Dance of the Apprentices
(*c*) Entrance of the Masters
(*d*) Homage to Sachs

In 1862 Liszt and some of his other friends arranged a concert tour for Wagner, and he traveled through Germany and Russia, conducting orchestral concerts. It was in Moscow that he heard the news that the Vienna production of *Tristan and Isolde* had been abandoned after fifty-four rehearsals. This was in 1863. He was fifty years old, had never had a production of four of his greatest works, and had no hope of completing two others that he had started. For a time he considered going to England with an English family, as a tutor, but finally decided to spend the rest of his life in Russia. First, however, he must finish the music of *Die Meistersinger.* An old friend, Frau Wille, took him into her house in Zurich, where he finished his great comic opera. One day at Frau Wille's he received word that his creditors from Vienna were on his track. Hastily leaving Zurich, he went to Stuttgart. There, he hoped, he might arrange to have one or two of his operas performed. If not, then Russia, and good-by to music. It was in Stuttgart, in May, 1864, that the messenger from the King of Bavaria found him.

In recapitulating these facts of Wagner's life I am, of course, repeating an oft-told tale. My apology for doing so is that I want to emphasize the contrast between the magnificent music and the hunted, poverty-stricken, debt-ridden life of the man who wrote it. It seems almost incredible that such worry and unhappiness could have gone hand in hand with this music's blazing vitality and eloquence. The fact that this is so is very reassuring. For a study of the lives of such men as Wagner, and Beethoven, and Mozart, and Moussorgsky does give us this assurance: that while the accidents of destiny may hamper, or even cut short, the career of a minor artist, nothing this side of death itself can keep a true creative genius from accomplishing what he was put here to do. We do right to encourage talent wherever we find it; but I do not believe that the world need have on its conscience any considerable number of mute, inglorious Miltons. If some powerful and malignant spirit had tried to devise every possible means of stopping Richard Wagner on his way, he could have found no more dreadful challenge than the troubles through which Wagner actually lived. As for Wagner's answer to that challenge—we have all heard it.

Five Who Died Young

"THIS side of death itself." There is a small band of composers who were confronted by the supreme challenge, the challenge to which no amount of single-mindedness and fortitude is an answer, and so died prematurely. In a way, it is hardly worth while to speculate as to what these men might have accomplished if they had lived longer, because there remains always the iron fact that they did not. Just the same, the temptation to do so is a strong one, if only because one man's guess is as good as another's. Let me yield to it and venture my own guess concerning the unlived years of a few of them. They are: Felix Mendelssohn, who died at thirty-eight; Frédéric Chopin, who died in his fortieth year; Wolfgang Mozart, who died at thirty-five; Franz Schubert, dead at thirty-one; and Charles Griffes, the American, who succumbed at thirty-five.

Suppose that Mendelssohn, for example, had, like Verdi, lived to be an octogenarian. Would he have left us not only more, but greater, music than he did? My guess is that he would not. With the possible exception of his E minor Violin Concerto, I don't think that any of his music comes up to his Octet for strings and the *Midsummer Night's Dream* Overture, both of which were written before he was eighteen. His later music is tremendously skillful and polished, but to me it never succeeds again

33

in saying the whimsical, imaginative, enchanting thing that is the young Mendelssohn whom we remember. After all, though we tend to forget it, during his lifetime he was important, not only as a composer, but as the famous conductor of the Gewandhaus Orchestra, and as one of the founders of the Leipzig Conservatory. If he had lived longer, I think you would have seen him less and less active as a composer and more and more as a conductor and educator.

Chopin was one of the greatest melodists the world has known, and, with Liszt, one of the most effective writers for the piano. But his genius was all for small forms, particularly those in which melody predominated. His piano works are unique; no one else has ever written anything quite like them. Whether they would have continued to maintain the level that they reach is almost entirely a matter of whether his melodic inspiration would have held out. A composer such as Beethoven, for instance, as he matures artistically, becomes less dependent upon the interest of his original themes than upon what he does with those themes, upon what you might call the architectural, the structural, and monumental character of his music. Chopin possessed little of that architectural quality. As I say, if he could have kept on inventing beautiful and wholly individual melodies, his music would have continued to be great. But failing that gift, he might have run into a blind alley, and spent the rest of his artistic life repeating what he had already said.

Concerning Mozart, I have to admit that I have no guess. I can say only that, considering the incredible quantity of music that he poured out in his thirty-five years of life, I don't see how it could be possible for him not to have burnt himself out, creatively, by the time he was forty. On the other hand, considering the quality and stature of the music he has left us, I find it equally impossible to conceive of that creative genius as ever burning itself out. In music, Mozart, to me, is like Keats in poetry. Of both men you can say that, at whatever age they died, the world would have been the poorer by their death.

Schubert, I am positive, died untimely. His inventive powers never flagged, and were obviously nowhere near their peak at the time of his death. And the very imperfections of his symphonic works are those of an artist who is on his way to complete mastery of his medium. I am sure that Schubert, leaving the world in his thirty-second year, took with him a mass of unwritten music that we should all have been glad to hear.

As for Charles Griffes, his early death is, I think, the greatest musical loss that this country has sustained. He died just as he was on the point of finding himself, of emerging as a strong, clearly defined musical personality. It is true that both *The White Peacock* and his longer, and best-known composition, *The Pleasure Dome of Kublai Khan,* are strongly influenced by Debussy and Ravel. Griffes himself made no secret of his admiration for these two men. But it is a natural and healthy sign for a composer, young in experience, to follow the lead of an older man. Offhand, I can think of no great artist, whether literary, graphic, plastic, or musical, whose early work does not show the influence of some older contemporary master. It is wise, before breaking away from the established order, to find out what you're breaking away from. And as Griffes's last works show, he was beginning to strike out entirely for himself, just as he died. After all,

I don't have to argue the worth of his music. The fact that *The White Peacock* and other works of his are still played, and enjoyed, nearly two decades after their composer's death, is the best proof of their vitality that anyone could offer. If he had lived, I am sure that Charles Griffes, today, in his middle fifties, would be world-famous, and his music would be a sign, admitted by all the world, that America had at last produced a composer of the first rank.

6

The Twilight of the Gods

SPEAKING of the longevity of great music, as we were a few chapters back, I had a letter not long ago from a correspondent who had been rather upset by reading a newspaper article that undertook to examine the trend of our musical taste. In it the authors analyzed the subscription programs of the leading American orchestras for the past sixty years, in an attempt to find out how certain orchestral works are, so to speak, wearing—in other words, to determine what composers are surviving and what composers are not.

According to my correspondent's summary, the investigation showed that Beethoven and Wagner, to name two, are not being played in subscription concerts today as frequently as they used to be. Bach, Brahms, Haydn, and Handel are being *more* frequently played. On the other hand, in popular series, Beethoven and Wagner are gaining. But, as the authors point out, it is the critics and the more experienced listeners who attend the subscription concerts and have the greatest influence in forming musical taste. Their conclusion is that every composer has a very definite span of artistic life; that sooner or later his work is doomed to be superseded by that of newer men, and to be forgotten; that our habit of referring to certain music as "immortal," is born of the fact that we *wish* the music we love to be immortal, and not having much historical perspective, persuade ourselves that it will be.

"In other words," writes my friend, "not only do the writers of this survey discredit the idea of the immortality of music, but they also imply that composers who have come to rank among the greatest in the world will be completely out of the picture in the comparatively near future, that even Beethoven will be dead in a couple of generations, to say nothing of Brahms and Bach. While every musical dog has his day, judged by the history of civilization over the past two thousand years or so, it is not a very long day."

Now if that conclusion is true, it seems a dismaying one to think about; and like myself, my correspondent is a bit depressed by it, and takes exception to it. He writes: "Now if today we can still be vitally inspired by looking at the Parthenon, the Venus of Milo, the Victory of Samothrace; if the Moses of Michelangelo is still a masterpiece, as are the portraits of Rembrandt; if the works of Sophocles, Homer, Aeschylus, Vergil, and Shakespeare are still potent forces in the world of literature, with little promise of reaching an imminent grave, how can we assume that the works of the greatest of all *musical* geniuses will be sunk in oblivion half a century, or even a century from now, simply because his works have been decreasing in prominence on the programs of American subscription concerts over the past sixty years?

"I think, for one thing," he continues, "that the authors of this survey have not taken into account the fact that America is a comparatively new country, and that it is only in recent times that a considerable portion of the public at large has paid serious attention to great music.

The very fact that Wagner and others are on the rise in *popular* series indicates this vast awakening of interest, and to my way of thinking it is this greatly extended popular support which will, in the long run, keep the great works alive, even if they may slip for a while in the subscription series."

I should like to supplement his remarks a bit. First of all, I agree with him entirely that in this country there is an enormously increased popular interest in serious orchestral music over what there was, not sixty, but only twenty years ago. The symptom of that increase in interest is the fact that today almost every American city of any size either has its own symphony orchestra or is apologizing for not having one. Its cause, in my firm belief, is the radio, the medium that has made it possible for almost any person living on this continent to come in contact with great music regardless of where he may be living or of how much or little he may be earning. The radio audience numbers, literally, millions, and to a large proportion of its membership music is a comparatively new experience. It will be a long time before the classics are an old story to such persons.

On the other hand, while Beethoven, Brahms, Wagner —all the so-called immortals—are not likely to sink into oblivion in any future that we can envisage, I am forced to believe that as time goes on we shall inevitably hear much less of their work than we do now.

In point of time, and perhaps in point of technique, music is the infant of the arts. Two hundred years before the Christian era, sculpture, for example, had reached a point of technical perfection that our own great sculptors may have equaled, but certainly have never surpassed.

Phidias was as completely a master of his medium as Michelangelo or Rodin or Jacob Epstein. There have been new sculptors, and they have managed, perhaps, to express a few new things in marble and clay and bronze, but they have found no new ways of handling their plastic materials. There will be new sculptors in time to come, but I think we can safely say that they will make no *technical* discoveries in sculpture.

The same is true of poetry and the drama. The language in which the Greek plays and epics were written, the language of Shakespeare and Molière, may be dead or obsolescent, but the ideas expressed in their works, the structure of their works, is as modern as it ever was. Painting is a younger art than sculpture and literature, but even in that field there are no radical discoveries to be made, I think. There are no greater craftsmen living today than were Michelangelo and Rembrandt. Painters of today may be expressing something different; but the old masters were just as completely *able* to say what they had to say.

The art of music is a very different story. Music as we know it today, that is, a combination of rhythm, melody, harmony, and counterpoint, has existed less than a thousand years, and music that has any appeal to anything but our archeological curiosity has existed less than half that time. The music of the Middle Ages is as primitive, as naïve, as are the drawings made by the cavemen of Les Eyzies half a million years ago. Music is an art whose growth was stunted by the stupidity of musicians for countless generations. An art that appeals to the ear or the intellect cannot develop beyond a certain primitive point unless it can be transmitted. Take, for example, the plays of Aristophanes. How could they have come into existence if there had been no *written* Greek language? How could a complicated dramatic structure be created and transmitted from one generation to another if its only medium was the memory of the author and the actors?

That is just what did happen to music. For centuries men tried vainly to devise some means of writing down music. The best they could do was to use letters of the alphabet to indicate the notes. This device was useful to convey the *pitch* of the sounds, but it gave no clue as to their *duration*. It was not until approximately the year 1000 that we discovered that in order to transmit music it was necessary, not to *write* it, but to *draw* it. We devised the musical staff, a ladder whose steps and spaces indicated the pitch of the notes. And on that ladder we placed symbols of various shapes and sizes to indicate how long the notes were to last. The minute we made that discovery we found that we could indicate and transmit various *vertical* combinations of sounds—in other words, harmony and counterpoint. Since we no longer had to depend solely on the memories of singers and players, we could create and write down, and *hand* down, compositions of far greater length and complexity than could be transmitted by the unaided ear. So that from the fifteenth century up to the present day music has progressed with incredible speed.

But—and here is the point of this rather academic discourse—how do we know whether that progress—I mean technical, not esthetic progress—has reached its goal? Here we have an art that is thousands of years younger than the other arts, and that has developed its technique in less than half a millennium. The gulf separating Monteverde from Beethoven is far greater than that between Praxiteles and Rodin. When I hear the music of Monteverde I hear the music of a man who is far from having mastered his medium, a man struggling to express ideas for which the language has not yet been found. Praxiteles was completely aware of what he was doing. Monteverde was not. How, then, can we be absolutely certain that two hundred years from now there will not be composers beside whom Beethoven will sound as naïve as Monteverde sounds to us?

There is still another factor that tends very definitely to limit the life of a musical composition, and that is the fact that music does not exist unless it is played. In this respect it is at a tremendous disadvantage compared with the other arts. A great painting or a statue *exists*. There it is. The only thing that threatens its immortality is actual physical destruction. (That risk may be ruled out here because we're discussing neglect rather than accidents.) The *Winged Victory* stands in the Louvre. We go to look at it, and it speaks to us direct. When a new statue arrives, we don't have to move the *Victory* out in order to make room for it. We put it in another wing. The *Mona Lisa* hangs in the Louvre, and as few or as many of us as wish to do so may go to see it, at any time of the day and as often as we wish. A book is equally accessible and even less destructible. Granted that we know how to read, the world's literature is open to us, to pick and choose as we please, and to read when we like. A set of Dickens stands on the shelf of a library. Since Dickens's time thousands of novels have been written, some of them as good as, or better than, his. But we don't have to throw Dickens out. We simply add more shelves. If only ten people in the world wanted to read Dickens we could still afford to keep him on the shelf for the sake of those ten. A play is supposed to be acted, but it doesn't necessarily die if it is not acted. How many of you have ever seen Shakespeare's *Cymbeline?* You don't absolutely have to see it. You can take it down off the shelf and read it for yourself, and libraries can afford the room to keep it for you.

But how many people can read music? And, of those of us who can, how many experience precisely what they experience when they hear it? Not one. Fully to enjoy music, even an expert score reader must hear it; and that means that somebody must play it or sing it. You cannot hear a symphony unless a group of men have rehearsed it under a conductor, and have come out upon a platform and played it for you; nor can you pick the time when you would prefer to hear it. A thousand people can't stroll through a concert hall, at all hours of the day, as they would in a museum. They must listen all at the same time —from three till five, say—or not at all.

All this means that a symphony concert is limited in time, and limited in repertoire. A great orchestra cannot afford to play music that is not to the liking of a reasonable plurality of its hearers. Consequently there exists, in the field of symphonic music, an incessant and merciless struggle for existence that hardly goes on in the other arts. As I said before, in order to make room for a new book in a library, you don't necessarily have to move an old one out. In music you have to do precisely that. The fact that a thousand good plays have been printed since Shakespeare's time affects Shakespeare very little. The fact that a hundred good pieces of music have been published since Beethoven's time affects even Beethoven very seriously.

There can be only so many concerts, and they can last only so long. In order to include a piece of new music on a program we must leave out a piece of old music. The first result of this condition is that a conductor looks at a piece of new music much more critically than a museum curator looks at a new picture. He must ask himself, "Is this *really* worth playing?" The second result is that when he does decide to play it, he must drop some other work to make room for it. And the day will come, inevitably, when we will ask, even of a work by Beethoven, "Is this truly irreplaceable?"

As a matter of fact, the day *has* come. The survival of the fittest is a very hard and inescapable fact in the field of music. Tchaikovsky's first three symphonies, Beethoven's first two, are seldom heard today. Why? Simply because some mysteriously reached consensus of opinion, among listeners to music, has agreed that there are other things more deserving of a hearing.

One answer to this, of course, is recorded music. You can have a library of records as large as any library of books, and can play them as often as you wish, and at any time you wish. And in that form, and in that form only, I believe, a great deal of music that we now consider immortal will continue to exist. The greatest composers, like the greatest playwrights, will be the only ones to survive in terms of actual performance. At least we can be sure that what works of theirs do so survive will be their masterpieces.

Or else—and this is not unthinkable—it may even be that those whom we now call the great masters will eventually disappear altogether. But they will never die. It may be that some day we shall have forgotten the music of Bach and Beethoven and Wagner. But we shall continue to hear it, in the music that comes from the hearts and minds of composers as yet unborn, composers who will say in a new way, a better way, perhaps, the things that the old masters said to us—but, nevertheless, the things that the old masters said first.

7

The Flood

A T FIRST glance it is rather appalling to observe the immense quantity of mediocre music that is written and published today. The new songs and piano pieces come from the presses by the thousands every year, and about one in fifty of them is worth hearing once, let alone twice. Yet the situation is probably not so bad as it looks. I have an idea that the proportionate amounts of good and bad music written today are about what they always were. We remember the highlights of a musical generation—Palestrina, Bach, Haydn, Mozart, Handel, Weber, Wagner—forgetting the countless ephemera that were their contemporaries. Bach was hired to run a church choir and write music for it, and so were dozens of other *Kapellmeister* of his day. They wrote just as much music as he did, and more; only, theirs was rubbish and his was great. So they died and he lived, and we have forgotten that they ever existed.

The essential difference between our day and his is largely one of production. Music was expensive to print in Bach's time, and could not be sold in large quantities. Nowadays a song can be published for about forty dollars, and it *may* sell a quarter of a million copies. So anybody can get his music published. The world has not produced a Bach or a Wagner recently, or even a Brahms, because we have fallen upon fallow times; but we are

46

writing our quota of good music, even if we are printing more bad than ever before. But the bad does not matter much. It will die, and be forgotten, and more will come to take its place, and will be just as unimportant. And the dismayed musician of 2039 will remark with despair the flood of mediocrity in which he seems to be engulfed, and will lament the brave old days of the early twentieth century, when music was still vital, when Strauss and Pizzetti and Respighi and Bax and De Falla and Ravel and Stravinsky and all the other old masters of the golden age were making musical history.

8

The Great Divide

WHY is it that a man who can write a successful symphony cannot write a successful aria? Or, to put the question in a little less oversimplified form, why is it that composers who are recognized as masters of symphonic music so seldom succeed in writing effectively for the theater? Tchaikovsky, for example, wrote nine operas, only two of which, *Pique-Dame* and *Eugen Oniegin,* have survived. Even these, although they are occasionally revived, have hardly won an enduring place in the standard operatic repertoire. Sibelius, another great symphonist, never got beyond the beginning of one opera (its prologue alone survives, as *The Swan of Tuonela*). Beethoven wrote one opera, *Fidelio.* Its music is greatly admired, and it is staged from time to time as a labor of love. But even the most devoted Beethoven partisan could hardly claim that his *Fidelio* has ever been a popular success—as his symphonies have been a popular success.

Now it seems a little strange, at first, that this should be so. For we are accustomed to being told that music is divided into two classes: absolute, that is, symphonic music, and program music; and opera is always catalogued as a branch of program music. Yet all three composers that I have mentioned have written program music that has been successful. The "Pastoral" has a definite program—a day in the country, so to speak, with a stroll by the brook, and a peasant dance and a thunderstorm, all complete. Tchaikovsky's *Romeo and Juliet* and *Francesca da Rimini* have definite dramatic bases. He admitted to definite programs for his Fourth and Sixth Symphonies. Even his Fifth is supposed to have a story behind it. Many of Sibelius's best-known works are based on Finnish legends.

Now if these men can write narrative music, why can't they write successful operas? The answer lies, I think, in the fact that our usual division of all music into two categories is too simple. Besides the two historic classes, a third kind of music has grown up during the past century and a half, and one that is becoming increasingly important: music of the theater. It differs from the other two kinds in many ways.

Composers like Beethoven, Tchaikovsky, Sibelius, Brahms, and Schumann, even when they are writing to an ostensible program, are always thinking purely in terms of music. Tchaikovsky's *Romeo and Juliet* may contain themes representative of Friar Lawrence, the quarrel between the Montagues and the Capulets, and the two lovers; but his handling, presentation, and development of those themes are purely abstract. We are told by its composer that the "Pastoral" Symphony has a definite program; and holding the program, as we listen to the music, we believe it. Actually, the music of the "Pastoral" is developed along strict symphonic lines. I would confidently challenge anybody who didn't happen to know its program beforehand to listen to the music and tell me with any degree of accuracy precisely what that program is. The scherzo is a village festival, yes—after you have been told that it is. But it is no more so than the scherzo of the

Ninth. The storm is fairly graphic; but it's a purely musical storm. With no great stretch of the imagination it might easily represent the fall of the Bastille, or Prometheus bringing down the fire from heaven. The best illustration I know of Beethoven's completely musical thinking is his descriptive piece, *Wellington's Victory*, in which he can think of no better way to suggest the opposing armies than the naïve device of having half the orchestra play *God Save the King* while the other half plays *Malbrouck s'en va-t-en guerre*. The weakness of *Fidelio* as an opera lies in the fact that Beethoven, the composer, stubbornly insists on developing his musical ideas as he conceives them, leaving the action to stand around on one foot, more or less, until he is ready to let it go on.

Tchaikovsky has much the same type of mind. Opera librettos apparently existed, for him, purely as springboards, as an excuse for him to write beautiful music, at whatever length he saw fit to write it. If it happened to be appropriate to the scene it accompanied, well and good. If it didn't, so much the worse for the scene. Sibelius, as I said, did begin one opera, but after he had been told that his libretto was too lyric and not dramatic enough, abandoned the idea. Brahms toyed with the idea of writing an opera, but never found a satisfactory libretto. That, at least, was the reason he gave for not setting one; but I've always had an idea that some instinct warned Brahms that his way of expressing himself musically would never be successful under the restrictions of opera.

What are those restrictions? Why is it that the purely musical thinkers so seldom succeed in opera, and, conversely, that the purely operatic thinkers are rarely successful in the symphonic field? One reason is that the approach of the symphonic composer to his task differs profoundly and fundamentally from the approach of the operatic composer to *his* task. Roughly speaking, it is the difference between the point of view of the novelist and the dramatist. The former tells his story by a leisurely narrative method, unrestricted by limitations of time or space, and at liberty to make any apparent digressions he pleases, so long as they contribute, however indirectly, to the general mood and structure of his book. The latter has no such freedom. He must tell his story in a series of crises, in which he gives you the words and actions of a group of people during certain crucial moments in their lives. Correspondingly, the symphonist is thinking in terms of the prevailing mood of an entire work, while the operatic composer must occupy himself primarily with the mood of a given moment or situation. One is the long shot, so to speak, and the other the close-up.

The operatic composer is concerned with *here* and *now*; the symphonist is concerned with life in retrospect, its contours softened, its colors mellowed, its implications pondered and understood. He says his say in measured terms, in a more or less formal arrangement, because he has the leisure to do so. He is the poet-philosopher; the other is almost the poet-journalist. Small wonder, then, that two such opposite temperaments and musical points of view seldom exist in the same person.

There is another aspect of the operatic form that the symphonic composer dislikes to face: the fact that the form his music must take is dictated by exigencies that are not primarily musical, but dramatic. He experiences the same difficulties in meeting these exigencies that a landscape painter would if he attempted to become a scene designer. As a pure musician he may feel the necessity for the recurrence of a given theme at a certain definite point in his musical structure; but if that theme, in an opera, has been associated with a given character or situation, it may be *dramatically* impossible to bring the theme back at the moment when he would like to hear it again.

Moreover, the length of time that it takes to develop a purely musical idea to its fullest significance has not, necessarily, the slightest connection with the length of time it takes to develop a dramatic idea or situation. Anyone who has ever listened to an opera or a play, and at the same time watched the audience, knows that any given scene has its own natural and inevitable length; and that it must not exceed or fall short of that length if it is to hold the attention of its hearers. As a consequence, the operatic composer is forced to take his musicianship almost for granted. While he is writing his music he must think, most of the time, not like a composer, but like a stage director.

He may have a magnificent theme for the scene in which the two lovers part forever, only to find, just as he has warmed to his work, and is ready to develop his theme to the utmost, that the scene is over. However it may hurt to do so, he must cut his beloved music short; on the other hand, he may have brought his music to its logical, *musical* conclusion, forty bars before the scene reaches its *dramatic* conclusion, and finds that he has to pad it out. In either case he must subordinate his music to the needs of the theater. If he cannot bring himself to do so, his opera will not hold the stage.

If he can do so, if he happens to be a born operatic composer, he is not likely to be successful as a writer of symphonic music; in fact, he must reconcile himself to the fact that very little of his music is likely to be played by symphony orchestras. As a rule, concert audiences will hear nothing of his beyond an occasional overture or en-tr'acte. The three most popular operatic composers today are Wagner, Verdi, and Puccini. It happens that the last two wrote very few introductions long enough to warrant their being called overtures, so that there is nothing of theirs to play in concert except music from the scenes of their operas; and that music, divorced from the action, sounds too undeveloped, too scrappy, for the concert stage. One movement of a symphony, developing two themes, may last twelve or fourteen minutes. In that length of time Verdi or Puccini would have got rid of two arias, a duet, and a short scene, employing seven or eight main and subordinate themes.

The apparent exception to this rule is Wagner, who wrote exclusively for the theater and whose music is as much played on concert programs as that of any sym-phonic writer, including Beethoven. But Wagner, I think, survives in concert through his invention of the leading motive. Almost any given scene from one of his music dramas may contain six or eight of these motives, all short, and all interwoven with such consummate mastery that he is able to follow the pace and changing moods of a dramatic situation and at the same time convey the *illusion* of thematic development. Consequently, when his music is played in concert it sounds like symphonic music, although, strictly speaking, it is not. The reason why the Wagner phenomenon is not more common is that, in order to use the leading-motive system successfully, a composer must have Wagner's genius for inventing short, unforgettable themes. Up to now, no other composer has had that particular brand of genius.

As a matter of fact, the only composer I know who has, with complete success, bridged the gulf between the operatic and the symphonic composer is Mozart, who was equally at home in the theater and in the symphony. And since it is generally conceded that every rule needs at least one exception to prove it, I shall elect to leave Mozart unexplained.

There is one composer who has been generally successful in the operatic field, who is equally successful in writing for the symphony orchestra: Richard Strauss. But Strauss, I think, rather helps my case. He does not think in terms of abstract music. His ventures into the field of pure music, such as his sonatas and concertos and his one symphony, are not the works upon which his reputation is based. His symphonic victories have been won by his tone poems, which are almost pure theater music. The whole list, from *Don Juan* through the *Domestic Symphony*, are dramatic works, each with a plot and a cast of characters. They are highly condensed orchestral operas, owing their apparently symphonic character to the fact that, not being handicapped by the exigencies of the physical stage, Strauss has been able to develop his material in terms of symphonic thought. He remains, always, a man of the theater. Beethoven and Brahms and Tchaikovsky would undoubtedly have admired his music; but the mental processes that produced it would have left them hopelessly bewildered. I think it is fairly safe to say to any composer: if you want to write a good opera, forget the development section. If you want to write a good symphony, keep out of the theater.

9

The Fruits of Condescension

A THIRD and fairly obvious reason why composers whose leanings are purely symphonic fail in the field of opera is the distressing flair most of them have for poor librettos. I do not know just why it is that a mastery of the sonata form should go hand in hand with an inability to appraise theatrical values; I know only that in nine cases out of ten it does. If Beethoven's *Fidelio* gets comparatively few productions, the cause of its neglect does not lie entirely in Beethoven's insistence upon developing his musical ideas at the expense of dramatic timing. It lies partly in the fact that the book of *Fidelio* is, if you will forgive my saying so, pretty dull. *Rosamunde,* upon which Schubert squandered some of his finest music (it is, technically, only incidental to the play, but the score is of almost operatic elaborateness), has long since been little more than a rumor. If Weber did have the lucky inspiration to select *Der Freischütz* as one of his librettos, he also chose the slightly absurd *Oberon* and *Euryanthe.*

Here is, possibly, one reason: opera, like the stage and the motion pictures, is a co-operative art, one that attains its ends through the combined efforts of not one, but several artists. Every successful stage director, scenic artist, librettist, and composer knows it, realizes that, to some extent he must subordinate complete freedom of expression in his chosen medium to the demands of the work as a whole. But the composer of "absolute" music is under no such restrictions. He can work as he pleases, and to please himself. He can write his music in the form of a symphony, a trio, a quintet, or a tone poem, with no one but his own sense of fitness to dictate the form. He may even, if he likes, begin a work as a tone poem and turn it into a cantata midway, saying "by your leave" to nobody.

Since his works achieve success solely on their musical merits he is likely, when he enters the field of opera, to do so with a subconscious conviction that the success of his opera, like the success of his symphony, depends solely on him; a libretto is a necessary evil, and almost any set of words, provided they are not so antipoetic as to impede the flow of his musical ideas, will do. So he picks something with pleasant words and no conflict or dramatic situations, sets them to his best music—and sees his opera fail.

And fail it will; for, on this side of the water at least, audiences, even opera audiences, will not take much interest in an operatic work that lacks dramatic effectiveness. The apparent exceptions, of course, are pieces like *Lucia* and *L'Africaine,* whose theatrical appeal is about zero. But these works, you will find, generally contain a number of famous arias that make ideal vehicles for the display of expensive voices. They contain moments that even the most unsophisticated audience knows enough to wait for; so that even though the amorous vicissitudes of Edgar and Lucy of Lammermoor leave one cold, the fun of waiting for the Mad Scene to come around furnishes a certain element of suspense. A modern *Lucia*—an opera consisting of five or six big scenes stuck like plums in the suety wastes of a childish and obvious plot—would not appeal thus to a present-day audience. It would be dead long before its big song hits had had a chance to become familiar.

Verdi, particularly in his earlier operas, has been the target of much criticism from commentators who find his librettos hack-written, prosy, improbable, and even sometimes downright illiterate. They are all of that, many of them. But they are something else, too. In the worst of Verdi's librettos you will find dramatic situations, suspense, and—however absurdly unbelievable—emotional conflict; all of them the indispensable ingredients of a successful play.

One can always pass for a humorist, in musical circles, by commenting wittily upon the average operagoer's supposed utter ignorance of the opera to which he is listening. But that is no longer a very good joke, if it ever was. My own circle of operagoing acquaintances is about as ignorant as the next man's, I suppose; yet most of them at least know something of the plots of their favorite operas, and some even know the names of the principal characters. They may go consciously for the sake of listening to the tunes and hearing the singers, yet it is noticeable that the operas they like best are those whose stories they can follow. Go over the list of works that hold the operatic stage today, and you will find that almost all of them possess dramatic interest. *Rigoletto* is still fairly entertaining as a play; *La Traviata* is, of course, our old friend, *Camille*. *La Tosca, Butterfly, L'Amore dei tre re, La Bohème, Louise, Pelléas*—all of them are good theater. Wagner offers less rapid action, but his librettos are none the less dramas. In all these works one finds the dramatic essentials of character, motive, suspense, and conflict. The fact that the average listener is probably conscious only of listening to singing and playing does not prevent his attention being caught and held by these dramatic essentials.

A prize example of what happens when the composer neglects to take into account the dramatic values of what is, externally, a purely musical entertainment is the failure of Russian opera to gain any secure place in the affections of our operagoing public. The stage works of Borodin, Moussorgsky, Tchaikovsky, and Rimsky-Korsakoff contain beautiful music, music worthy to rank with the operatic literature of any country in the world. Yet, with the exception of Rimsky's *Le Coq d'or* and Moussorgsky's *Boris Godunoff*, not one of them has ever achieved a genuine and permanent success in this country. I have often wondered why a nation that could produce the superb plays that Russian playwrights have written should turn out such dramatically formless operas. Russian audiences must have been lenient in their theatrical demands —in the opera house. Certainly Russian operas are dramatically uneventful to a degree that we hardly dream of. No Russian, given the *Nibelungen* saga as operatic material, would do what Wagner did—tie it together with an ethical idea. He wouldn't bother. *Boris Godunoff*, the most viable of all Russian operas, is dramatically interesting only because Boris Godunoff's own life was moving and dramatically interesting. Even so, its construction is so loose that the Metropolitan has produced it with the two final acts transposed, without seriously outraging our esthetic sensibilities.

The attitude of Russian composers toward the dramatic

aspects of their art is illuminatingly set forth in Rimsky-Korsakoff's delightful autobiography. He gives us a picture of himself and his confreres writing first acts of operas without the slightest notion of how they are going to end, beginning operas in the middle, taking an act of one opera and putting it into another, or taking an orchestra piece and turning it into an operatic scene—and all without the slightest idea that they were doing anything unusual or open to criticism. Tchaikovsky sets whole pages out of a novel, without an elision, in *Pique-Dame*, and the plot of Borodin's *Prince Igor* concerns a mythological prince who does nothing more complicated than go to war, get captured, escape, and arrive home again.

Or take, for example, Rimsky-Korsakoff's *Sadko*, produced at the Metropolitan some years back and quietly shelved after a few only mildly successful seasons. Let us take, specifically, the fourth act of *Sadko*, a typical instance of this happy-go-lucky method of libretto construction. A great fair is under way at Novgorod. Sadko appears and wagers his head against the wealth of the merchants that there are golden fish in the lake. The merchants take his bet; he goes out on the lake in a small boat, casts his net, and returns with the golden fish. Sadko, triumphant, bids his companions make ready to sail away in search of further treasure. At this point the action stops completely in order to allow a young friend of Sadko's to sing a lengthy ditty relating every detail of the happenings that the audience has just witnessed. Sadko now asks three foreign merchants to tell him about their countries, so that he may know which one to visit. Three long numbers follow, sung by a Viking, a Hindu, and a Venetian.

Everybody votes for Venice. Sadko, scorning to collect his bet, boards his ship and sails away to the tune of an ancient folk song, sung by all the people.

Strictly speaking, this chain of incidents, if it can be called dramatic at all, is a complete drama in itself. For all its apparent relation to anything that has gone before or since, one might imagine it to be the first act, or the last, of a drama, but certainly never the fourth of a six-act piece. The three songs of the foreign merchants are, dramatically speaking, totally superfluous, like the ode of the young *gusli* player. They halt the action, and are inserted merely to give Rimsky-Korsakoff a chance to write some delightful music. What pace the act does possess is so leisurely that it takes the better part of an hour to perform.

Unfortunately, delightful music is not enough for us. We demand the sense of steady growth, of motion, of getting somewhere that distinguishes every Western play from *Macbeth* to *The Little Foxes*. Particularly do we demand emotion of some kind. Find a good play that has failed in this country, and you will probably find a play that did not move its audience. The music of *Sadko* is beautiful, and its story is diverting. But it does not move us. A single act of the opera—say the fourth—done with scenery and costumes, would be irresistible. But six acts of simple entertainment, no matter how gorgeously appareled, are a bore.

10

Piotr the Great

SPEAKING of Russians, I had a letter a while ago from a young woman who is terribly worried about her musical taste. She writes, in part, "Did you ever hear anybody say that if you liked Tchaikovsky's music it was a sure sign that you were immature as far as music was concerned? Well, it's being said, and being said by people who are spending time and money taking music courses in well known colleges. Just because I like Tchaikovsky's Sixth Symphony, they tell me I am immature; and I won't be grown up, musically, until I've grown to dislike him."

I have heard that said a good many times, by a good many people, over a period covering a good many years; and I've often wondered just why it is that poor old Tchaikovsky is always singled out, not only by a certain proportion of the public, but by certain of the critics, as a sterling example of everything obvious, sentimental, and superficial, somebody who can be seen through by anybody possessing an adult musical intelligence. I thought once that possibly it was because Tchaikovsky wrote a certain amount of music that really is pretty bad. But then, so did most of the great men. If you have ever heard Beethoven's *Wellington's Victory*, or his *King Steven* Overture, you are aware that there were moments in even Beethoven's musical life, when he was somewhat less than divinely inspired. Then there is Wagner's *American Cen-*

tennial March—which you have never heard—concerning which the composer himself said that the only good thing about it was the five thousand dollars he got for writing it. And he was right. If Tchaikovsky had his off days, so had plenty of others. That, therefore, can't be the real reason why he is despised.

I think the truth is that a good many people who are suffering from exactly the complaint of which they accuse my correspondent—that is, musical immaturity—rather look down upon Tchaikovsky because he is so simple and direct that he sounds obvious. They tend to think that if he were saying anything really worth while, he ought to be more difficult to understand. As it is, he hardly ever said a complicated thing during his whole musical life. Take the way he writes for the orchestra, for instance. Compare a page from the *"Pathétique"* Symphony with a page from Strauss's *Ein Heldenleben*. Tchaikovsky asks for nothing more than the conventional symphony orchestra. Strauss's score calls for that, plus an extra flute, two extra oboes, an English horn, an E-flat clarinet, a bass clarinet, an extra bassoon, a contrabassoon, four extra horns, two extra trumpets, an extra tuba, and two harps.

Tchaikovsky's writing for the instruments is almost childishly simple. He uses scarcely a combination that a first-year student of orchestration wouldn't understand at a glance. The writing is so technically easy that almost any competent orchestral musician could play his part perfectly almost at sight. Strauss's score, on the other hand, makes demands upon the instruments such as no composer ever made before. He takes them from the bottom to the top of their register, and writes passages that require a perfect technique to negotiate. His part-writing is a maze of complex counterpoint that is as fascinating to study as it is difficult to follow.

On the other hand, these marvelous contrapuntal passages sometimes do come off, and sometimes don't. The score of *Ein Heldenleben* contains pages that are miracles of orchestral writing; but it also contains pages that are sheer "paper music"—that is, music that looks great in print and doesn't come out in performance. I remember one wonderful passage for the bass clarinet, that takes the player from his lowest clear to his extreme top register, in sixteenth and thirty-second notes. There's only one trouble with that passage: along with the bass clarinet, three trumpets, a couple of trombones, and thirty-two violins are playing something else—forte. For all the difference the bass-clarinet player makes in that passage, he might just as well be in the musician's lounge, having a smoke. The concluding chords of Strauss's *Also sprach Zarathustra* are marked double pianissimo. They have never been played that softly, and never will be, because two of the instruments on those chords are piccolos, playing in their extreme top register; and the piccolo player has not yet been born who can play his top D-sharp and F-sharp anything but pretty loudly.

But poor old Tchaikovsky, elementary as his scores may *look,* is just as great a master of orchestration as Strauss. He may not get all of Strauss's effects, but he doesn't make Strauss's mistakes, either. Every bar of his music "sounds," as the conductors say; that is, every note written for an instrument to play will, if it is played as he directed, be heard by the listener. I know of no composer, with the possible exception of Wagner, whose orchestral writing is so completely free of deadwood and occasional miscalculations as to balance.

Tchaikovsky is obvious, of course, in another way. He is incorrigibly melodious; and this, at a time when a good many composers seem to be running dry of themes, is not fashionable. The second theme of the first movement of the *"Pathétique,"* the main theme of *Romeo and Juliet*, the theme of the first movement of the B-flat minor Piano Concerto—why, they're tunes! Not only are they tunes, but they are tunes so simple and easily grasped that you can whistle them practically after one hearing. They can't be good.

Now I don't say that Tchaikovsky, in music, is to be compared with Shakespeare, in the drama. Just the same, let me draw a comparison between the two for a moment. Read any play of Shakespeare's, and you'll find him full of clichés—stock phrases and figures of speech that are so much the common coinage of the language that they possess no particular literary value whatsoever. Let me quote the sort of thing I mean—these are all phrases from *Macbeth*:

The milk of human kindness
Even-handed justice
The primrose way
What's done is done
Scotched the snake, not killed it
Can such things be
The slaves of drink
Make assurance doubly sure
The crack of doom

64

Those are all commonplace enough. Yet, to me, they are the most exciting thing about Shakespeare, because none of them had ever been said until he said them. They are a few out of hundreds of similar phrases that he invented and added to the English language—so many of them that I doubt whether any English-speaking person can carry on one day's conversation without quoting Shakespeare. They are Shakespeare's immortal contribution. The plays are great; but long after the plays are forgotten, those humble phrases will still be spoken, as long as there is an English language to speak.

Now Tchaikovsky, to a lesser degree, is like that. The themes—tunes, if you like—that form the backbone of his work are simple in conception, comparatively uncomplicated in their development, easy to grasp at a first hearing.

The theme that I mentioned from the *"Pathétique,"* for instance. You hear it once, and you say, "Yes, yes, I understand. Anybody could write that." The catch is, that nobody did, until Tchaikovsky wrote it. And nobody wrote dozens, scores of others, until he thought of them.

Anybody who tries to write music, as I do, approaches music—or, rather approaches composers—with a certain degree of professional intimacy. That is not a boast. I'm merely saying that even a bad actor has a keener appreciation of the fine points of good acting than most dramatic critics. I think I understand Tchaikovsky fairly well. I listen to his music, read one of his scores, and I have a fairly good general idea of what he was trying to do and how far he succeeded. But there's one thing about Tchaikovsky, as about any other first-rate composer, that will always be a mystery that I never shall know. *Where did he get those tunes?* And where could one get some more? I don't say that they are equal to Beethoven's or Mozart's or Wagner's finest inspirations. I don't say that any generation may not tire of them. But by the time it does, another generation will have come along, for whom they will still possess beauty and eloquence. So let young Miss Blank's musical friends be not too scornful of her immaturity. It may be that she knows instinctively something that they have not yet learned: that when a man has something to say, he is a true master of his craft if he can manage to say it simply and directly.

The Perennial Victor

"Songs for a summer night." Willow Grove Park, Philadelphia, on an evening some thirty-five years ago, the evening when I first heard Victor Herbert conduct a potpourri of airs from his new extravaganza, *Babes in Toyland,* which was running, currently, in Chicago. "In the Toymaker's Workshop" was the first selection, as I remember; and when that was followed by "Toyland," the "March of the Toys," and more of that adorable score—well, if you're Herbert-minded, you will understand how I felt. If you're not, this is not for you.

Babes in Toyland was not, of course, my first hearing of Herbert's music. The very first time must have been about 1898 or 1899, in the Montauk Theatre, in Brooklyn, where I heard Frank Daniels play a return engagement of *The Wizard of the Nile.* Frankly, I remember now only one tune from the score, "Starlight, Star Bright." It made a particularly lasting impression at the time because I had been singing it for some time (*The Wizard* dates from 1895). My chief recollections of the show are the name of the wizard, Kibosh, which struck me as inordinately funny at the time; and his running gag-line, "Am I a wiz?" But however vague my recollections of the details of the score, the music did one thing. It inspired me with a love and admiration of Victor Herbert's genius that the years have never lessened.

For this German-trained Dubliner who wrote like a Frenchman *was* a genius. Beginning with *Prince Ananias* in 1894, in the ensuing thirty years he wrote upwards of forty operetta and musical-comedy scores, the least successful of which are alive, *as music,* just as much as on the day they were written. I say "as music," for only a handful have survived on the stage. But that is not Herbert's fault. If he had had Sullivan's luck, and had found a Gilbert, there would be repertory companies doing Herbert and Blank as well as Gilbert and Sullivan: if you ask me to take sides, as between Herbert and Sullivan, Herbert's my man. The Gilbertandsullivan fans put no hyphens between the names, for the simple reason that the two are inseparable. Think of a song from one of the Savoy operas, and you think as much of the words as of the music. Think of something from a Herbert score, and ten to one you cannot quote the words beyond the first line. It's the music that counts, frequently in spite of lyrics that are appallingly pedestrian. You can parody Sullivan—the tonic-and-dominant harmony, the excessive use of six-eight time, the burlesque Italian ritornellos that were burlesqued so long that they became a mannerism. Try to parody Herbert, and you'll probably turn out nothing but an unconvincing imitation—the difference between champagne and ginger ale.

So this will be no dispassionate critique, no survey of "Victor Herbert and His Times." From me you will get the ravings of a Herbert addict, and little more, most of them beginning with "Do you remember?"

Do you remember, for instance, the summer of 1904, in Stamford, Connecticut? No, I suppose you wouldn't; but I do. I was the piano section of the three-piece orches-

tra that played at the Shippan Point Hotel. Our repertoire, obtained by cadging professional copies from the
publishers, was limited, but good. Selections from *Wood-
land, Piff Paff Pouff,* and *Little Johnny Jones* were our
staples. Those, and Herbert—*The Serenade, The Idol's
Eye,* the perennial *Wizard, The Fortune Teller,* and the
Babes, which by that time was as big a hit in New York
as it had been in Chicago. We played afternoon tea concerts, and evening "hops." The latter were simple—no
nonsense about rumbas and tangos and such; just two-
step, waltz, two-step, waltz. The waltzes were mostly Herbert. For the tea concerts, the "Gypsy Love Song" from
The Fortune Teller was our *pièce de résistance.* In fact,
we played it so much that we began to be afraid that the
rocking-chair brigade might notice its almost daily appearance on the printed program. So every third day we
used to call it "Golden Heart Throbs," by Zaboli, and
everybody was happy.

Do you remember the Sunday-night concerts in the old
New York Theatre, on—what was it?—Broadway at
about Forty-fifth Street, in 1905 and 1906, with Herbert
conducting his own orchestra? They were supposed to be
miscellaneous "pop" programs, but by the time we got
through demanding—and getting—*Badinage, Punchinello,
Pan-Americana,* and the *American Rhapsody,* they were
pretty nearly all-Herbert. And do you remember the opening of *Mlle Modiste,* on Christmas night of that same year,
1905? I think I could still play that score straight through,
by heart, opening choruses and all. Remember Claude
Gillingwater as Hiram Bent, the American millionaire?
And William Pruette, singing "I Want What I Want When
I Want It"? And that chorus of footmen that opened the

first scene of Act II? And "The Culture Club in Keo-kuk"? And do you by any chance remember Fritzi Scheff? Fritzi, of the eighteen-inch waist that strangled half the girls in New York in their attempts to emulate it? Fritzi, singing "The Mascot of the Troop" and beating her drum? Fritzi, singing the song hit of all song hits, now and forever, "Kiss Me Again"?

That "Kiss Me Again" had a curious history. As placed in the score, it was half a burlesque in intent. It was one refrain of a number, "If I Were on the Stage," in which Fritzi showed how, if she got a chance, she would sing a gavotte, a polonaise, and, finally, a sentimental love song. The audience took it seriously and swooned over it, from the start. In later years, Herbert wrote a new introductory verse for it, and posterity promptly forgot the stage version entirely.

Then the golden year of 1906, with two of his best scores, *It Happened in Nordland*, for Lew Fields, and *The Red Mill*, for Montgomery and Stone. Remember the "Absinthe Frappé" number from the former? And remember "Whistle It," "You Never Can Tell About a Woman," "The Isle of Our Dreams," "Because You're You" (in which the public got a duet in the form of a canon, and liked it), "In Old New York," and—oh, the whole of that *Red Mill* score?

In 1907 I met Herbert, and he changed my life for me. It was between the acts of a musical show that William Le Baron and I (the Le Baron who runs the Paramount Studios today) had written for New York University. It was called *The Oracle*, and Herbert had been dragged there (I can guess now how wearily) by our principal comedian, who was a friend of the family. He sent for me after the first act, and said, "My boy, you have talent."

(Did you ever have Victor Herbert tell you you had talent? Try it some time.)

"But," he continued, "you don't know anything about music, do you? I mean musical theory."

I admitted that I did not.

"If you want to write music you must study harmony and counterpoint. As it is now, you're like a man trying to write plays who doesn't know how to read and write. You can go just so far. If you want to go farther, you must study."

So I studied.

There was more, so much more, Herbert to come. *Algeria,* one his best scores, killed by its libretto. He had so much faith in the music that he bought the show and reproduced it, as *The Rose of Algeria*; but it merely lost him money. Then came *Naughty Marietta*. Remember Emma Trentini, late of the Hammerstein Opera, singing the "Italian Street Song"? And Orville Harrold, later to be of the Metropolitan Opera, singing "I'm Falling in Love With Someone" and "Tramp, Tramp, Tramp"? And remember *The Enchantress,* and *Sweethearts,* and the score that he loved best of all, *Eileen*?

The last time I saw him was in 1924, just after *The Dream Girl,* which was having only a mild success. The era of hot numbers was beginning, and the one thing in the world that Herbert was constitutionally incapable of writing was a hot number. He had tried to write a couple for *The Dream Girl,* but they were merely bad Herbert. He was very low in his mind.

"My day is over," he said. "Already they're forgetting

poor old Herbert"—and half believed it. On May 26 of that year he died.

I wish he could have waited a little longer. Two or three years more, and he would have seen the radio gradually emerging as the greatest purveyor of music the world has ever known, a medium that, from its very beginnings, needed Herbert. Today, on the air, there is no composer, serious or light, living or dead, whose music is more in demand. They haven't forgotten poor old Herbert.

12

The Fat Man of Passy

HERBERT was the latest, and perhaps the last, of a line of composers of comic opera that began with Mozart and included Rossini, Lecocq, Offenbach, and Sullivan. Of the six, Lecocq is the least important, and Mozart is the most gifted. The most picturesque, and to my mind the most misunderstood, is Gioacchino Rossini.

As we look back we can realize that he gave his contemporaries early warning that his was not going to be a life of the usual sort; for he managed to be born on the twenty-ninth of February, 1792. His father was the town trumpeter of Pesaro, a little seaport town on the Adriatic shore of northern Italy. (The office of town trumpeter, in the Italy of those days, was the equivalent of our own New England town crier.) In addition, Rossini senior earned extra money by playing the French horn in the town's theater band, and still further added to his income by getting himself appointed inspector of public slaughterhouses. Rossini's mother was the daughter of one of the local bakers, and had an unusually good singing voice. While he was still a very small boy, she and her husband, deserting the slaughterhouse business, embarked on a modest joint career of singing and playing, respectively, with various small-town opera companies in that part of the country. This kept them out on the road a good deal, with the result that young Rossini, left in the hands of an indulgent and helpless grandmother, spent a very spoiled early youth in the reluctant pursuit of an extremely sketchy early education.

In 1802, when he was ten, the family moved to Lugo, and two years later settled down in Bologna. It was in that town that the boy took up the study of music in earnest, after a brief and unsuccessful apprenticeship to a blacksmith. He studied the viola, horn, spinet—and singing. Later he took up musical theory, although his first successes were as a singer, and his early ambition was a singing career. He did, however, at the age of sixteen, compose a Mass at the request of a friend of his, and the same year won a commission from the local conservatory to write a cantata, which was duly performed, with no success whatsoever. In 1810, when he was eighteen years old, he got his big chance. A friend of his family's, a small-time opera singer named Morandi, had an engagement at the San Mosè opera house in Venice. The season was to consist of five one-act operas, written by local talent; but one of the composers had failed to deliver his score. Morandi managed to persuade the manager to write to young Rossini and ask him if he would like to try to supply the missing opera. Rossini didn't even wait to reply. He arrived. In a few days he had composed the score of a one-act opera called *La Cambiale di matrimonio* —The Matrimonial Bill of Exchange—which was successfully produced, and which earned its creator the staggering fee of forty dollars.

Opera, in the Italy of those times, was not the consecrated and expensive institution that it is nowadays. It was much more comparable to our modern motion pictures. Just as the main function of a motion-picture scena-

rio, today, is to provide a vehicle for the display of the
charms of a favorite movie star, the main function of an
opera, then, was to provide a vehicle for the display of
the voice of a favorite *singing* star. Every city, in fact
every town of any pretensions, had its local theater and
opera company, presenting three or four seasons a year,
either of existing operas, or works written to order. There
was, consequently, an enormous demand for new operas,
with speed and quantity much more desirable than artistic
inspiration.

Nothing was asked of a libretto except that it give an
excuse for scenery and offer the cast the opportunities
called for by the accepted formula. This formula was
strict and unvarying. The cast must consist of a prima
donna (who was frequently a male soprano), a tenor, a
singing bass, a comic bass, and one or two secondary
sopranos. The singing bass was not allowed to have any
principal arias, for these were the exclusive property of
the prima donna and the tenor. *Their* arias must be equal
in number and in length. The secondary soprano was allowed one aria in the second act. This was popularly
known as the *aria del sorbetto*—the ice-cream aria—because it was customary at that point to pass around sherbet
and ices among the more solvent members of the audience, who chatted and refreshed themselves while the unfortunate second soprano was holding forth.

The music was expected to be reasonably tuneful and
to offer the singers opportunities to show what they could
do in the way of trills, cadenzas, and roulades. These, by
the way, were almost invariably invented by the performers themselves. The recitatives must be accompanied only
by the harpsichord or piano. The arias were accompanied

largely by the strings, anything ambitious in the way of orchestration being confined pretty strictly to the overture, the entr'actes, and the ballet.

Now these rules, coupled with the haste with which operas had to be written, made the creation of any masterworks highly improbable. On the other hand, composing operas was a comparatively simple business, with no dramatic writing asked for, and no innovations in form or orchestration demanded—or even tolerated. Moreover, it was a reasonably profitable business; for as the scores were virtually never published, a composer could sell his opera to one theater after another. A young composer with a facile pen and a gift of melody, as Rossini was, could not only learn his business but earn a not uncomfortable living as well.

Rossini's life during the ensuing nineteen years is hardly more than a record of his travels and his operatic productions. Between 1810 and 1812 he wrote seven operas, which were produced in Venice, Bologna, Ferrara, and Milan. In the year 1813 he wrote four, for Venice, including *Tancredi,* which was popular for years afterward all over Europe, and *L'Italiana in Algeri*—The Italian Lady in Algiers—which established him, at twenty-one, as the most popular young composer in northern Italy. From Venice he went to Milan, where he wrote two for La Scala. Then back to Venice, from which he was summoned to Naples to write an opera, *Elizabeth, Queen of England,* for the famous prima donna, Isabella Colbran, whom he was later to marry.

His next opera, produced in Rome on February 20, 1816, when he was twenty-four years old, was destined to make him world-famous and to become one of the most popular operas in the world, even today—*The Barber of Seville*. He didn't call it that at the outset. A previous operatic version of Beaumarchais' comedy, and a very popular one, had been written by the composer Paisiello; and as Paisiello had great influence in Rome, Rossini decided to avoid antagonizing the Paisiello fans, as far as possible, by giving his version another title. He wrote it in about three weeks, some say two. Its overture, in which so many listeners have found an epitome of the whole story, is nothing more than the overture to the *Queen Elizabeth* opera that I have just mentioned. Time being short, he warmed it up and used it over again.

The opera was finally produced under the name of *Almaviva, or the Useless Precaution*. And a useless precaution it was; for Paisiello's followers, not at all mollified by the change in title, booed and hissed and laughed the first performance into a spectacular failure. For the second performance, Rossini pretended to be ill, so as to avoid the ordeal of presiding at the piano. But he needn't have done so; for with the Paisiello faction out of the way, the audience got a chance to hear *The Barber*— which was all that was necessary to make it an instantaneous success.

During the ensuing six years Rossini wrote sixteen more operas, of which *Otello, La Cenerentola* (Cinderella), and *La Gazza ladra* contained music that is still played. In 1822 he married Mme Colbran and went for his honeymoon to Vienna, where he was already famous. It was here that he first heard the *"Eroica"* Symphony, which inspired his lifelong veneration of Beethoven. He managed to get an interview with the great man, who liked *The Barber of Seville* and advised its composer always to stick to comic opera. He returned to Venice, where in thirty-three days he wrote the grand opera, *Semiramide,* for which he received the unheard-of fee of a thousand dollars. Then to London, where he met everybody of any importance, including George IV, with whom he used to sing duets.

From England he went to Paris, where he entered on another phase of his career by accepting an offer to run the Italian Theater—the equivalent of the present-day Paris Opéra-Comique. He took the job seriously, and made a number of important productions, including one of Meyerbeer's operas. Nevertheless, between 1825 and 1828 he managed to write four more operas of his own, two of which, *The Siege of Corinth,* a serious opera, and *Le Comte Ory,* a comedy, were popular for years. And then, in the following year, on August 3, 1829, he produced what he and many of his contemporary critics considered to be his masterpiece, *William Tell.* We don't hear much of *William Tell* nowadays, outside of "pop" concert performances of the overture. I heard the entire opera when it was revived at the Metropolitan about fifteen years ago; and to me it contains stretches of musical wilderness. But nothing quite so epic had ever been heard before, in Rossini's time, and it made a profound impression. Within a comparatively short time it was being performed all over Europe, and in Russia.

And then an extraordinary thing happened. Ten days after the production of *William Tell* in Paris, Rossini, at the age of thirty-six, left for Bologna. During the ensuing thirty-seven years of his life he never wrote another opera. The popular version of this strange renunciation is that Rossini, having made a lot of money, and being very lazy, simply quit, and spent the rest of his life eating and drinking and entertaining his friends. But it wasn't quite so simple as that. In the first place, although he never wrote it, he was planning an opera on the life of Joan of Arc when he left for Bologna. I doubt if he ever decided, at any particular moment, never to write another opera. He himself gave all sorts of explanations for his silence— among them, that the times were too troubled, and that he was too lazy.

But you can't exactly call a man who composes thirty-nine operas in nineteen years, "lazy." If I may make a guess, I think, for one thing, he was secretly disappointed in *William Tell*. Rossini was no fool, musically. He admired Wagner, he venerated Beethoven and Mozart, and he worshiped Bach. He knew great music when he heard it. He must have known that *William Tell* was hardly what the critics said it was—a truly monumental work. He realized, I think, that his true field, as Beethoven had said, was comic opera. And the times were certainly not ripe for comic opera. For another thing, I think he was simply tired out mentally. The strain of writing thirty-nine opera scores must have been terrific. He probably waited for inspiration, and when inspiration failed to arrive, he simply waited until it should arrive. It did arrive, in 1832, long enough for him to compose his *Stabat Mater*. Then, seemingly, it left him again.

Moreover, his health broke down. He seems to have been one of those morbidly sensitive men who try to avoid being hurt by beating everybody to it, by ridiculing themselves before anyone else has the chance. A famous anecdote relates that after the disastrous opening night of *The Barber* his friends, going to his lodgings to offer their condolences, found him already in bed and asleep. That yarn has always been accepted at its face value, and I have no good grounds for questioning its authenticity. It is quite possible that Rossini was so indifferent to the failure of his opera that he could fall peacefully asleep. On the other hand, a man who was so hurt by that failure that he couldn't bear to talk about it, even to his friends, might find it expedient to *pretend* to be asleep.

His laziness, gluttony, avarice, and cynicism were all legends that he started himself, and encouraged. He was not lazy; he was a gourmet, but not a glutton; and while he made and saved money, he was never avaricious; and no composer was ever more generous with encouragement and help for younger musicians. What finally gave way was not his body, but his nerves. The years between 1835 and 1855 were an almost ceaseless and vain search for health. His neurasthenia became so acute that at one time he was thought to be losing his mind. In 1855 he settled permanently in Paris, and in that same year, after taking the waters at Baden, he almost miraculously recovered.

From then on he lived a quiet and happy life. The French government gave him a summer home in Passy, and his musical evenings, in his apartment in town, were one of the features of Paris life. He even resumed composing, turning out a host of little piano and vocal pieces with absurd titles such as *A Little Pleasure Trip on the Train*, *A Word to Paganini*, *The Tortured Waltz*, and *A Hygienic Prelude for Morning Use*. Few of these have ever been published.

In the summer of 1863, when he was seventy-one years old, he composed his last ambitious work, a solemn Mass for orchestra, chorus, and four solo voices. It was first performed at the home of the Countess Pillet-Will, in Paris, on March 14, 1864, where it made a profound impression upon an audience that included Meyerbeer, Auber, and Ambroise Thomas. The original accompaniment was for two pianos and a harmonium, but in 1865 Rossini's friends induced him to score it for orchestra, on the ground that if he didn't, someone else, after his death, certainly would. I heard a performance of it in the spring of 1939, by the Westminster Choir and the New York Philharmonic-Symphony Orchestra. The only adjective for it is "delightful." It is a gay, featherweight little thing, full of charming part-writing and abounding in sparkling tunes in the best vein of *The Barber*—and about as much in the mood of a solemn Mass as *The Mikado*!

After the Mass he wrote only a few small, unimportant pieces. In 1867 his health failed again, and it became evident that he was nearing the end. He died at eleven o'clock on the evening of Friday, the thirteenth of November, 1868. On the twenty-first he was buried in Père-Lachaise cemetery, with all Paris, in fact all Europe, mourning him. Nineteen years later, in 1887, his body was moved from Paris to Italy's Westminster Abbey, the church of the Holy Cross in Florence. And there he lies today.

13

How Spillville Helped

IT IS highly improbable that the name "Spillville" will arouse any particularly vivid musical memories in the breast of my average reader; yet the town of Spillville, Iowa, U.S.A., is closely linked with one of the world's most famous and popular symphonies, and at one time played a very important part in the life of its composer.

Before we go into that, however, suppose we take a long jump across the Atlantic and back to the early middle of the nineteenth century, landing finally in the little town of Nelahozeves in what was then a part of German Austria called Bohemia. (We know it now as the late lamented Czechoslovakia.) One of the best-known citizens of the town was a young man named František Dvořák, who kept an inn and did pork-butchering on the side, and who had recently married the daughter of the manager of one of the big estates in the neighborhood. And there, on the eighth of September, 1841, innkeeper Dvořák served free beer to celebrate the birth of his eldest son. (Children, by the way, were to be no novelty in the life of the Dvořáks. They had eight altogether.)

There is an old Bohemian superstition to the effect that, if you place a silver spoon and a violin on either side of a newborn baby, you can tell what he is going to be. If he reaches for the fiddle, he is going to be a musician; if he reaches for the spoon, he's going to be either a rich man

82

or a thief. Apparently František's new son, whom he named Antonín, avoided both the latter calamities by reaching for the fiddle. At all events, we know that he was honest, that he certainly never became rich, and he did become a musician.

His musical training began early, and more by luck than by design; for it happened that the village schoolmaster, besides being the local repository of book learning, was also a musical Jack-of-all-trades, and had more than a nodding acquaintance with several instruments. Under the guidance of this teacher, whose name was Josef Spitz, the youngster learned to play the violin and the bagpipes, and became rather a local celebrity by playing for village dances and singing solos in church. Meanwhile, the Dvořák family kept growing larger and larger, while the Dvořák income remained stationary. Something had to be done. Finally, when Antonín was twelve, he was shipped off to live with an uncle who was located in a town called Zlonice. Here again he had the luck to attract the attention of the local schoolmaster, who was also the town organist. He realized that the boy had exceptional talent, and taught him the piano, the viola as well as the violin, a bit of musical theory, and also German, which was indispensable for anyone who had hopes of getting anywhere in Austria.

While this was going on his father decided to move the whole family to Zlonice and set up in business there. The business, however, lagged, and Dvořák senior decided that in order to save the wages of an assistant, Antonín must stop his schooling and serve as bar boy. Up to this time no one had suspected that he might have talent as a composer—that is, no one but himself. In the hope of getting away from the pork and hotel business he decided to impress his father with an original composition. The story is that he wrote a polka, orchestrated it, had some of his friends rehearse the instrumental parts separately and in secret, and finally assembled them for the performance that was to dazzle his father. Unfortunately he had neglected to realize that the trumpet is a transposing instrument—that is, an instrument for which, if you want the player to produce the note C, for example, you must write G, or D, or E-flat, depending on the kind of trumpet. But our young hopeful merely wrote the trumpet part in the same key as the violins. Consequently, when the performance finally took place, the orchestra was playing in two keys at once.

His father, ignorant of the fact that his son was merely eighty years ahead of his time, was not impressed. However, his uncle intervened, and finally, in 1856, at the age of fifteen, young Antonín Dvořák was allowed to go off to study at the organ school in Prague, on an allowance of $3.25 a month. Here he studied the organ, and what was more important, got a chance to play the viola in the orchestra of the St. Cecilia Society. What he earned in this way, plus his allowance, raised his income to the dizzy height of $12 a month. When his two years at the organ school were up he decided to strike out for himself, and stayed on at Prague. In '62, his twenty-first year, he got a place among the violas in the orchestra of the National Opera, and found a few private pupils. Incidentally, none of his teachers at Prague seems to have noticed anything unusual about his musical talents; but when he joined the National Orchestra he did meet the conductor, the great Bohemian composer Smetana, who inspired him by his example and also gave him some practical encouragement.

By this time young Dvořák was writing reams of music —chamber music, vocal music, instrumental solos, and symphonies, most of which he later burned. One of his great early influences was Wagner, and his first opera, a piece called *Alfred,* produced in Prague in 1870, was completely Wagnerian. His second effort, a year later, a comic opera entitled *The King and the Coal Dealer,* was much more Dvořák than Wagner. The Opera House offered to produce it, but he wasn't satisfied with it, and took it back for repairs. It was produced finally, first in 1874, then in 1887, and again in 1914, after his death. At no time did it have any great success. As a matter of fact, none of Dvořák's operas (he wrote ten of them) was ever what could be called a smash hit, chiefly by reason of his propensity, which amounted to genius, for picking bad librettos.

In 1873 the half-starved, thirty-two-year-old viola player and music teacher scored his first real success as a composer with his hymn for chorus and orchestra, *The Heirs of the White Mountain.* This was a lament for the disaster that overtook the Bohemians in 1620, when their revolt against Austrian domination was crushed at the battle of the White Mountain. Not only the patriotic nature of the work, but the flavor of the music itself, convinced his fellow countrymen that they had found a new Bohemian national composer.

From that time on Dvořák's artistic career was an ever-increasingly successful one. Financially, he was never a shining success. To give you an idea of his shrewd business sense, he married, in 1873, and deciding that he needed more time for composing, gave up his post at the opera to take a job as church organist at a salary of $1.25 a week. Money, of course, was worth more than it is now, but even so I cannot feel that Dvořák was being overpaid. In 1875 he managed to win a grant of about $165 from the Austrian government. It was good for only one year, but it helped a little, and was particularly important in his career, in that on the committee who had to examine his compositions, in order to see whether he was really deserving of help, were the famous critic Hanslick, and the composer Johannes Brahms. Neither, of course, had any love for Wagner, and they were favorably impressed at the outset by Dvořák's freedom from Wagnerian influences (he had long ago recovered from his attack of Wagnerism). But they were equally impressed by the freshness and individuality of his music. Brahms was especially kind to him, went about trying to get him performances, and put pressure on his own publisher to take some of Dvořák's music. Another good friend and active champion was Hans von Bülow, who conducted much of his music and to whom Dvořák dedicated his Symphony in F. In 1878, thanks to Brahms, the first of his Slavonic Dances were published, in the form of piano duets. He got $75 for them. In '79 he found a new admirer in the great violinist, Joseph Joachim, for whom he wrote a concerto.

In 1884, when he was forty-three, he went abroad for the first time, to London, where he had been invited to conduct his new *Stabat Mater* at Albert Hall. This was the beginning of his tremendous popularity in England, a popularity that still endures. There was hardly a year, from 1885 to 1891, that did not find Dvořák conducting some new work of his at one of the great English festivals.

Then came the great adventure of the National Conservatory in New York. I doubt whether there are many of us who remember Mrs. Jeannette Thurber, more's the pity. She was a great moving force in music here in the eighties and nineties. In 1885 she organized the American Opera Company, with a list of directors whose combined fortunes must have totaled half a billion dollars. She persuaded Theodore Thomas to become conductor of the new company, and proceeded to give two seasons of grand opera, sung in English, in New York, Boston, and other cities, that were a terrific artistic success and—need I add?—a financial disaster. Along with the opera company Mrs. Thurber had founded a National Conservatory—or rather, as she named it, *Conservatoire*—of Music, in New York. When the opera scheme went down with all on board Mrs. Thurber, nothing daunted, kept on with the Conservatory. In 1891 she made her most impressive gesture by inviting Antonín Dvořák to come to New York to be its director. He accepted. I am afraid the salary Mrs. Thurber offered had something to do with the acceptance. It was fifteen thousand dollars a year—and one can only imagine what that must have sounded like to a musician whose annual income had averaged about one twentieth of that sum.

He arrived here late in 1892, and was immediately taken to hear a complimentary concert at which there were a chorus of three hundred, an orchestra of eighty, speeches, and a silver wreath. Then he went to work. As a matter of fact, Dvořák's influence in America was stronger on individuals than it was on American musical life in general. He was not a trained teacher, and he was not an executive. He was, however, a great inspiration and influence for Henry Burleigh, the colored singer and composer, and Rubin Goldmark, the American nephew of the famous Austrian Karl Goldmark.

Dvořák stayed in America two and a half years. In the spring of 1895 he declined the offer of a new contract and sailed back to Europe. His life, thenceforward, was a tranquil and comparatively uneventful one. He died in Prague on the first of May, 1904, at the age of sixty-three.

And where does Spillville come in? Right here. Dvořák suffered desperately from homesickness all the time he was in America. Some friend of his told him that the town of Spillville, Iowa, eleven miles from the railroad, had a large Bohemian colony, and that it was just like home out there. So for two successive years the entire Dvořák family—Papa Dvořák, Mrs. Dvořák, six children, a cousin, a maid, and a secretary, migrated to Spillville, Iowa, to spend the entire summer. There Dvořák was perfectly happy. He played the organ in the village church while his wife sang in the choir; he played string quartets with the village schoolmaster and two of his children; he played the violin, and he inspected farms and barns and pigeon lofts—he was quite a pigeon fancier. Spillville was so proud of him that it named a road after him: the Dvořák Highway.

His famous symphony, *From the New World,* is, as I said at the beginning, closely connected with Spillville; for much of the orchestration of the work was written there. It is not, incidentally, the only music of Dvořák's that was composed and orchestrated in Spillville and elsewhere in America. During his stay here he also wrote his Quintet in E-flat, a piano suite, a sonatina for violin and piano, his Cello Concerto, some of his Biblical songs, and a cantata, *The American Flag*. He thought of writing an opera on the story of Hiawatha, but never got around to it.

But of all the music that he wrote in America, I have not yet named the most popular of all, the one that has made the name "Dvořák" known to millions who otherwise would never have heard of him; a small tune that has been the showpiece of many an infant pianist and embryo violinist. I need hardly add that I refer to Dvořák's *Humoresque.*

14

Branded

SPEAKING of Dvořák, and the remorseless manner in which his footsteps have been dogged by the incorrigible *Humoresque,* have you ever been struck by the fact that so many composers owe much of their fame, at least among the nonprofessional musical public, to isolated small works that are by no means their best? A composer writes a song or a short instrumental piece that happens to strike popular fancy, regardless of its actual musical merits, and is instantly doomed to wear that albatross around his neck, not only for the rest of his life, but even after he is dead. Ravel is another of the prize examples, with his *Bolero.* It's a brilliant, entertaining piece, not to be compared, however, with the *Daphnis and Chloë* suite, or the G major Piano Concerto, or half a dozen other works. Yet I think it's safe to say that literally millions of people who had never heard of Ravel before he wrote the *Bolero* now know him by that piece, and that piece alone. Almost offhand I can think of nearly a dozen other composers who are similarly tagged. Sibelius, for example, is famous, not for the Fourth Symphony, or even *Finlandia,* but for the *Valse triste.*

To millions of people the name Beethoven means— what? The Fifth Symphony? No, the Minuet in G. Out of all of Schubert's immortal songs, the general public had to pick one of the least important, the *Serenade,* as their favorite. Brahms means his *Cradle Song*; Schumann, *Träumerei*. Chopin has two trade-marks, I should say: the E-flat Nocturne and what is known as "the" funeral march. Among a few comparatively advanced music lovers the name of Edward Elgar is associated with the *Enigma* Variations, or *The Dream of Gerontius*. But if you want to know the piece for which he is really famous, go to almost any restaurant and hear the five-piece orchestra play his *Salut d'amour*. Mention Debussy's *Les Sirènes* or the *Ibéria* suite to the average person, and he never heard of them. But he probably does know the *Golliwog's Cake-Walk*.

Among living composers, the one who has probably suffered more real mental anguish over being thus hag-ridden is Sergei Rachmaninoff. I happen to know the intensity of remorse that he feels over having composed the C-sharp minor Prelude. It really hurts him to hear it. I once heard him say, piteously, to John McCormack, the great tenor, "John, *why* do they play that piece? Dot iss bod music!"

And then there is Wagner. One might think that his most famous composition would be something from *Die Meistersinger,* or *Tristan,* or *The Ring*. But it isn't. It is a piece that you will hear this month, and the next, and the next, played in almost any church, at almost any hour of almost any day. I often wonder how marriages could have been legal before Wagner wrote the *Lohengrin* "Wedding March." And then, of course, after the bride has been safely married, she comes up the aisle to the strains of another march that is responsible for keeping alive the name of Felix Mendelssohn.

15

Finders, Keepers

IF YOU have ever heard Balakireff's tone poem, *Thamar*, you may have noticed that in several places it bears a strong family resemblance to Rimsky-Korsakoff's *Scheherazade*. One passage irresistibly suggests the "sea" theme in the latter work, while another is very close to the "young prince" episode. If it were not for the fact that Balakireff was Rimsky-Korsakoff's teacher, and that *Thamar* was composed in 1881, while *Scheherazade* was not written until 1888, one might be tempted to accuse Balakireff of stealing Rimsky's stuff. Take another, a historic example of similarity. You are probably familiar with the broad, hymnlike passage that is the second theme of the last movement of Brahms's First Symphony. Now the second part of that passage is, for four bars, practically note for note the theme of the second half of the *Ode to Joy* that closes Beethoven's Ninth. The legend is that at the final rehearsal of the Brahms First, a wealthy young musical amateur who prided himself on his musical knowledge hurried up to Brahms, who had been conducting, and pointed out the reminiscence. What Brahms said—I shall tell you later.

There are plenty of such resemblances in music. To name two or three out of hundreds, the first few bars of the overture to *The Bartered Bride* bear an astonishing resemblance to the first few bars of the opening of

Madame Butterfly—possibly we'd better put it the other way around, since *The Bartered Bride* came first. In an ode written by Henry Purcell in 1682 there is a passage that is almost identical with a passage in the overture to Wagner's *Die Meistersinger*. The first notes of the themes of the Prize Song from *Die Meistersinger*, of Schumann's *Lied der Braut*, Opus 25, No. 11, and the slow movement of the Ninth Symphony are identical. The second half of the Habanera from *Carmen*, of one of MacDowell's *Sea Pieces*, and a song from Victor Herbert's *It Happened in Nordland*, have a theme that is, note for note, the same in all three. The third act of Puccini's *La Bohème* begins with a passage that is just like a passage in Giordano's *Andrea Chénier*.

As I say, there are dozens of these similarities. We all have our pet lists, and we call them anything from unconscious emulation to plagiarism. Just what is plagiarism? The dictionary defines "to plagiarize" as "to steal or purloin and pass off as one's own the ideas, words, artistic productions, etc., of another; to use without due credit the ideas, expressions, or productions of another."

That sounds simple and clear enough. Plagiarism is a sort of intellectual pocket-picking; and applying the dictionary definition strictly, we now discover that Rimsky-Korsakoff stole from Balakireff, that Puccini robbed Smetana, that Brahms cribbed from Beethoven, that Wagner picked Purcell's pocket, and that Wagner, Schumann, and Beethoven, and Bizet, MacDowell, and Victor Herbert, all stole from one another.

So far, so good. But wait a minute. In the eighteenth century nobody worried about such stealing. Handel, for instance, not only appropriated other people's themes, but sometimes stole entire tunes from other composers, and was never even indicted, let alone convicted. Well, we say, that shows that our standards of artistic morality are higher than they were in the eighteenth century.

But granted even that, here is another complication. While, theoretically, it is very immoral to steal a theme or a tune from a composer who can be identified, it is not only respectable, but positively praiseworthy to steal a theme from a composer whose identity is unknown. For instance: we talk of Brahms's Hungarian Dances and Liszt's Hungarian Rhapsodies. The "rhapsody" part is all right, but neither Brahms nor Liszt made up the tunes on which the dances and rhapsodies are based. Those are Hungarian gypsy tunes that existed long before Brahms or Liszt was born. The great Coronation Scene in Moussorgsky's *Boris Godunoff* is built on a traditional Russian hymn tune that is centuries old. (Beethoven used the same theme in one of his Rasoumovsky string quartets.) In fact the score of *Boris* is about one half Russian folk songs. So is the score of Stravinsky's *Petrushka*. The Coachmen's Dance, for instance, is a Russian folk song called *Down Saint Peter's Road*. The lovely theme of the *Andante cantabile* of Tchaikovsky's string quartet is a Russian peasant song, the words of which begin, "Little Ivan sat on a divan." The main theme of the finale of his Fourth Symphony is a Russian folk song called *The Little Duck in the Meadow*. The Grail theme in *Parsifal* is a traditional German amen, known as the Dresden Amen. Roy Harris writes an orchestral piece on a tune we all know, *When Johnny Comes Marching Home;* and Bizet builds one of the most popular movements of his *L'Arlésienne* suite on an old French folk song known as *The March of the Kings*. I could go on indefinitely listing this sort of borrowings. The interesting feature of them is that the appropriation was made without apology or attempt at concealment, and no critic would dream of accusing the composers of plagiarism. Quite the contrary.

Apropos of that attitude of music critics, I cannot resist the temptation to be autobiographical in order to illustrate it. When the Metropolitan produced my opera, *Peter Ibbetson,* some years ago, one critic—among others, I might add—found very little of merit in the score. That is putting it very mildly. I can't remember the entire list of the composers from whom he said the music was stolen, but it included Puccini, Massenet, Wagner, Debussy, and, if memory serves, Johann Strauss, to say nothing of Richard. In short, his verdict was that the only discernable merit in the score was my treatment of certain old French folk songs, "particularly the lovely old *Dors, Mignonne.*" Now it is quite true that I had employed a number of French folk songs in the score. In one scene in particular, I needed a folk song of a certain character, and couldn't find one that exactly filled the bill. So I invented my own folk song, including the words; and by a deplorable coincidence, that song, *Dors, Mignonne,* happened to be the one that he singled out for special commendation. In other words, the only music of mine that he liked, because it had not been borrowed from a known composer, was something that he thought I had stolen from an *unknown* composer.

Well, now that we have complicated the puzzle as much as possible, just what is the answer? Is Brahms a plagiarist when he writes a theme that Beethoven had already written? And if he is, isn't Tchaikovsky no less a plagiarist when he uses a theme that was invented by some unknown Russian peasant? And if they are, why don't we point the finger of scorn at them? And since we do nothing of the sort, why are we so very scornful when we discover that the popular song, *I'm Always Chasing Rainbows,* is a direct quotation of part of Chopin's C-sharp minor *Fantasie-Impromptu*? Just what *is* plagiarism?

The answer is not simple. The dictionary definition won't do, for it leaves out too many qualifying considerations. Perhaps the best way to approach the solution of the problem is to begin by realizing that we're very childish in our notions as to what constitutes originality in music. We're much more intelligent and grown up in our judgment of plays, for instance. Suppose a play should open tomorrow in which one of the actors had the line, "Now go to the door and stay there till we call." How many dramatic critics would point out that it was a direct steal from Shakespeare? But it is. It's straight out of the first scene of the third act of *Macbeth*. If a new symphony contained that much of a quotation from Beethoven or Wagner, the music critics would jump all over the composer.

Suppose a young playwright wrote a play in which a young man, talking to a friend of his, should say, "You know, I'm in such a state that I often think of committing suicide. As a matter of fact, the only thing that stops me from killing myself is the thought that, bad as things are, I've no idea whether I'd be better off, dead, or worse." Would the dramatic critics point out that this was obviously a barefaced steal from Hamlet's soliloquy, thinly disguised by being written in prose form? I doubt it.

How much fuss was made over the fact that the essential plot of *Abie's Irish Rose* was little more than the essential plot of *Romeo and Juliet*? Why not? Because we are mature enough, in our judgment of literature and the drama, to realize that a plot, an idea, is not *necessarily* important in itself; that the supply of original ones has long ago been exhausted, and that what matters is what an author or a playwright *does* with his plot or idea, how he develops it.

Take a literary example. The idea back of George du Maurier's novel, *Peter Ibbetson,* is probably as near to a brand-new, original story as the world has seen in a long time. Now Rudyard Kipling took the identical idea—that of a man and woman being able to meet, in their dreams, when their actual selves were far separated from each other—and wrote the story that is called *The Brushwood Boy.* Does anyone accuse Kipling of having stolen Du Maurier's idea? No. Why? Because what Kipling did with that idea was far different from what Du Maurier did with it. The fact that *Peter Ibbetson* is utterly Du Maurier's doesn't alter the fact that *The Brushwood Boy* is utterly Kipling's.

But in music we are still in the tune-detective stage. We've all done it. I've been a music critic, and I've certainly done enough of it in my time. It is very hard to resist the temptation to do it. When you point out that five notes in the second movement of Blank's new symphony are identical with five notes in Bach's B minor Mass, it proves to your astounded readers that you're a profound musical scholar, blessed with a prodigious musical memory and with the entire literature of music at your finger tips. At least, that is what you subconsciously assume that it proves. What it *doesn't* prove is whether Blank's new symphony is good or not.

I think there are three things that we must take into consideration in deciding whether or not one piece of music has been stolen from another. The first is that the alphabet of the language of music is exactly half the size of the alphabet of the English language. Our scale contains twelve notes; and out of various combinations of these twelve all music has been evolved. Musicians haven't even the advantage of being able to express themselves in different languages. There is only one language for all the musicians in the world. Consequently there are certain conventional turns of musical expression—the ifs, ands, therefores, and buts, so to speak—that are virtually unavoidable. Find one of these that has been stolen from Brahms, and you will find likewise that Brahms stole it from Beethoven, who stole it from Mozart, who stole it from Haydn, who stole it from Bach, and so on, back to the Pharaohs. Take the perfect cadence, for example, the resolution from the dominant to the tonic, that finishes more than half the music ever written. It's an extreme example, perhaps, but it will illustrate what I mean. The perfect cadence is like a period at the end of a sentence, and as a rule, when a composer tries to avoid it, he succeeds only in making it obvious that he *is* trying to avoid it.

The second consideration is the defendant's character and past history. Has he given any evidence of being able to think up themes on his own account? Sometimes that past history will be enough to convict him. When some obscure composer who has never succeeded in writing a bar of music that was of any particular interest to anybody turns out a piece in which there are eight notes that more or less duplicate something by Strauss or Debussy, we're quite justified in the suspicion that the resemblance is something more than just a coincidental meeting of two great creative minds. On the other hand, when we find Wagner, Schumann, and Beethoven all beginning a theme with the same sequence of notes, the countless evidences those men have given us of their real inventive genius compel us to conclude that the resemblance *is* a coincidence. Three great men happened to think alike about something.

I promised to tell you Brahms's reply when the similarity between his First and Beethoven's Ninth was pointed out. The reply was, *"Dass kennt jeder Esel!"*—Any ass knows that. I think I know what he meant. He was referring to the third thing we have to take into account before reaching a verdict. And it's the most important one: what has the composer *done* with his borrowed idea? Now in the field of popular music there is a great deal of very real plagiarism; for a popular tune is nothing *but* an idea. It is not put through any transformations or development. It lasts eight, sixteen, or twenty-four bars, and that's the end of it. Consequently, when somebody else appropriates it bodily, he is, definitely, stealing. I know of one popular composer, rather notorious for the haunting sense of familiarity that most of his tunes convey, of whom one of his colleagues remarked that "So-and-so writes the kind of music that people whistle as they go *into* the theater." When we find that *Chasing Rainbows* is identical with the C-sharp minor

Fantaisie-Impromptu, we are justified in scowling at it, because the composer of the former did nothing more with the tune than Chopin did. Not as much in fact.

But when we get into the field of symphonic music we must step a bit more carefully. Brahms was quite right in being indifferent to the fact that his theme was like Beethoven's. Why? Because what Brahms did with that theme was quite different from what Beethoven had done with it. Borrowed or not, it was Brahms. Brahms's Hungarian Dances may be based on gypsy airs, but what he does with them is something that no Hungarian gypsy ever did or could do. That is why we don't criticize composers for using folk music as the raw material of their works. What Stravinsky, and Bizet, and Moussorgsky, and Humperdinck do with peasant music is something that no peasant could conceivably do with it. Under their hands it becomes something new, and eloquent, something entirely their own. As a matter of fact, I have an idea that to a great composer any given theme is not nearly so important as we assume. The supreme illustration of this is Beethoven. Take the opening theme of the Fifth Symphony. What is it? It is two bars long, and consists of three repeated G's and an E-flat. Can you imagine giving that theme to an average composer and saying to him, "Out of these four notes I want you to build a large part of the first movement of one of the world's great symphonies"? He'd say you were crazy. And you would be— for picking the wrong composer.

A great work of musical art is like a cathedral—something built out of the mind, the imagination, and the spirit. It may be built of brick, like the Frauenkirche in Munich, or of limestone, like Notre-Dame de Paris. The material is not of primary importance. And neither, I am afraid, is it supremely important whether its builder quarried the material himself, or bought it, or stole it. What we ask, concerning him, is not "Where did he get it?" but "What did he do with it?"

16

Guest Speaker

Speaking of stealing things, this particular chapter is largely the work of Fraser Macdonald of Lacombe, Alberta, Canada. I have never met Mr. Macdonald, and he does not know that he is writing this chapter. The one that precedes it, the one concerning plagiarism, was originally delivered as an intermission talk during one of the New York Philharmonic-Symphony broadcast concerts. What follows is taken from a letter that I received from Mr. Macdonald, in which he commented upon my remarks. His own are so pertinent, and so well expressed, that I appropriate them herewith, with no scruples—or hardly any.

"You were saying, in effect," he writes, "that we tend to worry too much about the originality of a tune, and that we are quick to shout 'plagiarist' over the shadow of a likeness between two melodies. I not only agree with you, but I would go even further. Don't you think there is too much attention paid to the composer and not enough to the composition? That is to say, don't we too often listen to the man who wrote the music instead of to the music that he wrote? In short, don't we make too much of so-called originality? Instead of asking, 'Is this good?' we ask, 'Is this original?' Nor do I restrict the meaning of originality to the chance likeness of a tune; do we not insist too much on a composer's having a wholly original style?

"The early work of every composer is dismissed because it sounds like the music of some other composer whom he in his youthful ardor admired. Wagner's opera, *Die Feen,* was laughed out of rehearsal once because it sounded so much like Bellini; and I can appreciate the humor of the situation. Yet what if *Die Feen* were passed off as a genuine work of Bellini? Would it be so funny then? If the attitude we take toward a piece of music depends only upon our knowledge of who the composer is, then there is something wrong somewhere.

"Mind you," Mr. Macdonald continues, "I can't pretend to be free from such extra-musical influences myself; but I don't always claim that a bad habit is a good one just because I share it. For instance, if I thought that Stravinsky had written his *Piano Rag-music* as a satire on jazz, I might find it funny. But knowing, from his autobiography, that he took it seriously, I find the music painfully bad—and I am usually a Stravinsky cheer-leader! Incidentally, I've heard Stravinsky's own *Firebird* dismissed lightly as resembling Rimsky-Korsakoff in style. Which it undoubtedly does. But that doesn't make it any the less good music.

"And since we're on the subject of Stravinsky, do you not think that his *Apollo Musagètes* music might have succeeded if it had been composed by almost anyone else but the composer of *Petrushka?* Personally, I think it is one of the most beautiful things he has written. That it has little in common with the Stravinsky of *Petrushka, The Firebird,* and *The Rite of Spring* does not make it any the less beautiful. Yet I am aware that more than one listener has been left cold by the music. But what if—excluding the coda, of course—what if it had been passed off as the work of an eighteenth-century composer? As a matter of fact, the music of Purcell leaves me a little bit cold, too, although for some reason or other I would like very much to love it. Handel, too, has his cold side—but we don't call this cold in Quebec. We call it classicism. But because Stravinsky is an ultra-modernist who wrote a tremendous drama called *The Rite of Spring*, his *Apollo Musagètes* is condemned as the mistake of a composer who ought to keep on turning out *Petrushka*s.

"Too often one hears it said: 'This early work by X is important because it bears traces of his later style.' If a piece of music is good only because it bears an occasional likeness to something that its composer wrote later in life, then the piece is not good. A few years ago the Philharmonic-Symphony broadcast some excerpts from Wagner's *The Flying Dutchman*. As I remember the commentator's remarks,* we were given to understand that here was a curiosity from the early life of Richard Wagner—the equivalent of one of his baby pictures—that was, nevertheless, interesting because traces of the later Wagner were to be found in it. Well, believe it or not, I found *The Flying Dutchman* enjoyable music all on its own. If I got any coldly intellectual thrill out of it, it was because of its very lack of the usual Wagnerisms. I found that interesting. I like the later Wagner, too; but I'm not exclusive.

"It is true" (this is still Mr. Macdonald) "that when a composer reveals an attractive personality through his

* It wasn't I, please.—D. T.

music we look for that personality in his music. Brahms is an example. I like typically Brahmsian music just because it *is* typically Brahms. But, to find Brahms's early music interesting solely because of the occasional trace of the more familiar older Brahms is not only unfair to the composer but is also to miss the real enjoyment of the music itself.

"This prejudice, which elevates the creator at the expense of his creation, is also manifest when it comes to the question of the transcription of works. Bach, for instance. We hear a very free orchestration of a Bach organ prelude, or violin sonata, and at once become very worried about what Bach would have thought of it. Some cry, 'a desecration!' Its defenders reply, 'Bach would have done it like that if he had lived today.' Both sides are more worried about a dead composer than they are about living music. What if it isn't played exactly as Bach wrote it? So long as it is not worse than he wrote it, what does it matter? Perhaps a composer should know best how his own music should sound. As a matter of fact, does he, always?"

At this point, if I may interrupt Mr. Macdonald a moment, I should say that a composer emphatically does *not* always know best how his own music should sound. A talent for interpretation and performance does not necessarily go hand in hand with creative genius. Many of Tchaikovsky's finest orchestral works, for example, received their first performance under the conductorship of the composer himself; and it is notorious that many of them made a very poor first impression, and were not fully appreciated until they had escaped from Tchaikovsky's hands and had been played under the leadership of more talented conductors. I have heard Richard Strauss conduct performances of his own works that obscured many of his finest pages.

The trouble with the composer as an interpreter of his own work is that his mind is so saturated with what he meant us to hear that his imagination tends automatically to disregard the shortcomings of his own performance, or of his own interpretation. Sometimes he begins a composition with the idea of saying one thing, and sends it out into the world utterly unconscious of the fact that he has ended up by saying something quite different. To cite a very small and homely example: anyone who has ever heard Dvořák's *Humoresque* played in the fast tempo that he marked it to be played will agree, I think, that it is a different and far better piece of music when it is played in the slow tempo that Fritz Kreisler has made so familiar. It took Kreisler to show us that, whereas Dvořák thought he was writing a light, gay piece of music, he was actually writing a nocturne.

But to get back to Mr. Macdonald's letter. "Another thing," he writes, "—and this goes back to a previous remark of your own. You said that if a tenth symphony of Beethoven's were found, and palmed off on the world as the work of a modern composer, it would not be accepted by the critics as good, for the simple reason that it would not be written in the present-day idiom. I believe that that is an accurate prediction of what would happen. But is it just? If a modern composer were to write that symphony, and—just to reverse the situation—succeeded in imitating Beethoven's style so perfectly that he was able to pass it off as a newly discovered tenth symphony by that composer, would it be accepted by the critics as a masterpiece, and pass into the concert repertoire? Assuming that it was not only a good imitation but a good symphony as well, it undoubtedly would."

Again I interrupt Mr. Macdonald to point out that just that did happen, only a few years ago. For years Fritz Kreisler used to include on his programs short violin pieces that bore the names of little-known eighteenth-century composers. The public adored them, other violinists eagerly included them in their programs, and most of the professional critics agreed that they were charming, and that Mr. Kreisler had displayed excellent judgment and taste in restoring them to the violin repertoire. Then, not long ago, Mr. Kreisler calmly revealed the fact that all these pieces were his own compositions. He had written them for his own enjoyment, and considered them worth playing in public. On the other hand, he had no desire to have his name appear as a composer two or three times on every program, so he hit on the idea of ascribing their origin to other composers.

The yell of rage that went up from the critics and professional musicians was something that, to me, was very funny. They couldn't very well get around the fact that they had pronounced the pieces good; so they ignored that point, and comforted themselves by getting purple in the face and accusing Kreisler of being a forger, a liar, and a swindler, a traitor to his profession, a man who had deliberately set out to make fools of his colleagues. Well, in one sense, he did make fools of them; but only as experts, not as musicians. They had said the pieces were good, and they *were* good; and the fact that the wrong names were on them always seemed to me to be something that concerned only autograph collectors. I always wondered why, instead of losing their tempers, some of them didn't go about boasting of their ability to spot good music when they heard it. I might add that the pieces are now published under Kreisler's name, and the general public still happily listens to them.

And, as Mr. Macdonald goes on to say, "Once more we are letting our knowledge of the facts interfere with our enjoyment of pure music, which should be—because it is—independent of the facts of this world. Just as the enjoyment of a tune because of the associations it arouses is not the same as enjoying the tune because of its own merits. It is true that the former is very potent, and is a legitimate enjoyment, providing we don't claim to be enjoying it for the latter reason. The extra-musical facts can be highly interesting. But it is not right to confuse that interest with the enjoyment of music for its own sake."

It is hardly necessary to say that I agree wholeheartedly with Mr. Macdonald's plea that we listen to music for what it is, and not for what we know about it. Not that I think that is easy to do. In fact, I know of nothing in the world more difficult than to form a wholly unbiased opinion of anything. We are all of us influenced by those "extra-musical" facts that Mr. Macdonald mentions, by associations of ideas, and by the pressure of other people's opinions. You hear "taps," for instance, played on a bugle. Now I defy you, unless you never heard it before in your life, not to have your mood influenced by your knowledge that "taps" is played at bedtime and over the graves of dead soldiers. As a matter of cold musical fact, "taps" is no better or more eloquent music than is the dinner call. But your subconscious mind refuses to believe that. You hear a piece of music with the name

"Beethoven" attached to it, and against your will you are likely to hear it with a biased mind. If you're a Beethoven lover, you are anxious to find it good; if you don't like Beethoven, you are bored before you hear it. In neither case are you doing what I should call pure listening.

Eugene Goossens tells a story of a wealthy English musical amateur who had aspirations towards being a conductor. So he hired the Queen's Hall Orchestra and started rehearsing a program. The rehearsal didn't go very well, and after an hour or so both conductor and orchestra were pretty irritable. Finally the timpani player, completely befuddled by the conductor's rather vague beat, anticipated a cue by sixteen bars, and in the midst of a quiet passage suddenly came in—bang, crash, boom! —with a fortissimo roll on the kettledrum. Whereupon the conductor, in a rage, threw down his baton, glared at the orchestra, and demanded, "Now, who did that?"

That is what we all want to know. We no sooner hear a piece of music than we want to know who wrote it. If it has peculiarities of style that suggest, say, Strauss or Debussy, we aren't happy until we find out whether it really *is* by Strauss or Debussy, or by someone else; and not until we do find out are we quite sure whether we like it or not. I'm always a little bothered by the attitude of two or three of my friends who are experts in antique furniture. When they see a chair or a table in a shop window or an auction room, their first question is not, "Is it beautiful," but "Is it genuine?" They have some right on their side, of course, because they are also asking a commercial question that has nothing to do with art. But we take the same attitude regarding music; and we shouldn't. It's the attitude of a stamp collector. When you or I hear a piece of unfamiliar music, we ought to have the courage to say, "I like it," even if it is signed, Anonymous; and if we don't like it, we should have the courage to say that, too, even if it is signed, jointly, by Bach, Beethoven, and Brahms.

17

What Makes it Tick

A<small>N</small> <small>ENGINEER</small> writes: "Everyone is interested in the question of 'what makes it tick,' regardless of the subject. Also some of us, who are blessed—or cursed—with a mechanical mind, are likewise interested in the method of making the parts that do the ticking. What is the procedure followed by a composer in producing a symphony, an opera, or, in fact, any representative composition? Does he make a preliminary survey of the route as an engineer would do with a proposed road, mapping its various windings by scoring them, and then work out the orchestral embellishments? Or does he comprehend his work in its entirety? In other words, did Wagner score the music of The Forest Murmurs from *Siegfried* as he wrote it, or was the beautiful background laid in afterward, much as a painter fills in the background of his canvas?"

Well, that is a broad question that cannot be answered in precise terms, because no two composers work exactly alike, just as no two painters or poets work alike. But there are certain general methods of composition that have been followed, I think, by most composers, both of the past and the present. First of all, of course, the composer must have a theme. As to how he gets it, let me quote a brilliant contemporary American composer, Aaron

Copland, on the subject. In his valuable little book, *What to Listen for in Music,* Mr. Copland writes:

Every composer begins with a musical idea—a *musical* idea, you understand, not a mental, literary, or extramusical idea. Suddenly a theme comes to him (theme is used as synonymous with musical idea). The composer starts with his theme; and the theme is a gift from Heaven. He doesn't know where it comes from—has no control over it. It comes almost like automatic writing. That's why he keeps a book, very often, and writes themes down whenever they come. He collects musical ideas. You can't do anything about that element of composing. The idea itself may come in various forms. It may come as a melody—just a one-line simple melody which you might hum to yourself. Or it may come to the composer as a melody with accompaniment. At times he may not even hear a melody; he may simply conceive an accompaniment figure to which a melody will probably be added later. Or, on the other hand, the theme may take the form of a purely rhythmic idea. He hears a particular kind of drumbeat, and that will be enough to start him off. Over it he will soon begin hearing an accompaniment and melody.

Now having acquired his theme, or themes, in the manner described by Mr. Copland, what does the composer do then?—assuming, that is, that he is writing something more ambitious than a song or an etude, which is simply written through at one or more sittings. Suppose he is working on a symphony. Generally speaking, he does exactly what my correspondent suggests: he makes a preliminary survey of the ground he intends to cover. He goes to work very much, in fact, as a dramatist does. Structure is as important in music as it is in a play—the length of a given movement—or act—the alternation of moods, the gradual working to a climax in each movement, and beyond that, the working to one main climax of the entire play or symphony. In other words, our composer probably makes a rough sketch of the entire structure of his work, indicating his themes rather than working them out, before he proceeds to the development of his ideas. Once he is sure that the general skeleton of his symphony is properly constructed, then he does begin to work it out, one movement at a time. It's safe to say that a composer hardly ever orchestrates as he goes along. There are too many technical details to work out—the transpositions of the various instruments, the limitations of their registers, the necessity for giving wind players time to breathe, and for string players to put on and take off mutes—a thousand small mechanical problems that would interfere with his perspective on the music as a whole if he tried to solve them as he went along. To do so would be like trying to paint a house while you were building it.

On the other hand, I think most composers do have a distinct impression of the general *sound* of the orchestra as they are writing. Wagner once said that he never conceived a theme without hearing its orchestral color simultaneously; but that doesn't mean that he wrote down the orchestration as he worked out the theme. He did what most composers do—wrote a sort of extended piano sketch, on two, three, or half a dozen staves, indicating the movement of the various instrumental voices without necessarily deciding at the moment just what the instruments were to be. Only in solo passages would he be specific, in writing his orchestral sketch. To use an architectural comparison again, a composer may write "brass," "woodwind," "strings," and so forth, opposite a given passage in his sketch, just as an architect may write "stone," "metal," "wood," on *his* sketch, without stopping to decide whether the metal should be copper or steel or bronze.

I should say that, assuming the vitality and significance of his musical ideas, the composer's most important—though not necessarily his hardest—work is the work he puts in on his structural sketch; for if the general proportions of his symphony, its length, its interrelation of movements, and its climaxes, are not right, his symphony will be a failure. His hardest work, mentally and spiritually, is the working out of the tonal fabric, of the flesh and blood, so to speak, that goes over his skeleton—the music as it comes to the listener. The most tedious, and yet the most fascinating, part of his work is the orchestration. Tedious, because of the thousands of notes that he must put down on paper, and fascinating because it makes no demands upon his creative powers, and yet challenges his ingenuity and powers of invention.

. . . No, I was too hasty. The hardest work comes last: getting somebody to play it.

18

Music à la Carte

As far back as the late nineteen-twenties the, German composer Paul Hindemith and some of his followers announced that from now on composers must write what they termed *Gebrauchsmusik*—that is, "useful," or "utility," music; music that is a part of everyday life, to be composed, not for the sake of what it can say, as music, but to be an accompaniment either to some useful occupation or some other contemporary art form. For instance, the director of a gymnasium wants some rhythmic instrumental piece to help his pupils keep time in their setting-up exercises. So he comes to you, or Mr. Hindemith, or myself, and says, "I want four dozen bars of assorted gymnastic music by next Thursday, please. I'll give you a dollar a bar." So we sit down on Wednesday morning at nine o'clock, and by five we've turned out the required forty-eight bars, wrapped them up, and delivered them to the trade entrance of the gymnasium. Now that is *Gebrauchsmusik*—and don't think that what I have just written is meant as a burlesque. On the contrary, it is a pretty accurate illustration of what Hindemith means. He himself calls himself a craftsman, not an artist, and goes on to say that "a composer should never write unless he is acquainted with the demand for his work. The times of consistent composing for one's own satisfaction are probably gone forever."

Now of course, the second part of that statement, taken at its face value, is nonsense. Any composer who gets no satisfaction or pleasure out of his own output has no right to call himself even a craftsman, because he is probably a poor one. I know of no really competent worker in any trade or profession who doesn't enjoy at least doing a good job. Ask any first-rate carpenter whether he doesn't enjoy turning out a really fine dovetail joint, or a perfectly fitting mortise-and-tenon job. Ask a shoe manufacturer, or a maker of automobiles, if he doesn't derive great pleasure just in looking at his product. A composer who doesn't write for his own pleasure isn't likely to give much pleasure to anybody else. Besides, music isn't a *useful* commodity. If it's any kind, it comes under the head of luxury goods; and articles of luxury always serve an esthetic, as well as a utilitarian, purpose. For instance, you buy a pair of dancing shoes. They must, of course, serve the utilitarian purpose of keeping your stockinged feet from coming into direct contact with the ground. But it's equally important that they be beautiful shoes. If they are not, you don't buy them. On the other hand—or foot, rather, you buy a pair of shoes for heavy farmwork, and all you ask of them is that they be durable, heavy, and waterproof. You don't care whether they're ugly or not. Now music is like dancing shoes. It isn't enough that the forty-eight bars you write for the gymnasium class be written in strict time. They must also possess some element of interest in themselves. Otherwise, just a drum would be better, because it's easier to keep time to pure rhythm than to rhythm adulterated with something that merely distracts your attention without holding your interest.

The first part of Mr. Hindemith's statement is a little sounder, I think—that "a composer should never write unless he is acquainted with the demand for his work." Taken literally, of course, it hardly needs answering; for if it had always held good, if composers had always written *only* to meet a demand, we should lack about three fourths of the world's literature of music, including, among hundreds of others, Beethoven's symphonies, Brahms's, most of Debussy, and all of Wagner.

On the other hand, *Gebrauchsmusik* in its widest sense is by no means the novelty that Mr. Hindemith seems to think it is. We owe the existence of many great musical works to the fact that their composers had customers who ordered them.

Haydn, for example. For nearly thirty years he was musical director on the estate of Prince Nikolaus Esterházy. The Prince had a private chapel and a private theater, and devoted special days and special hours to operatic, orchestral, and chamber music. He maintained a private orchestra and a private company of Italian opera singers. Haydn's duties were not only to take general charge of this formidable music plant, but to provide a great deal of the music that it played and sang. And in these surroundings and under these circumstances he turned out a large proportion of his hundred and twenty-five symphonies, his numerous operas, his forty-five instrumental trios, and his eighty string quartets. When his patron died, and he was thrown more or less on his own resources, much of his income was still derived from music that he wrote to order for other patrons.

Bach is an earlier example. He was successively official organist at the court of the Duke of Weimar and cantor of St. Thomas's School in Leipzig, and at both places, he, too, was expected to compose much of the music that he directed and played. To that fact we owe many of his greatest organ and choral works. To a request from the Margrave of Brandenburg we owe the six great *concerti grossi* that still help to perpetuate his name.

Mozart was another who wrote to order. While he was in the service of the Archbishop of Salzburg he wrote for his ecclesiastical patron something like seven symphonies, five Masses, and a vast number of smaller choral and instrumental pieces. He composed his Requiem Mass to order for a customer who wanted to have it performed as his own composition.

Beethoven worked more as he pleased, partly because of his intensely individualistic temperament, and also because he found it possible to make a living without taking a regular position as choirmaster or musical director. Even so, had it not been for specific commissions from Prince Lichnowsky and Count Razumovsky, it is debatable whether or not his greatest string quartets would ever have been written.

Brahms wrote at least one important work, if not exactly to order, at least for a special occasion. When he was offered his degree of doctor of music by the University of Breslau, he simply mailed his thanks on a postcard. One of his friends remonstrated with him, pointing out that under the circumstances something a little more elaborate might fairly be expected of him. So he wrote the *Academic Festival Overture* in acknowledgment of the honor.

Tchaikovsky wrote very little to definite order. His only notable piece of *Gebrauchsmusik* is his "1812"

Overture, written for the consecration of a cathedral in Moscow. Opinions differ as to the merits of this piece. At least we know what the composer thought of it, from a letter he wrote to Mme von Meck, in which he says: "The overture will be very showy and noisy, but will have no artistic merit because I wrote it without warmth and without love." Incidentally, anyone who happens not to be passionately fond of the "1812" Overture might hold it up to Mr. Hindemith as an example of what happens when a composer isn't writing for his own satisfaction.

The most conspicuous example of *Gebrauchsmusik* in our times is the work of Igor Stravinsky. The ballets by which he has become world-famous, and which seem likely to prove the most viable—that is, *The Firebird, The Rite of Spring, Petrushka,* and *Les Noces*—were all written expressly for the great ballet impresario Diaghileff, and it is highly improbable that they would have been written without him. To Diaghileff also we owe the existence of *Daphnis and Chloë,* one of Ravel's finest scores.

Just what do we find from these examples, a few out of many others that I could cite? First, that at all times, composers of music, even the world's greatest, have been opportunists, have written music, not always from an inner compulsion, but in response to a demand from the outside. Score one for the Hindemith side. But we also find that the limitations placed upon these composers were those of *medium* and general *form,* not of material or musical content. The patron of one of these men said to him, in effect, "See here. I have a quartet of string players; I have a mixed choir; I have a small chamber orchestra; I have a symphony orchestra; I have an organ.

I need some music for these instruments and musicians to play. Will you write it for me?" Or, if he didn't say that, he said, "I have a special occasion that I wish to celebrate with music. Will you help me celebrate it?" He made no attempt to dictate the kind of music he wanted, except as its form was determined by the resources at his command. One other thing: the music was ordered, and written, *as music,* for its own sake. The special groups for which it was written were musical groups. They existed solely for the purpose of making music, and the people who gathered together to hear them play that music gathered for no other purpose. I don't say that they thought of nothing else, that they listened with concentrated attention to every measure, that they didn't occasionally whisper or cough. Audiences in those days were probably about as human as audiences are today. But with all their shortcomings, they did give the music a hearing. So, in the sense that Mr. Hindemith means, you cannot say that there was any such thing as "utility" music in those days.

Is there any now? Unfortunately, yes. To say that I disagree bitterly with Mr. Hindemith's whole idea of writing music for more or less utilitarian purposes does not say that such music is not being written. I can cite you two examples. One is the field of motion pictures. Do you ever go to see newsreels? If you do, you may or may not be conscious of the fact that the various news shots, no matter what their character, are accompanied by an almost continuous stream of music. An oil well burns in Texas. A burst of brass music heralds the first view of the catastrophe; and the remarks of the news commentator are interspersed with other, more or less appropriate, snatches of made-to-order music. A football championship game, an interstate beauty contest, a prize bull, a politician referring in favorable terms to the institution of motherhood, a trip through Picturesque Patagonia, the launching of a new ferryboat, or the completion of a pipe line—none of these is complete without its quota of music, music whose sole function is to keep the picture from being run in silence; music that some poor devil of a composer put on paper, knowing perfectly well that nobody was going to pay the slightest attention to it. The feature pictures handle music a little more considerately, and buy a good deal of it to use *as* music. In fact, if it were not for the haste with which a picture composer has to work (he is often allowed two weeks in which to write the score for a picture that it took eight or ten weeks to shoot), the musical motion picture might become a new and impressive art form. Under present conditions, however, a considerable proportion of the music that the pictures buy serves no better purpose than to be one of several sound effects.

Radio is another industry that uses a great deal of utility music. If you have ever listened to a radio drama, you may not have noticed, but you will remember now, that every change of scene was heralded by a few bars of music, music that was written for the occasion. Generally such music is written by the conductor of the orchestra, as part of his regular duties. I remember Robert Armbruster, the conductor, once telling me that his toughest assignment was to write sixteen bars of change-of-scene music that would convey the feelings of the county superintendent on learning that the appropriation for the high school had been vetoed.

Now, Mr. Hindemith to the contrary, this sort of hack writing is none too good either for music or the composer. The fact that the latter knows that nobody is going to pay any attention to him tends to make him uninterested and careless; and even if he remains a conscientious artist, the little scraps and rags of music that he has to write are too short to be worth anything. Beethoven himself couldn't make them valuable. As Constant Lambert says, "The whole theory of utility music is based on the misconception that one can distinguish between the esthetic and the useful in this particular medium. Music is only useful if it is good music, whether light or serious. Unless it provides one with some vital experience which no other art can convey, it is not only useless but a nuisance." So I don't think there's much hope of our being able to make useful citizens out of composers. The only use to which we can put them is the use to which they have always been put: to hire them, or just allow them, to produce music that is not a trimming, or a background, for something else, but is something to be heard, undistracted, for its own sake.

19

Aid and Comfort

No one knows, naturally, when and where the first public concert was given. But whatever the date and place, I am willing to wager that on the morning following that historic event the editor of the *Cro-Magnon Gazette* received an indignant letter, written on a clamshell, deploring the dearth of melody in contemporary music. This is the oldest and most widespread of musical grievances. As a correspondent wrote to me only a short time ago; "Why is it that melody—easily remembered bits of musical phrasing, if you prefer—is so rare, if not totally absent, in works of the modern school of composition? To put it another way: Any of us, even with elementary acquaintance with the masters, can recall snatches of song—pleasing bits of harmony—to hum, or whistle, or play, from their operas, their symphonies, even their lesser works. They come almost unbidden: a passage from Brahms, Beethoven, Wagner, Tchaikovsky, Saint-Saëns, Debussy. Consider the modern school: too often it seems that the theme, and the whole work, is one of, shall we say, 'harmonious discord'—a dissonance continuing through major and minor keys, or both; a musical crazy-quilt which, when spread, reveals few, if any, memorable designs or passages easy of recollection. Can we believe that musical historians fifty years hence will look upon the output of contemporary radical composers as 'mid-twentieth century classicism'? Will such music, can it, ever be ranked even with the lesser-known but vastly more lyrical works of those revered for generations past? I cannot escape the belief that music which lives longest is that which lives through its lyric charm—a charm not unlike that of our folk-songs."

Naturally I agree with the sentiments of the last sentence: that unless a given piece of music contains recognizable musical ideas, themes that make sense, so to speak, and that either remain in the memory or arouse the desire to remember them, it isn't music, and it won't survive. Now there is no formula for creating such a theme. It may be the undulating chromatic-scale passage for the flute that opens Debussy's *The Afternoon of a Faun,* or it may be the three reiterated G's and the E-flat that open Beethoven's Fifth Symphony. In either case, it is a group of notes that suddenly comes to life. And live music, in my opinion, must be made up of those groups of living musical cells. But there is no denying that to the ears of a vast number of persons, very little of the music being written today contains memorable or viable themes. Why is this so?

There are two answers. One is that there is a dearth of creative musical ability in the world today; that too many so-called composers are fooling around with experiments designed to supply a substitute for musical ideas. The other is that the themes are there, but that we don't as yet recognize them. It is not for me to say which answer is correct. I don't know. I do know, however, that music, like any other language, tends constantly to broaden its scope and increase its vocabulary and modes of expression. Perhaps the simplest way to

explain what is happening in music is to take an illustration from the art that is most closely related to music.
Let me give you two extracts that will illustrate what has
happened in *poetry* during the past hundred-odd years.
The first is a passage from *The Sunset*, written by Shelley,
about the year 1816. It runs as follows:

> *. . . The lady died not, nor grew wild,*
> *But year by year lived on—in truth I think*
> *Her gentleness and patience and sad smiles,*
> *And that she did not die, but lived to tend*
> *Her agèd father, were a kind of madness,*
> *If madness 'tis to be unlike the world.*
> *For but to see her were to read the tale*
> *Woven by some subtlest bard, to make hard hearts*
> *Dissolve away in wisdom-working grief;—*
> *Her eyes were black and lustreless and wan:*
> *Her eyelashes were worn away with tears,*
> *Her lips and cheek were like things dead—so pale;*
> *Her hands were thin, and through their wandering veins*
> *And weak articulations might be seen*
> *Day's ruddy light. The tomb of thy dead self*
> *Which one vexed ghost inhabits, night and day,*
> *Is all, lost child, that now remains of thee!*

There is a beautiful example of poetry of the early
nineteenth-century romantic school, the school that, in
music, produced, for example, the overture to Weber's
Der Freischütz. We still consider Shelley a poet, and his
work real poetry. But notice that it is typical of its period.
The regular and sometimes arbitrary rhythm, the exalted
figures of speech, the sentences inverted to make them
conform to a rhythmic pattern, the sudden apostrophe
to the subject of the poem—all these are characteristic.

Also, he uses a vocabulary that is more elaborate and euphonious than that of prose, and uses the second person singular, which even in his day was virtually extinct in the spoken language. Generally speaking, the average poetry-loving contemporary of Shelley would have said that poetry, to be poetry, must possess the characteristics I have named, must be something set apart, not only in its ideas, but in its form, from prose.

Now let me quote you a poem written 118 years later, by Edna St. Vincent Millay. It comes from her book, *Wine From These Grapes.*

Childhood is not from birth to a certain age and at a certain
    age
The child is grown, and puts away childish things.

Childhood is the kingdom where nobody dies.

Nobody that matters, that is. Distant relatives of course
Die, whom one has never seen or has seen for an hour,
And they gave one candy in a pink-and-green stripèd bag, or a
    jack-knife,
And went away, and cannot really be said to have lived at all.

And cats die. They lie on the floor and lash their tails,
And their reticent fur is suddenly all in motion
With fleas that one never knew were there,
Polished and brown, knowing all there is to know,
Trekking off into the living world.
You fetch a shoe-box, but it's much too small, because she
    won't curl up now:
So you find a bigger box, and bury her in the yard, and weep.
But you do not wake up a month from then, two months,
A year from then, two years, in the middle of the night
And weep, with your knuckles in your mouth, and say Oh, God!
    Oh, God!

AID AND COMFORT

Childhood is the kingdom where nobody dies that matters,—
*   mothers and fathers don't die.*

And if you have said, "For heaven's sake, must you always
*   be kissing a person?"*
Or, "I do wish to gracious you'd stop tapping on the window
*   with your thimble!"*
Tomorrow, or even the day after tomorrow if you're busy hav-
*   ing fun,*
Is plenty of time to say, "I'm sorry, mother."

To be grown up is to sit at the table with people who have
*   died, who neither listen nor speak;*
Who do not drink their tea, though they always said
Tea was such a comfort.

Run down into the cellar and bring up the last jar of raspber-
*   ries; they are not tempted.*
Flatter them, ask them what it was they said exactly
That time, to the bishop, or to the overseer, or to Mrs. Mason;
They are not taken in.
Shout at them, get red in the face, rise,
Drag them up out of their chairs by their stiff shoulders and
*   shake them and yell at them;*
They are not startled, they are not even embarrassed; they
*   slide back into their chairs.*

Your tea is cold now.
You drink it standing up,
And leave the house.

I am not sure just what Shelley would have thought of that poem. I am positive, however, that most of Shelley's contemporary readers would have been utterly revolted by it. If it left them able to speak at all, they would have pointed out that so far as their ears are concerned, it has no rhythm at all. It is written in the vocabulary of prose, in simple declarative sentences that have no beauty at all—no figures of speech, no grace of expression, no phrases worth quoting. It contains allusions that are ugly and shocking—one doesn't write about dead cats and fleas in serious poetry; you don't yell at dead people, or shake them by the shoulders. The main idea: that one loses one's youth, and first knows remorse, when one is confronted with the death of a beloved person—has poetic possibilities, but they are cheapened and obscured. In short, it isn't poetry at all.

As a matter of fact, there are many living persons who probably react the same to this poem. Yet there are thousands of people to whom it *is* a poem, a beautiful and moving expression of grief and vain regret. What has happened, of course, is that poetry has broadened its frontiers, and that a poet to whom these new vistas are familiar ground can still write poetry, even if it is not in the old forms, even if it is written in forms so much simpler and yet subtler than the old forms that they seem to be no forms at all.

The same thing, I believe, is happening in music. We are in the midst of a transition period, during which music is working itself toward an increased flexibility and expressiveness. What makes this evolutionary process a rather painful one—and it is rather painful—is that composers, consciously or unconsciously, are trying to broaden our conception of melody. Now melody has always been based on two things, scales and harmony. We have two scales in use in modern occidental music: the diatonic, that is, the piano white-note scale; and the chromatic scale.

We take the existence of these two scales so much for granted, they are so ground into our subconscious minds, that we don't realize that they are purely arbitrary sequences of notes. They are not inevitable, and the only thing that makes them seem so is that we're so used to them. There are plenty of other possible scales. For example, if you will play a scale on the black notes of the piano, beginning with F-sharp, you will have played the pentatonic scale. That scale is the basis of Scotch bagpipe music, and every primitive Scotch air contains only the notes of that scale. Yet it lacks two of ours, the fourth and the seventh. We find it incomplete. But to the Highlanders who composed those bagpipe tunes, it was *not* incomplete. They couldn't imagine a scale that had more than five notes in it. On the other hand, our scales sound absurdly incomplete to the Hindu, who plays and sings music based on sixty-three different scales.

The other thing upon which we unconsciously base melody is harmony. We think, in spite of ourselves, in terms of chords and keys. Try this experiment. Make up a tune for yourself. Hum a melody to yourself—anything that comes into your head. Never mind whether it's a good one or not. Now write it down, or get someone else to write it down, and nine times out of ten you'll find that it can be harmonized in a definite key, and that at least some of its notes will be the notes of a chord. More than half the themes in Wagner's *Nibelungen* trilogy are bugle calls—that is, they are various combinations of the notes of a simple tonic chord.

Now during the past half century composers have begun to try to break away from these old scales and chords, to compose melodies that don't belong to definite keys, that are, in some instances, based on quarter-tone scales. The reason their work sounds so floundering and meaningless is that most of them are not yet familiar enough with their material. You can't make a melody stick, merely by putting some notes together in a combination that isn't like any other combination ever heard, or that is based on some new chords. You have to *think* in terms of your language before you can write anything worth while in it, whether the language is music or English; and most contemporary composers, in my opinion, are not yet sufficiently *un*conscious that they are saying something new. On the other hand, every once in a while I hear new music by some man who is obviously really thinking in terms of new music without consciously trying to do so. What he writes may or may not sound pleasant to my ear; but I have to admit that it is music. Don't let the experimenters shut you off from the real innovators. For every Edna Millay in poetry there are a hundred would-be poets writing free verse that *looks* like hers, but is nevertheless nonsense. True. But there is also Millay. The time will come when we shall begin to hear clearly enough to keep what is worth listening to, and throw away what isn't. Meanwhile, I should say, get plenty of fresh air and exercise, eight hours' sleep, cut out desserts, and don't worry. Everything's going to be all right.

PART TWO

The Givers

The Necessary Evil

ONCE upon a time—although this is no fairy tale—a young American composer was invited to conduct a performance of one of his works by the Chicago Symphony Orchestra. Naturally he accepted, delighted at the opportunity to hear his music played by a great orchestra and also rather elated at the idea of conducting it himself. By the time he arrived in Chicago, however, his elation had subsided considerably; for he had had time, on the way, to reflect that he had never conducted a symphony orchestra in his life, his previous slight experience in that field having been confined to directing a twenty-piece theater band.

He was a little relieved, upon his arrival, to learn that Dr. Frederick Stock had already given the piece two rehearsals, so that the players were thoroughly familiar with it. All that remained for our hero to do was to put in the finishing touches at the final rehearsal, and conduct the actual performance.

None the less, when the time came for him to take over the rehearsal he mounted the podium in a state bordering closely upon panic. To his relief, the musicians knew their job so thoroughly that they obviously were going to give a splendid performance if he could manage to keep time. The rehearsal over, they tapped and applauded politely, and sat waiting to be dismissed. Feeling that there remained something yet to say, the young guest conductor hesitated a moment; then, clearing his throat, he said:

"Gentlemen, if anything goes wrong at tonight's performance—for God's sake don't look at me!"

I know how he felt. I was that composer. I think of the incident whenever I receive a letter (and I receive a surprising number of them) inquiring as to the functions of an orchestral conductor. Some of my correspondents really seem to believe that all conductors are as superfluous as I was. As one of them wrote, recently:

"In concerts which I have attended since my recent arrival in New York, I have found myself so utterly absorbed in the activity of the conductor that he gets in the way of my enjoyment of the music. Would it be possible so to train an orchestra that it could reach the point of performing without being led by a conductor, much as a football coach does not go out on the field to manage his team? Could a system of signals be evolved, such as lights, invisible to the audience, which would effectively start and end the orchestra, and yet rid us of the presence of the conductor?" My correspondent adds, rather cynically, "The conductor could come out at the end of the performance and receive his due applause."

As a matter of fact, if it were just a matter of starting and stopping the orchestra, of course it could be done. The conductor could fix up a small traffic light on his desk. When he pressed one button, a green light would come on, and the orchestra would begin the Third "Leonora" Overture. He wouldn't need a red light, because when the players got to the end of the piece—granted they arrived together—there wouldn't be any more notes left, and unless they wanted to go back and play it all over again, they'd *have* to stop.

But that isn't quite all there is to it. Theoretically, it is quite possible for a conductor to rehearse a program so exhaustively that his orchestra could play it through without him. They say that Hans von Bülow, for instance, brought his orchestra to such a pitch of perfection that it could play some works entirely from memory; and that on one occasion, when he was late in coming out on the platform, the orchestra did begin without him, and gave a brilliant performance of the *Tannhäuser* overture. But the endless hours and days that Von Bülow was able to put in on rehearsals would bankrupt any symphony orchestra today, to say nothing of reducing the schedule of concerts to about one every two or three weeks.

As things are, a conductor is vitally necessary to an orchestra in performance, even if he does nothing but beat time. It is very seldom that a piece of music, other than dance music, is played through from beginning to end in strict, unvarying rhythm. There are held notes, and pauses, and quickenings and slackenings of pace, all of which it is virtually impossible for the orchestra to achieve cleanly unless the players can watch the conductor's stick. There are also cues to be given, and a balance to be struck and maintained among the instruments. Remember that an orchestra player is under two handicaps: he can't see and he can't hear. That is to say, he hasn't the full score before him as he plays. He has only his part, and has no way of knowing what relation it bears to all the other parts that are being played. If he has a long rest, he can't see what the other players are doing. He can only count bars. Being a skilled musician, he'll probably count them right.

On the other hand, he will play with more confidence and with better tone if he has the conductor in front of him to indicate his entrance with a nod of the head or a wave of the hand. Also, as I say, he can't hear. While he is playing he hears only his own part and that of the man next to him, or possibly that of his own section. In general, however, the rest of the orchestra is just a blur of sound to him. Consequently he can only guess as to whether he is playing too loudly, or too softly, or just right. It is part of the conductor's job to keep his various sections balanced, to bring up a soloist who is too weak, or subdue an accompaniment that is too loud. In other words, while the conductor *is* the coach of the team, as my correspondent points out, he is also the quarterback. He not only drills the plays, but calls the signals.

Besides, I think my correspondent is an exception. I think the average listener *likes* to see the conductor. I know I do. Not because I'm interested in calisthenics, but because he gives me a convenient, visible source for the music. After all, sight, I think, is our strongest sense. Only when our eyes are at rest, or closed, do our other senses function to their highest degree. The great disadvantage of broadcast music, for instance, is that one must listen to it blind. I find it harder to concentrate upon music that comes out of a radio set than upon music that I hear in a concert hall, simply because I haven't anything to look at except the loudspeaker, which is lifeless and immovable, and has no visible connection with the music. On the other hand, in a hall, the conductor—to me at least—has just enough apparent connection with the music to keep my eyes occupied. And once my eyes are satisfied, my ears can listen without distraction. If the conductor wasn't on the platform I would probably start wondering where he was hiding, and worrying for fear the orchestra was going to break down, no matter how good it was. I think that for the average person it is, paradoxically, easier to forget the conductor when you can see him, than when you can't.

2

A Little Rope, Please

WHETHER you forget the conductor or not, he hasn't forgotten you. He is giving you a performance that he has conceived, planned, and rehearsed. It is he who raises the music from the printed page and brings it to life. If he is not its creator, he is at least its re-creator. How much leeway shall we allow him in that re-creative process? Shall we allow his interpretation of an orchestral work to be colored by his own personality, or shall we insist that he confine himself to conducting the music strictly as the composer conceived it?

That question has been bitterly debated through the years, and will never be settled—for the simple reason that it's a debate over something that doesn't exist. A conductor *must* be given leeway in his interpretations, simply because you can't avoid giving it to him. Certain members of the music-loving public are never weary of saying that a conductor should express exactly what the composer intended to convey. After which statement they sit back and fold their arms in the triumphant conviction that they have said something.

Well, they haven't said much. Finding out exactly what the composer intended to convey is perhaps the most difficult problem that any interpreter has to face. To explain why, let me be a little more specific. The admirers of almost any famous conductor will tell you that the secret of his greatness resides in the simple fact that he has the orchestra play the exact notes, and follow exactly, and literally, the composer's markings in the score. Very good. Suppose he is conducting some music by Henry Purcell. What were Purcell's markings in the score? None at all. No fortes or pianos, no accelerandos or *ritenutos*; none of the *andante, con alcuna licenza*, or *allegro quasi presto*, that you find in more modern scores. No slurs, no phrasing indications of any kind. The same is largely true of Bach's music. The expression marks and tempo indications with which his scores are peppered today were put there, most of them, by Bach experts; but not by Bach. To talk of expressing exactly what Bach or Purcell or any other seventeenth- or eighteenth-century composer intended to convey is to talk of something that is a virtual impossibility. Follow their scores literally and you are merely following somebody else's *guess* as to what they intended to convey.

Ah, but that is all changed. From Haydn and Mozart on down to the present day, composers have been much more meticulous in indicating how they wished their music to be played. True enough. But their indications do not convey any absolutely *precise* meaning. Music is often compared to architecture; and there is a certain analogy between the two arts. A sheet of printed music, for example, is much more comparable to an architect's blueprint than to a sheet of printed words; for whereas the words convey a thought, whether they are read in silence or read aloud, the printed notes convey nothing by themselves. They are a set of directions. They tell the performer to blow or pound or scrape or sing, so as to produce certain sounds; and not until the sounds are produced does the musical thought emerge. In this respect they do resemble a blueprint, which is also a set of directions to carpenters, masons, and engineers. But there the resemblance stops. Read the blueprints for a building, and you can determine the precise dimensions of every stone, the exact length and width and thickness of every wall, down to a fraction of an inch.

But a sheet of music conveys no such precise information. Suppose a given movement in a symphony is marked "*andante*." All right; what does "*andante*" mean? Literally, it is the Italian for "walking"—in other words, an easygoing pace, neither very fast nor very slow. But how are you to determine what any given composer means by "an easygoing pace"? How fast was Beethoven's idea of walking? Is a walking speed, to him, as fast, or faster, than it is to Brahms, or Mozart, or Schumann? And when he writes one passage in two-four time, and marks it "*andante*," and another passage in four-eight time, and marks that also "*andante*," should the first passage be taken exactly twice as fast as the second, and if not, why not? Both contain exactly the same number of eighth notes to the bar; but, theoretically, the easygoing pace applies to quarter notes in the first passage and to eighth notes in the second. By this time, I imagine, you're getting a little bit muddled by these technicalities. So am I. And so will anybody be who attempts to assign a precise and infallibly accurate meaning to just one simple tempo indication.

Take another example: expression marks. Here is a page from a score by a great composer. It contains a passage in which the flutes are playing in their lower middle register, the violins in their upper middle register, and trombones and trumpets sustaining a chord at about the middle of their range. All the parts are marked *"mezzo forte."* Now *mezzo forte* is the dynamic equivalent of *andante*, that is, a sound that is neither very loud nor very soft. It is, I may say, the curse of the orchestra, and the bane of conductors. And this is why. *Which* of the three sections of the orchestra is supposed to be the most prominent in this particular passage? The violins? Very good. Then the brasses will have to play *mezzo piano* rather than *mezzo forte*, if they are not to blur the sound of the strings. The brasses? Then play the passage as marked. The flutes? Then the violins will have to play much softer than *mezzo forte*, and the brasses will have to go almost to *pianissimo*. The tone of a brass instrument is so much more powerful than that of a stringed or woodwind instrument, and that of a woodwind so much weaker than either of the other two, that the marking, *"mezzo forte,"* if followed literally, results in three totally different intensities of sound. Perhaps that is what the composer wanted, and perhaps it isn't. In any case, it is a very rare composer who differentiates his expression marks so as to balance the orchestra automatically. Even when he does, his guess is likely to be no better than that of any outsider. As a matter of practice, the composer almost invarably puts the problem of detailed orchestral balance up to the conductor, without even bothering to say so. I could show you many a passage from the works of the masters that would be merely muddle and chaos if it was conducted precisely as its creator marked it.

But what of living composers, or the surviving interpreters who knew certain composers during their lifetimes? Surely the creator of a work knows best how his work should sound? Certainly he should, and I am not at all certain that he invariably does. Don't forget that a piece of music may sound, to its composer, far different than it sounds to anyone else. He knows, so utterly, so in detail, exactly what he was trying to convey, that even at a performance he hears, not the notes that are being played, but the notes that he heard in his head when he wrote it. Some passage that is obscured in the playing may be perfectly clear to him because he knows it's there. In matters of tempo, particularly, composers are notoriously unreliable. The speed at which much of Wagner's music was first played at Bayreuth, under his direction was, I am told, much slower than the tempo at which it is taken today. And naturally enough. Remember that he was hearing some of this music for the first time in his life, music that had been buried in the written pages of his scores for twenty years. If occasionally he was so intoxicated with the sound of it that he hated to let any of it go, it is nothing to wonder at.

Suppose there were living today, a man who was directly descended from a descendant of a man who had been present at the first performance of Beethoven's Ninth Symphony, and who undertook to tell us exactly how loudly and how softly the various movements of that symphony were played, under Beethoven's baton. What would his testimony be worth? Exactly nothing. Beethoven was deaf when he wrote and conducted the Ninth Symphony; and what do *piano, crescendo, fortissimo* mean to a man whose ears are filled with nothing but a buzzing and a roaring, day and night, who has never heard his music except in some secret chamber of his brain? It is common knowledge that Maurice Ravel strongly objected to the speed at which Arturo Toscanini conducted his famous *Bolero*. Was Toscanini right, or Ravel?

My answer to that would be—both. The wonderful thing about a work of art is that if it is truly a work of art it doesn't necessarily mean just one thing. Beethoven's symphonies have meant a great deal to many millions of people since they were first played; and I imagine that they have conveyed a great many meanings to these generations that Beethoven never consciously intended them to convey. That is a tribute, and not a fault. Why shouldn't music mean slightly different things to different conductors?

I remember once hearing Henri Verbruggen, the late conductor of the Minneapolis Orchestra, say, "In my opinion, a conductor should be an actor. He should try to penetrate the spirit of the composers whom he conducts. When I play a Beethoven symphony, I must be, for the moment, Beethoven. I must try to understand what he was feeling and thinking when he wrote that symphony, and play it accordingly." And that, I think, is a just summing up of a conductor's duty. Three different conductors may give three different performances of any given work; and if their interpretations are sincere, intelligent, musicianly, and, above all, convincing, all three are right. Remember that the printed score is only a highly imperfect mechanical transcription of musical ideas that no composer can ever hope to set down with complete accuracy in written notes and words. The way the music sounds is much more important than the way it looks. Music is for the ear, not the eye. We should look a little less, and listen a little more intently.

3

How Right Is "Correct"?

Aᴌᴌ of which does not relieve the conductor of the obligation to try to determine just what the composer's intentions are, and to carry them out as faithfully as he can. After all, the composer did write the music, and he did know what, musically speaking, he wanted to say. Any conductor who deliberately tries to make him say something else is doing a dishonest job. But knowing his intentions, even hearing them explained by the composer in person, does not, in my opinion, obligate the conductor to abject obedience to the composer's *directions,* when, in his honest opinion, they interfere with the carrying out of those intentions. That is a rather involved sentence, and reads suspiciously like heresy. Let me simplify it by giving a concrete example.

Any composer's fundamental intentions, I think we all agree, are twofold: to move his hearers, and to hold their attention. Both must be carried out if his work is to be successful. If he holds their attention without moving them, his success is only superficial; if he moves them occasionally, but does not hold their attention throughout, he has defeated himself. Now the latter failing is one from which even the greatest composers are not wholly free. It generally takes the form of being repetitious, one of the most common, and most fatal, of all human faults. A speaker may have arguments at his command that are absolutely irrefutable; but the more convincing they are, the greater is the danger that he may drive his points home once too often, and lose the interest of his audience. A composer can, and does, run the same risk. The work of the great symphonists, up to the middle of the nineteenth century, are full of "double-bar" passages—that is, passages in which the composer indicates that a sequence of sixteen, twenty-four, or even seventy-two bars, is to be repeated verbatim, without any alteration in expression or orchestration. I've often suspected that eighteenth- and early nineteenth-century audiences were less attentive, or less musically quick-minded, than ours; for many of those repetitions, if played today, make the composer sound unbearably long-winded. The consequence is that you seldom hear a Beethoven or Mozart symphony today played without cuts. They are cuts only in the sense that the conductors elect to ignore some of the repeat signs. None the less they do result in suppressing something that the composer directed to be played; and the conductor who makes such a cut is deliberately disregarding the composer's explicit directions. Yet practically all conductors do it, and we accept it—in fact, few of us know it, except those who may be following the performance with a printed score; and a vast number of worshipers at the shrines of Beethoven and Mozart feel that such cutting helps, rather than handicaps, the composer. Why? Because in this instance the composer's intentions are better carried out by not paying too strict attention to his directions.

But aside from these more or less academic considerations, there is another reason why there can be no such thing as a provable, uniquely correct performance of any composer's music; and that is, simply, that a composer's work is never quite complete. A painting, a book, goes to its public direct from its creator. There, in paint or words, is his whole story, precisely as he chose to tell it. But a composer or a playwright reaches his public only at second hand. Until a large group of musicians have blown, or bowed, or plucked, under the direction of a conductor, until a group of actors have uttered words and made gestures, under the guidance of a director, a symphony or a play does not exist. A piece of music comes to you filtered, so to speak, through other personalities that stand between you and the composer, and there is no hope of its not being colored by those personalities.

There are, for instance, two schools of oboe playing, the German and the French, which produce two recognizably different qualities of tone. Which is the better? It's a matter of taste. If I were forced to choose between the German and the French tone, I should choose the latter. The fact remains that an oboe passage in a Beethoven symphony, played by a Frenchman or an Italian, does not sound like the German oboe for which Beethoven wrote it.

Now if the player, doing his best to be *mechanically* faithful to the composer's notes, can produce variations in their effect, how infinitely wider those variations are likely to be when we come to the conductor, to whom is intrusted, not just the playing of the notes, but the interpretation of the indefinable and utterly intangible spiritual values that the music may possess. That is not a matter of the conductor's sincerity. Leaving out a few freak performers, I think we may safely assume that every conductor honestly tries to grasp the essential meaning of the music that he conducts. But when he conducts Brahms's Fourth Symphony, no matter how profound, how intelligent, how musical, how utterly sincere his interpretation of Brahms's musical intentions may be, he cannot possibly escape from his own personality and temperament any more than he can change the color of his eyes. In the last analysis, you are seeing Brahms, not face to face, but through other eyes. That can't be helped. People talk about a great conductor's "selfless absorption in the music." I think that is nonsense. How can a man turn a faucet and shut off his own essential self—his own soul, if you like—just by mounting the conductor's platform? If he is an artist at all, you will hear him conduct *his* opinion of Beethoven.

I remember once hearing my friend Percy Rector Stephens, the famous vocal teacher, say, "You know, every once in a while I come across a pupil who starts to talk back, to argue with me about vocal methods. And I always stop him, and say: 'Now wait a minute. You're not here to exchange opinions with me. You're studying singing with me to learn facts. And while you're here, a fact is something that *I think*!' "

And Stephens is right. The virtue of any fine orchestral performance is that it bears the stamp of conviction of the conductor's belief in his own rightness. If a dozen conductors have a dozen sets of convictions, all the better for music. The crowning glory of any great work of art is just the fact that it says an infinite number of things to an infinite number of people. I have seen seven Hamlets in my time: Forbes-Robertson, Walter Hampden, John Barrymore, Basil Sidney, Leslie Howard, John Gielgud, and Maurice Evans. Now which was the *one* correct performance of Hamlet, the one that you could prove to be right? What is the one accurate, authentic, perfect performance of the Mozart "Haffner" Symphony, and how are you going to prove it? In the end, you'll find yourself saying that you like one particular performance better than any others, for reasons that you will proceed to give. But that is still only your opinion.

Of course there is a line to be drawn, and the need for drawing it is implicit in the very fact that the conductor is, in a way, the composer's fellow creator. A piece of music is not a book. It dies with every performance; and when it is not being played, its essential self is dead, until the orchestra gathers again in the hall, and the musicians and the conductor resurrect it. But it is one thing to raise Beethoven from the dead, and it is quite another to resurrect him and then proceed to make a sort of Charlie McCarthy * out of him, for the expression of some conductor's ideas. There are conductors whose creative impulses are so much stronger than their intellects that they use a musical composition as a springboard from which to dive off into a sea of self-expression. But there are not very many of them, and they betray themselves.

On the other hand, most conductors wander about in a musical no man's land, where A is infallible to his own followers, and anathema to the partisans of B. How are you to determine which of them is right? You can't. When Jones tells you that Smith conducted a perfect performance of the Franck D minor he is only telling you that Smith's conception of the Franck D minor coincides ex-

* For the benefit of posterity, be it said that at the time this book was being written, Charlie McCarthy was the wildly popular dummy of the famous ventriloquist, Edgar Bergen.

actly with Jones's. There is only one way of knowing whether you agree with Jones: form your own conception of the Franck D minor. Study the music that the orchestras play. If you can't read the scores, listen to it. Hear the same piece played by half a dozen different orchestras, under half a dozen different conductors, and you'll be amazed at the different ways one symphony can sound. But, as you grow familiar with any given piece of symphonic music, you will find that you begin to have your own conception of what the composer of that music was trying to say. In simpler language, you'll find yourself having your own idea of how a given piece of music should sound. Don't ignore what people say whose experience as listeners may be greater than your own. Your conception of a certain symphony *may* be based on the fact that you never heard a really great performance of it. But when you find yourself with a definite opinion concerning the interpretation of a composition, don't be talked out of it. We so-called musical authorities are far from being the source of all eternal truths. When you find a favorite conductor, don't be too partisan about him. Don't think that you're being unfaithful to him by admitting that other conductors may be equally great. It is hard to eradicate the incorrigible human desire to give the first prize to somebody. But first prizes don't mean much in the field of art. One man may be the supreme interpreter of Beethoven; which does not prevent another man's being the perfect Wagnerite. There is more than enough music to go around. Don't forget that even the Bible has never suffered by having too many interpreters.

4

The Devil and the Deep Sea

THERE is one phase of his work concerning which any conductor may confidently count upon finding no difference of opinion among his hearers. When he comes to make up his programs for the subscription series of the coming season, he may rest assured that, no matter what works he elects to put on the list, his choice is *bound* to be wrong. If his programs contain a preponderance of contemporary works he is denounced as a poisonous radical; if the moderns and the classics are about evenly balanced, he is an opportunist, truckling to both camps. If, on the other hand, he leans toward the classic and the familiar, he—well, listen to one of my correspondents.

"I would greatly appreciate a discussion, or some reasonable explanation," he writes, "of the rigid eclecticism practised by those worthy gentlemen who make up symphonic programs. Just what is the unassailable criterion that commands them to choose their selections from the conventional repertoire of two hundred-odd works, with only a rare performance of works that do not happen to be in that repertoire? As a music lover, I add my libations regularly at the shrines of Beethoven's *"Eroica,"* Fifth, "Pastoral," and Seventh; to Brahms's First and Fourth, Mozart's G minor, Tchaikovsky's Fifth and *"Pathétique,"* Dvořák's *From the New World,* etc. . . . But does nobody know that Beethoven wrote symphonies number One, Two,

Four, and Eight, that Brahms has a *second* symphony, and has actually written other things besides Hungarian Dances? Ditto with Dvořák and the Slavonic Dances? And why is his Fourth Symphony doomed to one performance every two years? Is Borodin to be forever a synonym for nothing but Polovtsian *Prince Igor?* Did Chabrier write nothing besides *España,* Debussy only *The Afternoon of a Faun,* César Franck only the D minor Symphony? Are the more serious works of the minor masters, and the less-known works of the classic masters, really so bad that their performance would be a disgrace to an orchestra?"

As a matter of fact, if the programs of any given symphony orchestra offer less variety than some listeners would like, the person responsible is usually not the person who generally gets the blame—that is, the conductor. Theoretically, perhaps, a conductor makes up his programs to please himself, offers them as an expression of his particular taste in music. As a matter of cold fact, while the *arrangement* of his programs is left to him, he has virtually no choice regarding three quarters of the music that goes into those programs. Music is not like the theater, where we have a constant stream of new plays being produced and old ones dropping out. It is like literature, in that an enormous proportion of its classics are still in active circulation. In the theater we have Shakespeare, a little Ibsen, a little Shaw—and there the active classic repertoire practically ends. But in music we have Bach, Handel, Haydn, Mozart, Beethoven, Wagner, Brahms, to say nothing of Strauss, Rimsky-Korsakoff, and Debussy; and there are many works by these composers that the subscribers to any symphony orchestra insist upon hearing every season. And those works are "musts" on the programs of every conductor. Personally, he might like to give Beethoven, Wagner, and Brahms a season's vacation some year; but let him try it—and see how soon his orchestra has a new conductor! The consequence is that the only real freedom of choice that he has is in deciding what new or seldom heard music he will play in the little time left to him. He must inevitably resign himself to the fact that he can't please everybody, and must let the innovation-loving minority—of whom he is one—go partly unsatisfied.

Now that radio has made so many orchestras accessible to all of us, the unfortunate conductors have a fresh complaint to face. The necessity for including a large number of the classics makes for an inescapable duplication in symphony programs. And radio listeners don't like it. They seem to think that the conductors are either deliberately ignoring each other's existence, or *trying* to conflict in their selections, in order to show off their own particular interpretations of certain works. Neither assumption is true, nor are overlapping programs peculiar to radio. There was overlapping long before broadcasting; only, we didn't notice it. In former days, the people in a town or city that had a symphony orchestra heard their own, local organization, and, with the exception of an occasional visitor, no others. The programs of two neighboring cities could be exact duplicates, with no one the wiser. Now, with so many orchestras on the air, we *are* the wiser.

Nobody plans this duplication. It is an unfortunate phenomenon that just happens. Programs are made up a long time ahead. By the end of August, for example, the average symphony conductor has a pretty clear idea of exactly what works are going to be played on every program of the season ahead of him. The last thing in the world that he wants to do is to conduct a given piece during the same week that it is being conducted by one of his colleagues. Nevertheless the duplications do occur, and they occur, curiously enough, even in the case of comparatively unfamiliar works.

A sort of unwilling telepathy seems to operate among performers and conductors in their choice of selections. I remember one season, years ago, when I was writing for the New York *World,* when every other pianist in New York, it seemed, played César Franck's *Prelude, Chorale, and Fugue.* The following year they dropped Franck like a hot poker and all played Schumann's *Carnaval* to death. During one season, the local and visiting orchestras in New York gave a total of eleven performances of Brahms's last two symphonies and none of the first two. The only way that I can see of avoiding such duplications would be for all the orchestras to pool their programs before the opening of the season, and have some Judge Landis or Will Hays of music tell every conductor what he could play and when he could play it. And just as soon as you can visualize a group of temperamental symphony conductors allowing some superconductor to tell them what they may and may not play, such an arrangement will be brought about—and not until then.

5

Bill of Fare

Just what does constitute a good orchestral program? What elements must a conductor consider in making up the list of numbers that he will conduct at a given concert? The best clue to the answer lies, I think, in a field that at first blush doesn't seem to have much connection with music, and that is—cooking. What makes a good program is precisely what makes a good dinner. Analyze that statement, and you will find that it isn't nearly as foolish as it sounds. After all, what does make a good dinner?

Let us see. We begin with something mildly nourishing and easily digestible—oysters or soup, for example, or both. Next, if the dinner is an elaborate one, we have something a little more solid and highly flavored—good, but not too much: an entree. Then comes the main course, whose principal object is nourishment. After that, something green, perhaps, and then something sweet, or, if you like cheese, something sharp and exotic. In any case, something to hold the attention of an appetite that has lost its edge, that is more interested in flavor than substance.

In short, a good dinner provides the elements of variety, cumulative interest, climax, and relief; and those are just the elements that should be present in a good concert program. By the way, when I say "concert" program I mean just that: a program designed to hold the interest of an audience of average listeners, possessing average good musical taste. I am not concerned here with special audiences, who bring a ready-made interest in some one kind of music. After all, there are people who can make an entire dinner out of Swedish *smörgåsbord,* or caviar and champagne; but they're not sufficiently numerous to play any important part in this present discussion.

Take first the question of variety—which includes contrast. A good symphony program, in my opinion, should not be confined too strictly to one style, one composer, or one period. It shouldn't be devoted entirely to works of the middle seventeenth century, it shouldn't be all suites, or all marches, or all symphonies. Nor should it, as a rule, be confined to the works of a single composer. For my tastes, the only composer who can stand the strain of providing an entire program is Wagner; and all-Wagner programs are generally popular for the reason that he covers so much territory, expresses so many different moods, conveys so many different atmospheres, writes in such a wide variety of forms, and has such an extraordinary command of orchestral tone color. Outside of Wagner, any other one-composer program is likely to be dangerous, because there is always the risk that, hearing just a little too much of one man, you begin to be conscious, not only of his genius, but of his mannerisms.

The question of cumulative interest is even more important, and is the element whose neglect makes bad program makers out of so many great conductors. A program, again like a dinner, should have a beginning, a middle, and an end. The heaviest number, like the heaviest course, should not come at the beginning; first, because the audience may not be quite settled down to serious listening, and second, because even if the audience is receptive, it is liable to find the rest of the program an anticlimax. Nor should it come at the end, because the audience, having been listening for an hour or so, is growing tired. Its attention is beginning to flag, so that Beethoven's Seventh or Strauss's *Ein Heldenleben* may find its listeners restless instead of absorbed. Somewhere just past the middle of the program, in point of time, is the best place for it, the place where musical appetites are whetted, and not yet jaded.

To retain the interest of an audience, two works whose prevailing mood—particularly if it is a quiet one—is identical shouldn't come together. Nor should an obscure, or highly ultramodern piece come too near the close. The longer people listen, the less tolerant they grow, the less willing to bother with musical riddles.

One of the most important problems that a program maker must face is that of fatigue. An audience does grow tired. No matter how wrapped up you are in the work, no matter how anxious to pay strict attention to every note, you cannot concentrate fully on a given piece of music after the lapse of a certain length of time. One of my favorite stage works is Wagner's *Tristan and Isolde*. It was years before I could sit through the second act without falling asleep. Because it bored me? Certainly not. I had listened so hard to the first act that I was exhausted. Now that I've reached the point where I know the first act almost by heart, I can really hear the second act. In fact, last year I even heard the third act.

So much for theory; now for practice. Suppose we analyze an actual program—in my opinion, an admirable one—that was played by the New York Philharmonic-

Symphony Orchestra, under John Barbirolli, during the spring of 1938. It began with a suite of dances by Purcell. These possessed the element of novelty, which is always a good beginning, but a novelty only in matter, not in style. The themes were new, but the style and idiom were more or less familiar, and so didn't demand too close *analytical* attention. Then we had a Chopin concerto. Here was beautiful music, written in a manner that was in strong contrast to the somewhat archaic style of the work that preceded it. It was lengthy, but its length was counterbalanced by the fact that, in addition to hearing the music itself, the audience had the interest and pleasure of hearing a beautiful performance of the solo part by Josef Hofmann.

Then a recess—the intermission, a few minutes in which to relax our concentration upon the music. The second half opened with Schubert's "Unfinished" Symphony, the heaviest number on the program, and placed in exactly the right spot. We had had a rest, our minds were warmed up, and our faculties of attention were at their peak. After the symphony, we were, whether consciously or not, a little fatigued. We needed something to stimulate us a little. So Mr. Barbirolli gave us the *Shepherd's Fennel Dance* of Balfour Gardiner, in other words, a complete novelty. We were immediately interested, because it's always a little exciting to meet a new musical personality, or a new expression of a known musical personality. Moreover the piece was not so drastic in its modernity that we became worn out trying to tolerate it. Then, the end of the program. For this we needed something not too old-fashioned in its idiom, because our minds must be kept awake by now; not too modern on the other hand, because we were in no mood to solve puzzles; not too quiet, because by now we were easily depressed. So Mr. Barbirolli, being a superb program builder, gave us the theme and variations from Tchaikovsky's Third Suite: music that has no cosmic message, that presents no problems, that asks nothing of us but to sit back, listen, and enjoy. Which, as I well recall, is precisely what we did.

6

The Irrational Art

O F ALL the arts, music is the one that exasperates the scientists the most. Once in a while a chemist may shake his head over the unsound combinations of pigments that the painters employ in the course of producing their pictures; but otherwise painting, sculpture, and literature jog along without much technical criticism from the laboratories. But music—! Hardly a week goes by that some acoustician doesn't rise and point out, either in speech or in print, the appalling number of things that are the matter with music, not as an art, but as a science. I sometimes wonder, considering all that is wrong with it, how any music manages to get written or played. In general, there are two main counts in their indictment. One is, that our scale is all wrong, according to the science of acoustics; the other is, that many of our instruments are simply absurd, from a scientist's point of view. I must say that, so far as they bring these charges *as scientists*, they are right. Let me elaborate a bit.

Take the violin, for instance. It is a patchwork instrument at best, made of three or four kinds of the most perishable of materials, wood. It is unnecessarily fragile, it is affected by heat and cold, and it is needlessly difficult technically. For example, the player has not only to determine the pitch of a given note, but at the same time must determine its quality. It ought not to be difficult to apply electric tone building and amplification to the instrument in such a way that the violinist wouldn't have to bother about tone any more. It would be made for him. Moreover, the instrument is ill-adapted for mass production. It has to be made on a tedious and expensive handwork basis, and even so, its manufacture is such a gamble that its maker can't determine beforehand whether its tone quality is going to be good or bad.

The same objections hold good for the cello, and more so for the double bass, which doesn't even belong to the violin family, being the sole survivor of the otherwise obsolete family of viols. The viola is even worse. It is mechanically ridiculous, having a set of strings that are too long for the size of its body, with the result that it emits a rather hoarse, hollow tone that makes it neither a violin nor a cello.

The piano is the worst of all. It, too, is made largely of wood, instead of metal, as it should be. But worse than that, it not only gets out of tune with distressing frequency, but even when it *is* in tune, it's *out* of tune. That, because it is tuned to the so-called tempered scale. To explain what that is will put me under the disagreeable obligation of becoming somewhat technical; so rather than lose your attention at the very outset I'll postpone the technical discussion for the moment. Let me list a few more things that are wrong with music.

One of the worst jumbles is the technique of our orchestral instruments, and the way in which composers write for them. When a student takes up the study of the French horn, for instance, the so-called horn in F, he is taught that his bottom note is the note C, on the middle line of the bass clef. So, with that fundamental C scale firmly fixed in his mind, he goes ahead and learns the instrument. But when he undertakes to play in an orchestra, we all suddenly discover that that *written* C note of his actually comes out as the F just below the *bottom* line of the bass clef. As a result, if the composer of a symphony wants his horn player to sound the real note C, he must write it as the G a fifth above. If a symphony is in the key of C for the violins, the horn parts must be written in the key of G.

Is all this a little confusing? If it is, don't think that you are the only one to be confused. To add to the troubles of the horn player and the composer, the horn part is always written without any key signature. No matter what key the rest of the orchestra is playing in, the horn player is always in the theoretical key of C, with all the sharps and flats written in as accidentals. There are two theories to account for this. One is that horn players are not bright enough to remember a key signature. That I rather doubt. The other is, that in the old days, horns had no valves, so that the musicians could play only the natural harmonics of the instrument—that is, the notes that can be played on a bugle. Consequently, in order to go from one key to another, the player had to insert an extra piece of tubing, called a crook, which would throw the instrument into the desired new key. Beethoven, for example, wrote for horns in F, E, E-flat, D, and even B-flat. The introduction of valves did away with all that, except that to this day certain composers—Richard Strauss, for one—still write for the theoretically different varieties of horns. When, on page 73 of the score of Strauss's *Don Quixote* we find the third horn playing in F, and on page 74 find him playing a horn in E, it doesn't mean that he inserts an E crook in his instrument. He probably doesn't own one, and he wouldn't have time to adjust it if he did. What he must do is transpose the part half a tone down, at sight. By another convention, which nobody can explain, whenever a horn part goes into the bass clef it is supposed to be written an octave lower than the actual notes the player is supposed to play. Perhaps you understand now why so few people get to be good horn players.

The horn has the worst time, but he is not the only sufferer. The lowest note on the clarinet is low E—except that it isn't. If it's a B-flat clarinet, it's really low D, and if it's an A clarinet it's really low C-sharp. On a bass clarinet it's a D, but sounds nine notes lower than the player reads it. Orchestral trumpets were formerly in F, but instead of sounding a fifth lower than the written notes, like the horns, they sounded a fourth *higher*. Trumpets are now in B-flat and A, like the clarinets, except that trumpet players never use an A trumpet, and their parts are usually written in C anyhow. There are five varieties of saxophones in common use, and their notes are all written in the treble clef, with the result that the written note E can mean any one of three varieties of D and two of G. This makes it easy for the player to pass from one instrument to another, the only headache being that of the composer.

Now crazy as this system is, it possesses a certain technical logic, except that it isn't applied consistently. The flute's natural scale is D; and it is written, not C, as you'd think it would be, but as what it is—D. The trombone and the bassoon are normally, like the clarinet, in the key of B-flat, but their written notes actually sound as written.

Our system of writing down music is still extremely unsatisfactory. Modern polytonal and atonal music is extremely chromatic in character, and must be written in a system of notation that bristles with sharps and flats and double flats and naturals until, however comparatively easy it may be to play, it is almost impossible to read.

Now, to get back to our tempered scale, I'll try to be as untechnical as possible. First, suppose we keep clearly in mind just what a scale is. If you will listen analytically to that rather seasick effect that people insist upon producing on a Hawaiian steel guitar, you will realize that it is a progression from a low sound to a high one that passes through an infinite number of notes of increasingly higher pitch. Now the human race, in the course of learning to sing and play, has elected to pick out certain tones along that infinite progression of tones, and sing or play those, leaving out the intervening gradations. The result of that selection is what we call a scale. There can be any number of scales. In East Indian music, for instance, there are about sixty-three, employing intervals that are much too close for us to enjoy. In the Occident, however, we have instinctively only three scales: the five-note, or pentatonic, the seven-note, or diatonic, and the twelve-note, or chromatic. The first is the scale upon which, for instance, all Scotch bagpipe music is played. The others are our ordinary scale, subdivided into major or minor.

Now granted that you have picked a seven-note scale for yourself, how are you to determine just how far apart those notes are to be? . . . And here comes the difference between the natural and the tempered scale. If you produce a certain note by vibrating a column of air or a string or a piece of wood or metal, you produce, not only that fundamental note, but a series of fainter notes known as the natural harmonics, notes that are higher, and that vibrate so many times a second in the perfect mathematical relations of two, four, eight, sixteen, and so forth. Again to simplify, the notes that can be played on a bugle are the natural harmonics of that instrument. Now however perfectly those harmonics are related to one another, they are *not* in perfect relation to the harmonics of *another* key. Put in more simple language, the note D-sharp is, scientifically at least, out of tune with note E-flat.

Now up to Bach's time, composers used the natural scale. This did very well while music remained comparatively simple in character, and stuck fairly consistently to a single key or to one that was closely related to it. But as music began to broaden in expressiveness, and composers began to feel the need of shifting from one key to another, they found that they couldn't do it without producing painful discords. That D-sharp, for instance, was all right if you were playing in the key of E; but if you suddenly decided to go to the key of E-flat, you sounded out of tune. So in Bach's time they developed the so-called tempered scale. Taking the octave as their basis, they arbitrarily made the scale the same for all keys. They tuned the D-sharp down a little, and the E-flat up a little, until the two became synonymous. The result was a scale, very imperfect from a scientific point of view—to this day you'll notice that the top notes of a piano are a little flat in relation to the middle notes—but which gave the composer the inestimable advantage of being able to modulate from one key to another with the utmost freedom. The subtle and complicated harmonies of Debussy's *Pelléas and Mélisande* would be unthinkable—because our ears couldn't stand the resulting sour notes—in the natural scale. All of our music, from Bach's time up to the present day, has developed as a result of the invention of the tempered scale.

But the scientists still tell us that we are wrong, that we should go back to the natural scale because it would give us more and subtler intervals; that we should perfect the mechanism of our orchestral instruments along scientific lines, that we should write for them according to a rational system, and that we should make our system of notation simpler and more logical than it is. Why don't we do those things? Scientists are usually right, and certainly so, theoretically, in this case. What's wrong?

I think the answer lies in an experience that I had many years ago, when I was in college and running on the track team. One day I came to Mike Cann, our trainer, in a state of great excitement, and said, in effect, "I think I've hit upon a wonderful idea. Suppose, today, I run, say, fifty yards at top speed. Anybody can sprint fifty yards. Then tomorrow I sprint fifty-one yards. The next day, fifty-two yards; the next, fifty-three. Suppose I keep that up, increasing the distance by one yard a day, every day for about four and a half years. At the end of that time, why shouldn't I be able to *sprint* a mile—in other words, at the rate of a hundred yards in eleven seconds, why couldn't I run a mile in about three minutes and fifteen seconds, nearly a minute faster than anybody has ever done it?"

Mike thought that over gravely, and finally said: "Well, I don't see any reason why you couldn't. No reason at all—except that you're a human being, and not a horse, and you can't do it."

And that, I am afraid, is the answer. Science deals with

facts, and proofs. Art deals with instincts and intuitions, things that have nothing to do with science, and seldom anything to do with logic. You can prove that the relation of the number of vibrations of the seventh harmonic to those of the fundamental are absolutely correct. But why that seventh harmonic always sounds out of tune to the hearer is something you cannot prove. And out of tune it sounds. The human ear is a very primitive, and a very stubborn instrument. Up to now, the average person derives only discomfort from listening to intervals closer than the twelve semitones of our tempered scale. We may change. The day may come when we can distinguish, and produce, with profit and enjoyment, quarter tones, or eighth tones, or sixteenth tones; but I doubt if you or I will be alive.

We may eventually reform our system of instrumental technique. Meanwhile, unless we can provide that on a given day every teacher and conservatory in the world shall agree to inaugurate a new system of teaching, and every orchestra player will learn it overnight—unless we can do that, we shall have to wait for things to straighten out gradually, over the years, by a process of evolution. The day may come when violins will be made of stainless steel and will be equipped with electric amplifiers, and violas will be built in their proper acoustical proportions, and the double bass will lose its round shoulders. Meanwhile, the average, pigheaded human animal persists in having a sentimental fondness for the structure and tone of the violin as Stradivarius, in his illogical, rule-of-thumb way, managed to put it together. The trouble is that the progress of art—any art, is a progress of growth, not of manufacture.

7

Sir James's Umbrella

ITS TEMPERED scale is not the only crime for which that eternal musical whipping boy, the piano, is belabored. Not long ago the famous astrophysicist, Sir James Jeans, made some further rude remarks about the unfortunate instrument in the course of a paper that he read before the English Music Teachers' Association. It was entitled, *A Scientist Looks at Music;* and in the course of discussing the subject of touch and tone on the piano he referred to a series of experiments conducted by Professors Hart, Fuller, and Lusby of the University of Pennsylvania. Working in conjunction with the American pianist, Abram Chasins, they found that the sound waves produced by the pianist's fingers, and those produced by a mechanical striker hitting the keys, were identical. "The moral," he said, "for piano teachers, is that so far as single notes are concerned, it does not matter how the pupil strikes the key, so long as he strikes it with the requisite degree of force. If this is right, the tone quality will be the same whether he strikes it with his fingers or even the end of his umbrella. As far as the scientist can see, that is all there is to the much debated problem of piano touch."

Instantly several famous pianists jumped into the fray to differ violently with Sir James. The consensus of their remarks, stripped of their esthetic verbiage, was to the effect that he was talking through his hat. But was he?

Just to clear the ground, suppose we define our terms. By "touch" on the piano, I am assuming that we mean the quality of sound that the performer produces—in short, what we mean when we speak of a violinist's "tone."

How does a violinist produce sounds on the instrument he plays, and how does he control their quality? He does the first by drawing his bow across the strings. But he can do more than that with the bow. By altering, not only the pressure of the bow, but also its position as it crosses the strings, he can affect the quality of the sound itself. His left hand also has great control over the quality of the sound. Depending on the sensitiveness of his ear and the skill of his fingers, he can play in perfect tune—or out of tune, as you well know if you have ever heard a beginner play the violin. By vibrating the finger that touches the string he can also produce a singing tone. Incidentally, when he is playing notes of very short duration, the violinist obviously has no time to produce this so-called vibrato effect. Under those circumstances, whatever control of tone that he has is then up to his delicacy of bowing. Consequently, if you listen to the playing of two violinists of equal skill, you will find that they are much harder to tell apart in fast passages than in slow ones. Even so, the violinist always has considerable direct control of the quality of tone that he produces.

Now how much comparative control has the pianist? He is playing an instrument that produces sounds by *hammering* upon strings. The mechanism that does the hammering is called the action, and involves the use of four devices. It might be worth our while to study them for a moment. The first is the key, which is pressed or struck down by the player. The key then operates a sort

of trigger mechanism, which throws the felt-covered hammer against the string. At the same time the key also
operates to raise a felt-covered wooden piece called the
damper. Ordinarily the damper rests on the string and
stops its vibrations. When it is raised it allows the string
to vibrate freely. The fourth mechanism, the pedal, when
it is pressed by the player's foot, raises all the dampers at
once, allowing all the strings to vibrate more or less in
sympathy with those actually struck. The other two ped-
als, the sustaining and the so-called soft pedal, I'm leaving
out of consideration for the moment. All this is rather
dull, I know; but I'd like to have it fresh in your memory.

Let us go back to what Sir James says, which is: *"So
far as single notes are concerned* [italics mine], it does
not matter how the pupil strikes the key, so long as he
strikes it with the requisite degree of force." Well, that is
quite true, for, as I've said, the trigger mechanism of the
key *throws* the hammer against the string. At a certain
point in its passage from its resting place to the surface of
the string the hammer is a missle. The pianist has no
more control of its flight than does a hammer thrower,
once the hammer has left his hands. All the pianist can
do is to determine whether the hammer shall strike the
string gently or with force.

So we must admit that Sir James is absolutely right.
It is quite true that in the playing of any given note the
pianist can only determine the *volume* of sound produced.
The hammer flies out of his control, and hits the string
always at an angle that has been mechanically predetermined. If the felt covering of the hammer is hard, the
tone will be more brilliant than if it has been softened;
but that degree of brilliance cannot. be altered by the

player. Also, if the sounding board of the instrument is defective, and the tone is dull, he cannot change that. And if the piano is out of tune, he cannot play *in* tune.

But Sir James Jeans, being a great scientist, has been very careful to say only what he means. He says, "so far as single notes are concerned." And in that statement, whether knowingly or not, he determines the point at which the scientist must step aside to allow the artist to step forward. If playing the piano consisted of playing one note, and no more, on the piano, there would be no use in trying to argue with Sir James. If you placed Rachmaninoff, Hofmann, Chasins, Horowitz, myself, and a piano tuner behind screens on the stage of Carnegie Hall and had each of us strike a single note on the piano, you would be absolutely unable to tell us apart.

May I digress long enough to tell you a story that I once heard Professor William Lyon Phelps tell, and which I have never forgotten? It seems that on a certain voyage of a tramp steamer the first mate, who had always been noted for his abstemiousness, had a regrettable experience, one evening, with a bottle of rum. Unfortunately a violent storm arose on this particular evening, and as a result of the mate's condition, the ship very nearly foundered. The next morning the captain summoned the mate to his cabin and said, "I am sorry to say that I'll have to make a note of your condition in the ship's log."

The first mate begged him not to do so. "After all," he said, "it was my first offense in a long life of following the sea. If you do this it will ruin my career. I'll never be able to get another ship."

"Sorry," said the captain. "It's my duty to put this in the log. Facts are facts, and I must put them down." So he wrote in the ship's log, "The first mate was drunk last night."

The mate made no further protest. But the following week it became *his* turn to keep the ship's log. So, after long deliberation, he wrote: "The captain was sober last night."

In other words, the facts are not necessarily the truth. Sir James Jeans's statement is a statement of absolute fact—but hold a minute. "So far as the scientist can see," he says, "that is all there is to the much debated problem of piano touch." But that is not as far as the artist sees. Outside a lunatic asylum, nobody has ever yet sat down at a piano and given a recital consisting of a single, isolated note; and nobody ever will. A recital consists of many notes, thousands of them, produced one after the other. And in art, at least, the minute you place one form or color or word or sound next to another you introduce the element of relativity. In other words, at that point Professor Einstein comes in at the door and Sir James Jeans flies out of the window. When you tell me that a pianist does not *actually* change the quality of tone that he produces on the piano, I am not interested. You might as well tell me that Maurice Evans is not really Hamlet. Whatever the physical facts of piano playing may be, the psychological fact is that a fine pianist can produce a complete illusion, in the ears of his audience, of a variation in tone color.

Now how does he do this? First, by dynamic variation. A great pianist has complete control over the force with which his fingers strike the keys, a control so absolute that it extends to every individual finger. He can touch the key just strongly enough to make the hammer strike the string at all; or he can hit the key with all the strength of which his shoulders and arms, working through his fingers, are capable. Between these two extremes his control of power is practically limitless. The striking machine used in the experiments was capable of playing the notes with all the degrees of loudness and softness that are at the command of a concert pianist. Nevertheless, I doubt whether any machine has or will have the delicate, *selective* control over its striking mechanism that a good pianist has over his fingers. Thanks to this control, he can pick out certain notes in a chord or passage and play them more loudly than the others. And very often, in thus emphasizing a theme, he plays it at such a small dynamic level above the other notes that you are unconscious of the fact that it *is* louder. You receive the impression that it is being played with a different quality, rather than intensity, of sound.

But there's another thing he can do. Don't forget the damper that is above every string. So long as he keeps his finger pressed upon the piano key, the damper remains raised, allowing the string to vibrate and the sound to continue. When he lifts his finger, the damper falls, and the sound is cut off. In other words, if he strikes a short, sharp blow, the sound is produced only for a fraction of a second—what we call a staccato sound. If he strikes and holds, the sound lasts longer. Whatever the physical facts, in terms of sound waves, may be, another fact is that the sounding board of a piano vibrates more completely to a held note than to a short one, and the impression that its vibrations make on our ears varies accordingly. Whether or not it is actually different in quality, it *sounds* different in quality. A skilled pianist can hold every key down until the exact moment when he strikes the next one. This we call true legato playing. It is very difficult, and only a really good pianist can do it; but when it is done well, the singing kind of tone that it produces is unmistakable.

Equally unmistakable is the kind of tone produced when the player presses down the damper pedal, thus allowing the unstruck strings to vibrate also. Regardless of the actual *physical* facts, the apparent richness and sonority of a chord thus played is greater than those of a chord played with the damper pedal up. Likewise, if, in an effort to fake legato playing, he plays a melodic passage with the damper pedal down, the resultant blurred, fuzzy sound produced reaches our ears as an unpleasant *quality* of sound.

In other words, let no aspiring pianist be discouraged by Sir James Jeans. If you have spent years in practicing to produce a decent tone in your playing, don't think that you've been wasting your time. Remember that when you give your first recital your audience will consist, not of a battery of sound-wave candid cameras, but a group of human ears that are dying to be fooled into thinking that you have a beautiful touch. On the other hand, don't be too much *en*couraged. Don't think, just because Sergei Rachmaninoff can't sound his A any better than you can, that you can automatically become a box-office attraction in the concert field. Beauty is in the eye of the beholder. That is true of music, too. The actual sound waves that beat upon our ears do not greatly concern us. What matters is what our ears *tell* us we are hearing. If they do not happen to be telling us the literal facts—that is not very important.

8

First You Hear It

SPEAKING of imperfect musical instruments, there is always that prize example, the human ear, especially
when it is confronted by the problem, not of listening to
music, but of helping to produce it—in other words, as
part of a singer's equipment. We tend to think of a
singer's sound-producing mechanism as the only physical
apparatus that he has to worry about, when as a matter
of fact, his ears have almost as much to do with whether
he sings well or ill as have his vocal cords. Particularly is
this true in the case of choral singing. The amount of harmonic complication of which an *a capella* chorus is capable still remains small, and the choral composer who tries
out atonality and polytonality and suchlike ultramodern
experiments on unaccompanied singers—or even accompanied ones—is only laying up trouble for everybody.
There is much talk of writing for voices "just as for any
other instrument," but the fact of the matter is that the
human voice has one limitation from which every other
instrument is free. The violinist looks at the written note
and stops a string, the oboist presses a key, the trombone
player draws a slide, and out comes a corresponding
sound. The singer cannot do this. He cannot produce accurately any note whose sound he has not already imagined. He must think the note, in his mind's ear, before he
sings it. Consequently the singer feels his way through a

series of imagined sounds while he produces them.

All vocal music is, whether the singer is reading notes or not, played fundamentally "by ear." The moment the vocalist loses this mental image of the sound he is about to produce, he either misses the note altogether, or produces a faulty approximation of it. That is why choruses singing unaccompanied music that is extremely dissonant, chromatic, or otherwise harmonically complicated, tend to go off the pitch. The singers are unable to imagine the sounds accurately. Training and musical sophistication help a good deal, of course, but even the most sensitive vocal imagination lags about half a century behind instrumental harmony. This is the essential and ineradicable difference between choral and orchestral music, and if composers would face it with more resignation they would have fewer disappointments.

9

The High-Polish Question

To DROP into a motion-picture palace such as the Radio City Music Hall after attending a few musical recitals is to receive a lesson in the difference between achievement and intention. The amateur spirit is a beautiful thing, and music, of all the arts, owes most to it. Nevertheless, I cannot help feeling that the great curse of our musical life is amateurishness. A season spent in attending recital and concert halls is a season spent in hearing a few performers accomplishing what they set out to do and a host of bunglers offering good intentions as a substitute for professional skill. One gets so tired of listening to singers and players and conductors whose attitude seems to be that so long as they offer good music they are absolved from doing it well. The halls are full of these musical "halfways"—singers who sing good songs but cannot handle their own voices; singers who can sing but have nothing to say; players who have sensibilities but no technique; players who have technique but nothing else; conductors who manage to keep an orchestra from falling apart through the Tchaikovsky *"Pathétique"* and think they have produced art. A slogan is not a guarantee, and "Art for art's sake" is frequently the last refuge of the incompetent.

Now the big movie houses have little concern, consciously at least, with art. Their chief business is entertainment, and entertainment differs in this wise from culture: that whereas the consciousness of receiving culture will frequently lead a man to praise what he does not enjoy, or tolerate a sloppy performance of good material, no extraneous consideration can keep him from feeling entertained if he is being entertained, or from feeling bored if boredom be his portion. If movie patrons like the show, they come again; if they don't, they stay away. Consequently, anything the big motion-picture houses offer in the way of entertainment is done as well as skill and experience can make it. Their directors have firmly grasped at least one great canon of art: that almost anything done supremely well is interesting. Not long ago I heard some Russian folk songs done as one unit of a movie-house program. They were not put forward as anything extraordinary—all the larger houses offer similar units every week as a matter of course—but they offered a rather impressive illustration of what a first-class professional job ought to be. Everything about their performance was right. The costumes of the singers were appropriate and crisp and well fitting; the stage setting was well designed, striking in color, well painted, and beautifully lighted; the voices were good and the singing was alert, musicianly, and intelligent.

Not that it would necessarily be a good idea for all song recitals to be given in costume, with light effects. But almost any recital artist could learn a great deal from the movie houses in the matter of timing. The average song or instrument recital begins from three to twenty minutes late, and lasts from fifteen to forty minutes too long. If the performer be an old hand, he will prolong the applause after every group (it can be done) so as to take as many

bows as possible before offering the nearly inevitable encore; if he is a novice he rushes out with his encore almost
before the slightly startled audience is aware that it
wanted one. In both cases he has probably fatigued his
hearers to gratify his vanity, and will probably bore them
before he is through. Nothing like that is allowed to happen in a motion-picture house. There, no one's vanity is
nearly so important as giving a show. The Russian folk
songs that I heard were part of a schedule that was as
closely timed as a railway timetable, and a good deal more
reliable. They began upon one scheduled minute and
ended upon another; the curtains closed, opened again
long enough to allow the performers a single bow (picture-
house directors know better than to weary an audience
with encores). Then the lights changed, the orchestra began afresh, and another act was on. There was other music
on the afternoon's program, some of it good, some of it
cheap. All of it was performed with smoothness, technical
competence, intelligence, and unhurried dispatch. The
picture-house musicians are not necessarily masters, but
they are at least professionals; and that is something that
so few aspiring concert "artists" ever manage to be.

There is, on the other hand, such a thing as applying
showmanship appropriately. After a season or so of attending recitals and concerts in which women appear, one
begins to wonder whether some of them are more interested in music or dressmaking. Theoretically, at least, a
singer or pianist is on the stage primarily to make music.
In a sense, the performer is an instrument, much less important as a person than as an artist. Yet here are ladies
trailing clouds of flame-colored chiffon or dazzling in silks
and spangles. It is a wonder some of them do not have the

piano painted pink, or carry a gilded violin. They are clever, though, the ladies, and absolutely right in their estimate of what their audiences want. At one very smart musicale last season a famous prima donna made her first appearance of the year. I interviewed four separate feminine members of the audience that heard her, and not one of them could tell us whether she sang well or ill. They were, however, unanimously rhapsodical over her Turkish trousers.

There is something unfair about all this. Why should women musicians have such an advantage over their male coevals? Why shouldn't Jose Iturbi be allowed to come upon the stage in, say, a purple silk dressing gown with a green sash? He would look no sillier in it than many a woman pianist we have seen clad in her idea of an appropriate costume for playing the piano. The best artists generally dress, I notice, with reasonable simplicity. When they are less than best they sometimes assist the ear by dazzling the eye.

10

Hoking It Up

ANOTHER practice rife among recitalists, designed to make life easier for the audience, is known as Lightening the Program. It consists in giving three quarters of a concert of serious music, music that is worthy of the artist's best efforts, and suddenly offering a closing group composed of high-class trash that any night-club singer or instrumentalist could perform better. This is supposed to perform the double function of (*a*) relieving the hearers of the strain of listening to the kind of music that they ostensibly came to hear, and (*b*) proving that the artist is a good fellow, after all, possessing just as bad taste as any of us.

Singers are particularly prone to this sort of musical baby kissing. There seems to be a curious assumption among them that serious music is always heavy and solemn. I once heard a famous baritone assure me that while he hated cheap ballads as much as I did, a recital program made up of the best songs in his repertoire would be a doleful affair, "since lighter verse doesn't inspire a composer to put forward his best efforts." This, despite the fact that one of the most charming songs ever written, and one of the most effective in his own repertoire is Grieg's *Lauf der Welt*. And what about Schubert's *Heidenröslein,* or Moussorgsky's *The Siege of Kazan,* to name two out of fifty?

HOKING IT UP

"The sentimental ballads lighten the program." Yet I know nothing on earth quite so lugubrious as the text of a sentimental ballad. The themes most harped upon are three, all very sad. First comes the bent, white-haired mother, more beautiful than any queen, into whose arms the world-weary, disillusioned singer would love to creep, there to rest his tired head. Next we have a little road, or a little lane, or a little street (a big one would never do) that leads to an equally little house, or cottage, or home; generally there is someone of the feminine gender standing in the doorway with a welcoming smile in her eyes of blue. And oh, if the singer could only go back to it, and her! (Would God he could.) Sometimes, in the last verse, he *has* gone back, and they are both gray-haired. Last of the trio is contrasting in its moods. Yesterday the sun shone, and the birds sang their heads off, and the grass was green, because you were here. Now it is cloudy, and the birds are all dead, and the wind is keen, because you are gone. "Lighten," indeed!

11

Bach in the Groove

THERE was a great uproar, not long ago, over the question of the desecration of the classics by jazz bands. It all started when the president of the Bach Society of New Jersey sent a letter to the Federal Communications Commission, complaining of the practice of playing the music of the classic masters, particularly Bach, in swing time. He said specifically, that on two recent occasions he had heard a jazz orchestra giving its own rendition of Bach's Toccata in D minor. "All the beautiful fugue effects," he wrote, "were destroyed by the savage slurring of the saxophone and the jungled discords of the clarinet." His proposed remedy was—I quote from his letter—"that any station that violates the canon of decency by permitting the syncopating of the classics, particularly Bach's music, be penalized by having its license suspended for the first offense. A second offense could be punished by revocation of the license."

Somehow I cannot help feeling that the proposed penalty for the offense is a little out of proportion to the enormity of the crime. If you're going to suspend the license of a broadcasting station for permitting Bach to be played in swing time, what are you going to do to a station for permitting swing music to be played at all? (You might offer the owner of the station his choice of either listening to nothing *but* swing for, say, twelve hours, or else spend-

ing a month in jail.) You can't legislate against bad taste.
The minute you start regulating people's likes and dislikes
in music, or books, or whatnot, you are confronted by the
question of *who* is to decide what is good and what is bad?
And you soon discover that there is no Emily Post of the
arts.

Besides, I am not so sure that Bach himself would fall
to the floor in a fit if he heard a swing version of his
Toccata in D minor. If there's one thing of which I am
certain, it is that the so-called classic masters were not
aware that they were classic masters. As Gilbert Seldes
once wrote, "the Japanese are not Oriental to themselves."
The casual way in which Bach and Handel and Haydn
and Mozart turned out suites and fugues and symphonies
seems to me to indicate that they didn't take themselves
with quite the deadly seriousness with which some of us
take them. They wrote good music, and I think they knew
it, but I don't for a minute think that they looked upon
every note that they composed as a direct message from
Heaven, never to be touched or altered.

Take, for instance, Bach's Third Suite in D major. Of
what does it consist? First, an overture, in the style that
a then ultramodern French-Italian composer named Lully
had made popular. Next an air. This particular one happens to be one of the greatest melodies ever written. But
it happened to be written because, in the suite of Bach's
time, a slow melody was usually the second number. Then
follow two gavottes, a *bourée,* and a *gigue*—or, if you
want to spell it in modern English, a jig. Now much as I
hate to point it out, those last four pieces were the equivalent, in Bach's era, of jazz. They were popular dances of
the day. They may sound very dignified to us, but the fact

remains that when Bach wrote them he was thinking, not in terms of immortal music, but in terms of dance tunes. If there had been such a thing as a rumba or a tango when Bach was living, you may be sure that a Bach suite would have included a rumba and a tango.

Don't misunderstand me. I am not saying that it's a laudable thing to play swing versions of the classics, or that anyone ought to try *not* to be revolted by hearing a piece of familiar and beautiful music distorted. But the distortion itself, while it may be a nuisance, is hardly a crime.

Furthermore, if you're going to be completely consistent about this question of altering a composer's original work, where are you going to stop? After all, a so-called "swing" version of a piece of music is merely a debased form of a set of variations; and if it's wrong for a jazz-band arranger to write his particular variations on a theme by Bach, why is it right for Brahms to write *his* particular variations on a theme by Hadyn? There is a very obvious answer to that, of course, which is that the Brahms variations are great music and the jazz band's variations are trash. But while you and I may believe that, we can't prove it. We can only say, in the last analysis, "That's what *I* think." Most people would agree that we were right, in an extreme case such as I have chosen. But cases are not always extreme. There is, for instance, a swing version of a Bach prelude and fugue that Paul Whiteman frequently plays, called *Thank you, Mr. Bach*. To me, it is a delightful and witty piece of music, and does Bach no harm. As a matter of fact, I'm sure that Bach would have been enchanted with it. But I have no doubt that a vast number of persons, whose opinions are just as good as mine, would find that particular piece a horrible desecration.

I believe in letting people hear these swing monstrosities because I believe that it's the best method of getting rid of them. Occasionally, out of morbid curiosity, I, in common with the president of the Bach Society of New Jersey, have listened to some of those arrangements; and what strikes me about them is their spectacular dullness. There is—or was—one in particular that you probably heard— the one that goes: *Martha, Martha, dum-de-dum-dum* —and so forth. You don't have to know that that is a distortion of *"M'appari,"* from Flotow's *Marta,* to know that it's bad. The most harm it can accomplish is to give a few innocent people the impression that *"M'appari"* is equally dull; but that impression will last only until they hear the real *"M'appari."* Meanwhile, the swing arrangement will long since have been one with Nineveh and Tyre.

A great deal of this hatred and denunciation of swing arrangements rises, I am sure, from a fear that they will do lasting damage to the music upon which they are based. I don't think there are any grounds for that fear. A real work of art is a good deal tougher than we assume that it is. Great music, like great painting and sculpture and literature, can stand an incredible amount of mauling. In fact, I would go so far as to venture the opinion that one test of the greatness and vitality of a work of art is whether or not it can stand being burlesqued. A recent musical-comedy hit in New York was an opus by Rodgers and Hart, entitled *The Boys from Syracuse.* It was nothing more or less than Shakespeare's *The Comedy of Errors* adapted for the musical stage, and the title will give you a rough idea of just how respectful that adaptation is. Yet nobody, up to now, has claimed, or will claim, I think, that *The Boys from Syracuse* harmed Shakespeare.

The same is true of music. You can't spoil anything really great. If you could, think of what the motion pictures have been doing to the music of the masters ever since the first silent films. In putting together scores for the pictures, the arrangers long ago discovered that Bach and Beethoven and Tchaikovsky and Wagner and the rest had written much more graphic and colorful and dramatic action music than they could hope to contrive. So they used their music without scruple—and still do—to go with any and all kinds of films. And what has happened to the masters? The answer is summed up very well, I think, in a letter from one of my correspondents, a college student. He writes:

"What if Cab Calloway should, for a change, decide to arrange the B minor Mass as he arranges the *Hi De Ho Miracle Man*? Has any permanent or temporary harm come to Bach? I, for one, would hate to admit it. I am quite confident that the B minor Mass will last longer than Mr. Calloway. And so with the movies. What matter if they do use the second movement of the Beethoven Seventh and make 'hurry up music' out of it? How long is the life of a film? If Beethoven can't stand such competition, I'll take Hollywood. But that will not be necessary. I, for one, will still climb to the top shelf of Carnegie Hall and feel lucky to have a seat."

Yes, but as we all say, "It isn't that I mind so much. I can hear that stuff without harm, because my taste in music is already formed. It can't be corrupted. But think of the others. Think of the thousands of children whose taste is being ruined by that jazz stuff. Think of the thousands of men and women who are eager to hear music but don't yet know the good from the bad. It's the damage to *their* taste that worries me."

So far as the children are concerned, if you don't want your child to be corrupted by listening to jazz and swing arrangements, keep him out of night clubs. If, on the other hand, he insists on listening to them over the radio—may I point out that the average parent is physically stronger than the average child? Whether or not he is to listen to any given program is partly, at least, your problem. As for the grownups, nine times out of ten, while you are busy worrying about what's happening to somebody else's taste, you would discover, if you could meet him, that he is engaged in worrying about what's happening to *your* taste. So don't waste too much energy worrying about other people, or becoming indignant over cheap music. If your favorite night club or radio set insults your ears with a swing arrangement of Bach, don't get red in the face, and roar, and write to the *Times*. Just exercise the right of individual censorship that is the glorious privilege of every American. In the first instance, call for your check, pay it, rise, and stalk majestically out into the night—not forgetting to tip the hat-check girl. In the second, just lean over, and unostentatiously turn that small knob marked STATION SELECTOR.

12

Beethoven Goes to Town

WHILE we are on the subject of swing music, I wonder if the so-called jitterbugs, to whom it has come as a new and stunning discovery, realize just how old it is. As the result of considerable philological research, I find that one must draw a sharp line between jazz and swing. The former, as it is known today, is a term applied loosely to almost any form of popular vocal and dance music except, possibly, the waltz. Swing music, on the other hand, is music that doesn't exist in any permanent form whatsoever. When they speak of a trumpeter or a clarinetist "swinging" a tune, they mean that he undertakes to execute a series of impromptu variations on a given air. These variations are never written down, and are never twice alike, and the players who invent them are very scornful of what they call "paper men," that is, players who perform from written or printed notes.

That practice, of course, is as old as the hills. In the Neapolitan school of opera, about the middle of the eighteenth century, it was accepted as a matter of course that opera singers should make up their own trills and ornamental passages and cadenzas as they went along. In eighteenth-century concertos for piano and violin, the cadenzas were seldom written out. Usually, the composer simply came to a stop at some point in the work, wrote *cadenza* in the score, and tacitly invited the player to make up his own cadenza, based on the main theme—in other words, to "swing" it.

Even great composers and virtuosos like Mozart and Beethoven did it as a matter of routine. In the closing years of the eighteenth century, Beethoven's great rival as a pianist was a virtuoso named Wölfl. The two used to meet at soirees given at the castle of Baron Raymond von Wetzlar. Let me quote you a line or two from Thayer's monumental biography of Beethoven, as to what used to go on:

"There," writes Thayer, "the interesting combats of the two athletes not infrequently offered an indescribable artistic treat to the numerous and thoroughly select gathering. . . . Now one, and anon the other, gave free rein to his glowing fancy; sometimes they would seat themselves at two pianos and improvise alternately on themes which they gave each other, and thus created many a four-hand *capriccio* which, if it could have been put upon paper at the moment, would surely have bidden defiance to time." In other words, Beethoven and Wölfl sat down and had what, at the Onyx Club in New York, would be called a "jam session."

The only difference between the two is the possibly not unimportant one that one of the swing players was Beethoven.

13

Hands Across the C's

CLARA SCHUMANN was, if I am not mistaken, the only famous woman pianist of her generation. Today, of course, a woman pianist, violinist, or singer, or even a woman conductor, is no particular novelty. But turn back only a few pages of musical history and you will find that except in the field of opera, professional women musicians were a rarity up to within comparatively recent years. The reason why is no mystery, except that we don't think about it nowadays. I was forcibly reminded of it not long ago by hearing of a conversation that took place between a young singer and one of her friends.

Before embarking upon singing as a career she had led a very active social life. But singing, as she discovered— as any singer discovers—is a form of rather severe physical exertion, and no one can hope to become a successful vocal artist without keeping in training, more or less like any other athlete. Consequently, during the past few years she has seen a good deal less of her former intimates than she used to, simply because she hasn't been able to attend the midnight parties and noonday breakfasts where they were to be found.

Her friend, as I say, called her on the telephone and talked to her very seriously. He said, in effect: "Why do you waste your life like this? Think of the fun you're missing, the good times, the friends you're not seeing any more. Leave singing to the women who need the money. You're an attractive girl, and a clever girl; and you're doing a foolish thing. If you want to sing, sing for us, your friends. Look at the audiences that you sing for now. Just think: how many of those people would you dream of inviting to your house for dinner?"

Now to any professional musician—as a matter of fact, to most of you, I imagine, musicians or not—that point of view probably sounds fantastic. In this day and age it *is* fantastic. But we wouldn't have thought it fantastic as recently as a century ago. It is a prejudice that dates from the earlier days of the art of music, when the only people who had the money and the culture to be able to enjoy music were of noble birth. And since no titled person could take up any profession other than the church or the army without becoming a social outcast, the ranks of the musicians were necessarily recruited from the lower classes. Wellborn people simply didn't become professional singers or players or actors. Consequently there was a ready-made social abyss yawning between the audience and the performer. The friend whom I have quoted comes of a very old French family. It is quite within the range of possibility that one of his eighteenth-century ancestors may have given a party one night, at which he had young Mozart to play the piano. If he did, I am quite sure that young Mozart, granted that he was even invited to dinner, sat either at the extreme lower end of the table or, more probably, in the kitchen, with the servants.

I am quite sure that his attitude would be quite different if his young friend had decided, not to sing music, but to compose it, or to write novels, or paint pictures. Why? Because literature, composition, and painting are respectable and private callings. They are followed in the privacy of one's home or studio, so that it is possible to become a successful creative artist without coming into contact with socially undesirable people. On the other hand, I know that his point of view regarding the interpretative artist— particularly the feminine one—is shared by a great many persons—particularly in Continental Europe, which still considers a professional career pretty rough work for members of a sex so sheltered that it cannot even be allowed to vote. It is a point of view that results from two causes. One is the inherited prejudice that I have just mentioned, the habit of looking upon the singer or instrumentalist strictly as a hired entertainer. The other is a hopeless misunderstanding of the relation of the artist to the public.

That relation is a very important one and, quite truly, a very close one. I have often heard people say: "Suppose you were to put Heifetz, and Elman, and Kreisler, and Spalding, and Zimbalist on the same platform, and had them play behind screens. How many people would be able to tell them apart?" I can answer that. I'm quite sure that a vast number of people, including a fair sprinkling of music critics, would *not* be able to tell them apart. But that sort of thing is quite beside the point. Just as a blindfold cigarette test is more or less meaningless, for the simple reason that most people can't taste cigarette smoke in the dark, just so is any hearing of musical artists that ignores one of the chief distinguishing traits of a great musical artist—personality.

Any of you who have ever heard a really great violinist, or pianist, or singer, in an auditorium, must know the mysterious, exciting, electric emanation that flows from the artist to you, that grips you even before he begins to sing or play, and that immeasurably heightens your enjoyment of his performance. That is personality, something that is none the less real however much it may defy analysis. And it is a legitimate and vital part of the equipment of any artist. That is why I have never shared the apprehensions of people who are afraid that the radio will destroy concerts and operas. It won't destroy them. A great deal of an artist's personality does come through on the radio; but not all of it. No matter how long your friend may talk to you over the telephone, you are no less willing and eager to talk with him in person.

Conversely, anybody who has ever stepped on a platform knows only too well the feeling of having an audience with you or against you. It is a feeling that has nothing to do with whether the people laugh or cry, applaud or hiss, whisper or keep silent. It is a very definite current that passes, for good or ill, between the two halves that go to make up a complete performance: the performer *and* the hearer. The relation of a singer or an actor to his audience is the closest of all; for in the case of each, the instrument upon which he plays is his own voice and his own body. He is both the violin and the violinist.

But however close the relation is, it is a purely psychic one; *never* a personal or social one. It is the amateur, or the not quite complete professional, who smiles or nods to his friends in the front row. The real artist has no friends or relatives when he steps upon the platform. He has in front of him a monster that must be tamed; a thousand-headed monster that can be warm and friendly, or cold and murderous. In either case, once the performance is over, the monster dissolves. It is merely a lot of people. To ask a singer if she would care to invite a member of her audience to dinner is equivalent to asking her if she would care to invite one of her friends' fingers to dinner. In both cases it is the assumption that a part is the equivalent to the whole.

14

Too Good to Learn

YOU may think that I made too much of the incident that I cited in the last chapter. After all, in this democracy we have no such snobbish ideas about music. I wish that were true. Let me point out one form of musical snobbishness in this country that has been a real handicap in our development.

One question regarding American musical conditions that is probably asked more often than any other is: "Why are not our symphony orchestras being conducted by Americans?" Thinking about that question the other day, I thought I would try an experiment. I said to myself: "Granted that most of our symphony conductors are foreign born, how did they get that way? What were their professional beginnings?" So I looked up some of them. Here is a list of sixteen. It doesn't pretend to be complete, of course, but every man in it is a foreign-born conductor, well known in this country today. Here are their names, together with a description of what they were before they became orchestral conductors:

John Barbirolli: cello player in an orchestra
Georges Enesco: violin virtuoso
Vladimir Golschmann: orchestral conductor
Eugene Goossens: violin player in an orchestra
Willem van Hoogstraten: violin ensemble player
Jose Iturbi: piano virtuoso

Hans Kindler: cello player in an orchestra
Sergei Koussevitzky: double-bass player in an orchestra
Pierre Monteux: viola player in an orchestra
Eugene Ormandy: violin player in an orchestra
Fritz Reiner: conductor of comic opera
Artur Rodzinski: choral conductor
Alexander Smallens: timpani player in an orchestra
Frederick Stock: viola player in an orchestra
Leopold Stokowski: church organist
Arturo Toscanini: cello player in an orchestra

Do you see what I see? Sixteen conductors. Just two
of them, so far as the records show, actually began their
careers as conductors. One learned his trade conducting
choruses, another, training choirs. Two were famous and
experienced virtuosos before, comparatively late in their
careers, they took up conducting. The other ten learned
their business in the best place to learn it—at a player's
stand in an orchestra. It was there that they became
familiar with the orchestral repertoire, learned the various readings of various conductors, learned the standard
tempos and dynamics of the standard works, learned the
difference between a clear beat and a confusing one,
learned what an orchestra player needs from a conductor
—learned, in short, the things that any musician must
have at his finger tips before he can hope to be a competent conductor.

How many Americans are learning the business of conducting by that method today? If you want to know why
our conductors are foreign born, look at the roll call of
the musicians in our symphony orchestras. I think you
will find that eighty per cent of them are either foreign

born, or are the sons of foreign-born orchestral musicians. The plain truth is that the average young American who wants to be an orchestral conductor is far too willing to begin at the top. It is beneath his dignity to start as a common, ordinary, union orchestra player. No. If he studies any instrument at all, he does so in the expectation of becoming a successful concert artist. If he discovers that that ambition has no probability of being realized, he either gets out of music altogether, or tries to become a conductor because he knows how to beat time. But get a job in an orchestra? In most cases, no, thank you. Meanwhile, the foreign-born instrumentalist, who comes from a country where an orchestra player is accepted as a musician as readily as a singer would be, does get a job in an orchestra, and does learn to be a conductor.

That is all the fault of our snobbish attitude toward orchestral playing. It's rather a social distinction to be able to say that your son is at a conservatory studying to be a concert pianist or violinist. But you would rather hesitate to admit that your boy is at the conservatory studying the tuba or the contrabassoon.

Luckily, things aren't quite as bad as I paint them. Such *was* the case, but the situation is rapidly changing. One of the most striking phenomena of our musical life has been the incredible growth of school bands and orchestras during the past few years. Boys and girls are being encouraged to learn to play orchestral instruments, and to play them well. The word "piccolo player" is rapidly ceasing to be a term of reproach. I believe that during the next ten years we shall see an amazing increase in the numbers of American-born players sitting at the desks of our symphony orchestras. And when that happens—and, I think, not *until* that happens—we shall begin to see some American conductors.

15

Woman's Place

THERE is one class of our citizenry, however, and a very considerable class at that, who, no matter how willing and anxious they might be to begin a career at a desk in a symphony orchestra, would find it difficult, if not impossible, to find a position. I refer, of course, to the female sex. Just why is it that there are not more women players in our orchestras? If one could just reply, flatly, "Sex discrimination; they don't want women in orchestras"—that would be, at least, a definite answer. But one can't say that. As a matter of fact there are, if not many, at least a few women playing today in symphony orchestras. I should say that at least eight out of ten orchestral harpists are women, and that scattered throughout the country one can find numerous women violinists, violists, and cellists. Nevertheless, it is true that male orchestral musicians are in an overwhelming majority. Why is that?

I'm afraid there is no one answer. For one thing, there are physical reasons why women don't perform well on certain instruments. The average woman is not likely to possess sufficient lung power and sheer muscular strength to play the tuba, just as the average woman's hands are not likely to be large enough to finger a double bass satisfactorily. But, ruling those out, the question still remains unanswered. What about the other instruments?

Prejudice, custom, and tradition, I think. The one instrument that almost always *is* played by women in orchestras, the harp, is one that for centuries has been accepted as a woman's instrument. Playing the harp, a century ago, was one of the accomplishments of almost every properly brought-up young woman. While that is no longer so (I can scarcely imagine a present-day debutante entertaining her boy friends by playing the harp), it is still no shock to see a woman harpist in an orchestra.

I think social and family pressure have been very strong in keeping women out of orchestras. Think of the prejudice that existed, less than half a century ago, against so-called "nice" girls going on the stage. The stage won out, for the simple reason that it simply had to have women to play feminine roles in plays and operas, and was willing, therefore, to offer a young woman more money than she could make in almost any other profession. Moreover, on the stage she was appearing more or less as an individual, as a center of attraction. This was gratifying both to herself and to her family. To this day, while the average parents are reconciled to seeing their daughter become an opera singer or concert artist, they don't like the idea of seeing her a member of an organization, of submerging her personality to become a member of the chorus or the orchestra. This may sound a little silly, but I think it is so. A prejudice doesn't have to be intelligent in order to be binding.

Once, I remember, I asked the conductor of a famous Midwestern orchestra why he had so few women players. "Ten years ago," I said, "when I first heard your band, you had at least ten women in it. Now you have only one. Why?"

"Discipline," he said. "For a while I thought the experiment was going to work. But when the second flute ran off with the fourth horn, and the third oboe and the second cello staged a hair-pulling fight at rehearsal, and the bass clarinet horsewhipped the husband of the second double bass—I decided that the trouble wasn't worth the results. So I let them go." I add, hastily, that I didn't believe a word of what he said, and am quoting him only to show to what lengths some people will go in an effort to be funny.

The principal reason why we have so few women orchestral musicians is, I think, the simple one that so few of them play wind instruments well enough. They don't play well enough because they haven't had the proper training; and the reason for that lies in the history of orchestral music in the United States. Less than half a century ago in this country it was virtually impossible for a would-be orchestral player to get any instruction worthy of the name, on a wind instrument. Even our string players were studying, not for the orchestra, but for the concert platform. In consequence, a majority of the string players in our orchestras, and practically all the members of the brass and woodwind sections, were imported from Continental Europe, from France, Italy, Germany, and Russia. Now these men brought with them the Continental attitude toward women, which was that a woman's proper spheres were social and domestic, never professional or political. Such a thing as a woman orchestra player was a monster of which they never would have dreamed.

Playing orchestral instruments, on the Continent, is not only a strictly masculine occupation, but also, to a striking degree, a hereditary one. You will find famous European families of bassoon players, clarinetists, or oboists. These early, imported musicians of ours taught their sons to play the family instrument; and you will find the sons of many of these men in our orchestras today. Their sons; but never their daughters. If they had any other pupils, those pupils were boys, not girls. And to this day, while American women vote, hold public office, and practice all the professions without shocking our sensibilities, in this particular field, the orchestra, our attitude toward women still remains, I think, rather a Continental one. Woman's place may not be the home, but it certainly isn't among the trombones.

However, that prejudice is rapidly crumbling, and is likely to disappear entirely in a few years. For this we have to thank our high-school bands and orchestras, which offer instruction, practice, and experience in playing all orchestral instruments to boys and girls alike. The American father no longer averts his eyes at the sight of his daughter pounding a bass drum, nor does the American mother shudder at the sight of lipstick on an oboe reed. Of that, more in our next chapter.

16

To Play's the Thing

IT WAS, in a phrase that Mrs. Carrie Jacobs Bond has made almost too familiar, the end of a perfect day. We had driven over to the Sound for a swim before lunch, watched the local ball team achieve a victory in the afternoon, and demolished a picnic supper. Now we were sitting on the terrace in the waning light, preparing to enjoy one of those perfect, windless, not-too-hot-or-cold summer evenings that the Connecticut countryside provides to perfection when it feels like it.

The evening was silent—"silent," that is, in the rural sense of the word. Which is to say that there was not a sound to be heard save the roulades and cadenzas of thousands of tree toads, the complaints of a distant whippoorwill, the remote rumble of an electric dishwasher, and the faint creak of a neighbor's windmill. But we country folk don't hear those sounds, any more than city people hear busses and taxicabs. The evening, I still say, was silent.

But not for long. Suddenly I found myself musing on the essential sadness of life. The world, I reflected, is a pretty tragic place, after all. I thought of bombings in Spain, of slaughter in China, of purges in Germany. Why, I pondered, do I think of these things? Why, on this divine night, in these perfect surroundings, do I suddenly seem to hear the wails of the widowed, the crying of the orphaned, the groans of the dying?

Then I knew. It was a sound, a new sound, far-off and yet all-pervasive; a low moan that began as scarcely a whisper, then rose to a shriek of agony, trembled, broke, and then sank to a sobbing wail of despair. I sat, rigid, turning a pallid, questioning face towards my host and hostess. Was I going mad, or had they, too, heard this grisly thing?

They had. My host sprang out of his chair with a stifled oath, and disappeared into the house. In a moment the sound ceased as abruptly as it had begun. My hostess smiled apologetically.

"It was only Junior practicing his saxophone," she remarked, mildly. "It won't happen again."

Nevertheless, I am on Junior's side. Granted that an imperfectly played saxophone is one of civilization's scourges; admitted that the sound of a minor dependent practicing the B-flat clarinet or the trumpet in C is something not easily borne; conceded that there is nothing comparable to the tortures that can be inflicted by a young violinist who can play almost in tune; even so, I believe that every child who is not entirely tone-deaf should be encouraged to play some musical instrument. And if for "encouraged" you wish to substitute "coerced," I for one have no objection.

Why? Why, during the very period of a person's life when he is busy acquiring the education that is to fit him for making a living—or a home—when his body is developing and needs exercise, when, in short, his or her waking hours are already occupied with a multiplicity of tasks whose complexity would bewilder an adult—why, during these critical, crowded years, should he be asked or allowed to devote time to learning to play an instrument, an occupation that in most instances bears not the slightest relation to the practical side of the life for which he is supposed to be preparing?

The question I have just quoted is not a rhetorical one. I have been asked it many times. I can answer it, in part, by asking another. Just how many of the subjects that a child studies in school bear any direct relation to the so-called practical side of life? Outside of arithmetic, spelling, and grammar, how much of what we study do we really employ in making a living or running a house? Is a knowledge of the principal exports of Brazil, or the date of Milton's death, or the French for "Oh, I am, am I?" of any very definite use to the average wage earner or housekeeper?

Why do we study these things? Why bother with literature, and geography, and history, and composition writing, when, except in a few special cases, they are not particularly useful weapons in the so-called battle of life? The question is as old as the hills, and so is the answer. Which is, that what we call education exists not only to enable us to make a living, but to help us get some fun out of life. An educated person does not necessarily make as much money or cook as well as an uneducated one, but he has a better time. His topics of conversation are not limited to what went on in the office today or what the grocery boy said about Mrs. Gimmick. He reads a newspaper with more understanding and enjoyment; he can talk to other people about something besides himself; when he is tired of going to the movies or listening to the radio he can read a book, or look at a picture—or attend a concert.

Anyone who cannot listen to music with some degree of

interest and understanding is missing a lot out of life. I mean serious music, of course. Anyone can understand jazz, chiefly because there's nothing to understand. All you have to do is expose your ear to it. That is nothing against jazz; when it is mildly stimulating your nervous system, and doing things to your feet, it is doing all its creators ever intended it to do.

But serious music takes serious listening. It is much subtler than dance music, follows a less rigid pattern, is less easy to grasp. Once you do understand it, do gather what it is driving at, it is, of course, much more exciting. Thanks largely to radio, every one of us has a chance, as we never had before, to hear the world's greatest music, played and sung by the world's finest artists, for the mere turning of a switch. And any child who is not brought up on it is being neglected by his parents.

But why learn an instrument? Why not just see to it that he listens, or, at the most, takes some sort of course in music appreciation? Why should he learn to *play* music as well as listen to it, unless you expect him to become a professional?

There are two resons why—only one, really, that has any importance. The unimportant one is a social reason. You know those advertisements for courses in piano lessons by mail, the ones that begin "How they laughed when I sat down at the piano"? They go on to relate how the other young folks at the party were simply bowled over when they discovered that our hero could actually play dance music, with the result that he became the most popular member of his set. Don't laugh. There's a certain degree of good, sound, snobbish truth in those ads. It is quite true that anyone who has a parlor trick, whether it is doing imitations or playing jazz, is an amusing and desirable person to have around. I might add, in passing, that what the advertisements *don't* mention is that our hero, once his gift was discovered, was kept at the piano all evening, playing for the others to dance, and had to sit, miserably banging out "Kiss Me Again" while his best girl glided about the room in the arms of his rival, who later married her.

No, what I am discussing is what a child gains, not socially, but inwardly, by playing a musical instrument. And this is what he gets:

Do you play tennis? baseball? golf? football? If you have ever played any of these games you must have realized that when you watch your particular specialty being played you not only enjoy the spectacle, but you derive an additional keen pleasure from recognizing a thousand fine points that are entirely missed by the nonplaying onlookers. At a tennis match, what they see and applaud is A's brilliant line drive that caught B standing in his tracks. That's an exterior pleasure. But if you're a tennis player you also have the interior pleasure of appreciating the skill with which A, three rallies ago, began to trick B into getting out of position.

Music is like that. Teach a child to play a musical instrument, and he begins to know music *from the inside,* begins to learn about it in the easiest and pleasantest way that I know. When he listens to music he will derive a threefold pleasure from it. He will appreciate the skill of the player, having struggled with the instrument himself; he will enjoy the pleasant sounds, just as you do; and he will also recognize and appreciate the structure and details of the music himself, because he has played it for himself, and so become familiar with every note of it. No need to give him lessons in music appreciation. If he has learned to make his way through the second clarinet part of a Beethoven scherzo he knows more about Beethoven than a year of music-appreciation courses could teach him.

One word of advice: whatever instrument your child shows signs of wanting to play, insist that he or she acquire at least a rudimentary acquaintance with the piano. For the piano, outside of the organ, which is expensive, and the harp, which is limited, is the only complete musical instrument, the only one upon which one can play not only the melody but the harmony of a piece of music. It is, consequently, the ideal and indispensable instrument for becoming acquainted with the whole of a composition.

That acquaintance can be begun, by the way, at an astonishingly early age, as early as his third year, when you can encourage him to sit at the piano and bang. It sounds like a horrible thing to do, and for your sake as well as his own I wouldn't advise you to overdo it, but it does familiarize him with the idea that pleasing sounds can be drawn from that mysterious black thing with the white teeth. At the same time play him, or sing him, folk songs, simple tunes that are still good music. Get a cheap phonograph, and play him folk-song records, then start him at trying to pick out his favorite airs on the piano keys.

The minute he begins to show any aptitude at all, unless you play fairly well yourself, get him a piano teacher. The teacher need not be expensive, and the lessons need not be numerous, but you must avoid the mistake of letting him begin real piano playing without correct technique. If you don't, and later on he should decide to take the instrument seriously, he will have to spend laborious months unlearning the bad playing habits that you let him form as a small child.

When he is old enough to make any decisions of his own —say in the upper grades of grammar school—if your offspring wants to go on with his piano studies, let him. If, on the other hand, he still wants to play the oboe, or saxophone, or violin, or whatnot, by all means let him do that, too. For there exists today a medium for utilizing that instrumental technique of his that was not even dreamed of when I was a youngster: the school band or orchestra. There are vast numbers of them in existence today (undoubtedly there is one either in or near your home town), and outside the radio, they constitute the most important agency for spreading musical appreciation that I know. They offer, first of all, an incentive to children to learn to play, and play well; and they offer a priceless opportunity to study music, as I said, from the inside, to get to understand it, not by analyzing it, but by making it.

There must be thousands and thousands of American school children today who are playing in these bands and orchestras. Not one in a thousand of them, I imagine, has any chance or desire to become a professional musician. But the other nine hundred ninety-nine are not wasting their time. They are learning to know music, to live it, and to love it; and their lives will be the richer for it.

17

Portrait of an Artist

YEARS ago, when portable typewriters were more of a
novelty than they are now, I carried one with me to
France. On the way over, I showed it one day to the ship's
purser, who had never before seen one. He examined it
admiringly, exclaimed over its lightness and compactness,
and finally relinquished it with a sigh, remarking regret-
fully, "But, of course, Monsieur, such a machine would
be of little use to me. I never go anywhere!"

I thought of that incident when Heifetz and I were discussing this chapter.

"What about the biographical part of it?" I asked.

"I wish you'd keep it short," he answered. "Just make
it: 'Born in Russia, first lessons at three, debut in Russia
at seven, debut in America in 1917.' That's all there is to
say, really. About two lines."

And so, obediently, I give you Jascha Heifetz's autobiography, exactly as dictated. In a way, he is right. That
is about all there is to say. A man can run away to sea at
an early age, work as a cook in a lumber camp, serve with
the Foreign Legion, boss a railroad construction gang, and
finally emerge as a first-rate novelist. Most assuredly he
will never end up as a great violinist.

No concert artist can afford the sort of personal life
that makes melodramatic reading for the layman. Heifetz,
who, like so many musicians, is fond of figuring, will tell

you that up to now he has spent upwards of 66,000 hours
—about two fifths of his waking life—in playing the
violin. In the course of spending them he has been around
the world four times and has played in almost every country on the face of the globe; at thirty-eight, he has already
traveled a distance equivalent to two round trips to the
moon, and is well on the first leg of a third. Nevertheless, his career, stripped to its essentials, has inevitably
been one of: practice—travel—rehearse—play—sleep, repeated, with slight variations, year after year, for thirty-
odd years. The important things about him are not "Where
has he been and how did he get there?" so much as "What
has he done and who is he?"

You know the short and simple answer to the first question. He has played the fiddle; played it in a manner that
few men, living or dead, have ever equaled. Ranking artists is a silly business, and "the greatest in the world" is
nothing more, in the last analysis, than the expression of
somebody's opinion. But as far back as that fabulous
twenty-seventh of October in 1917, when a slender, seventeen-year-old Russian boy first stepped on the stage of
New York's Carnegie Hall, we all knew that the ranks of
the living masters of the violin had received another recruit.

The most obvious aspect of his playing was, and still is,
his incredible technical mastery, a mastery so complete
that the lay listener becomes unconscious of it. It takes
another violinist, I think, fully to appreciate Heifetz's
technique, just as it takes an engineer to appreciate the
silent perfection of a smoothly running piece of machin-
ery. He is one of the comparatively few musical artists,
even among the great ones, who can be described, somewhat inadequately, as "safe," the master craftsmen upon

whom you can rely to accomplish, completely, whatever they set out to do. Once in a while you run across a singer to whom you can listen without wondering whether or not he is going to manage that tricky chromatic passage or whether she is going to hit that high B-flat; a pianist upon whom you can count not to muff that run in thirds; a horn player who, you know, isn't going to blow a bubble at the end of Siegfried's fanfare.

Heifetz is one of those. You may differ with his interpretation of a given piece of music, but so far as concerns his ability to play it, you can settle back in your seat without misgivings. You can count on the crystal purity of his intonation, the perfection of his harmonics, the evenness of his tone, and the dazzling surety of his bowing. He will never let you down.

Not that this technique of his affects everyone alike. There is a story connected with his New York debut. Since it is a true story, I shall suppress the names of the principals, relating merely that sitting in a box at that debut recital were a world-famous pianist and an equally famous violinist. As the program progressed the violinist began to show signs of distress. The longer Heifetz played the more uncomfortable his listener became. Finally, running his handkerchief around his collar, he turned and whispered: "It's awfully hot in here, isn't it?"

Upon which his companion remarked, simply, "Not for pianists."

I thought of that story as I sat in a projection room on the Goldwyn lot in Hollywood, one afternoon last year, watching—and hearing—a sequence from his picture, *They Shall Have Music*. It showed Heifetz, on the platform of a concert hall, playing Saint-Saëns's *Introduction* and *Rondo capriccioso,* and, in accordance with motion-picture technique, showed the player, not merely as one would see him from a seat in the auditorium, but from many angles and at varying distances—long shots, medium long shots, close-ups, and what one might call close-close-ups, views of the bow and the wonderfully controlled arm that propels it, glimpses of the flashing fingers of that miraculous left hand. I thought then, with what despairing admiration a violinist must watch those fingers; but I thought, too, how the violinists, amateur and professional alike, were going to haunt that picture, for the sake of seeing, as no one ever saw before, how Heifetz does it.

But sheer mechanical perfection would never have brought Heifetz to the place he occupies in the world of music. There are other great technicians. It is the use to which he puts his technique that entitles him to the adjective "great." The versatility of his style, the breadth and nobility of his interpretations, are traditional. The only serious criticism that I have ever heard leveled against his playing (generally by people who had heard him very little) is that it lacks warmth. He is too Olympian, too detached, they say; he touches your head too much, and your heart not enough.

I am pretty sure that, in part at least, that opinion has a subconscious physical basis. People are childishly dependent upon visual impressions, and, watching Heifetz, they might easily confuse the sound of the playing with the appearance of the player. And Heifetz is the least demonstrative of any concert artist I know. Even among his friends, although he laughs readily, curiously enough he seldom smiles. On the platform, almost never. His attitude to his listeners is one of perfect, unsmiling courtesy, and when he plays he does so with such complete absorption in the music that, looking at his remote, almost mask-like face, one might make the mistake of thinking, "Here is a cold man."

It is not coldness. What it is—but let me come to that later. Whether or not his playing touches your heart is a matter of what you mean by "heart." Did you ever hear of *Schmalz*? It is a German word, meaning, literally, "grease," which has long been in the vocabulary of musicians. (Brahms is said to have used it in voicing his opinion of Mendelssohn's music). They use it to describe singing or playing that insists upon buttering sentiment with sentimentality. The wailing of self-pity of a radio crooner "interpreting" the latest torch song; the greasily voluptuous tone of a self-styled "gypsy" restaurant violinist—those are *Schmalz*.

Now if there is one predominant element in Heifetz's playing it is a complete absence of *Schmalz*. He never tries to drag out of a given piece of music more drama or emotion than there is in it. When the music demands it, he can give you a singing tone that is thrillingly beautiful; or, on the other hand, icily brilliant. But never dry, mind you. He has an amazing variety of tone color at his command, and it is his subtle application of this color to the musical canvas, so to speak, that gives his playing its never-flagging variety and eloquence.

One of the most familiar Heifetz anecdotes relates that after his first recital in London George Bernard Shaw visited him in his dressing room, and warned him against playing too perfectly. "Nothing may be perfect in this world," he said, "or the gods become jealous and destroy it. So would you mind playing one wrong note every night before you go to bed?" I have often thought of the appropriateness of Shaw's visit. For the styles of the two men, in their respective fields, are curiously alike. Shaw, to me, possesses the most nearly perfect literary style in the world, in that it approaches a complete absence of "style." He knows so wholly what he wants to say, and says it with such clarity and simplicity, that his writing is like a sheet of flawless glass that allows the reader to look straight through the words to the ideas that they convey.

Heifetz's playing is like that. At his best, he plays with such a complete grasp of the meaning of the music, such effortless mastery of his instrument, that you tend to forget him. You are no longer hearing violin playing; you are hearing the music, hearing it as the composer hoped you would hear it, unconscious of any instrumental barrier between you. It is given to only a few artists in any generation to achieve this selfless perfection of communication; and Heifetz is one of those elect few.

To give an idea of the man himself is not so easy, chiefly because he has so few eccentricities that would make picturesque reading. Two trivial memories of him may give you a vague picture of him. One is of a late party at Neysa McMein's studio, back in 1923, I think it was, when Jascha, about four in the morning, played as I have seldom heard him or anyone else play in concert. I told him so, and he explained. "I was using the Strad tonight, and she's never played so well as since I bought the Guarnerius. You know, she's jealous!"—and half believed it. The other is a recollection of Jascha, backstage at an absurd revue a crowd of us were putting on for charity— Jascha, with his music stand propped up in the wings, jostled by stagehands, tripped up by electric cables, nervous but determined, playing unaccompanied off-stage music for a burlesque melodrama with the devotion and earnestness that he would have given to a command performance before royalty.

There, exemplified, are what to me are his two most striking characteristics: a simplicity and directness that are almost childlike, and a complete seriousness about his art. He gets along wonderfully with children. Not that he is a head-patter. For all I know, he may not even care much about them. But he meets them on an equal footing, and they accept him as an equal. A children's orchestra figured prominently in the story of his picture (an amazing aggregation, by the way, recruited and trained in Hollywood by a devoted Russian musician named Peter Meremblum). When Heifetz first saw and heard them on the screen he refused to believe that they were doing the actual playing, and had to be taken to hear them in person before he could be convinced. The studio heads had hoped to induce him to appear with them on the screen, and spent anxious hours debating the most diplomatic way of asking him to do so. When he had heard the youngsters, *he* asked to be allowed to play with *them*.

I was on the Goldwyn lot the morning that he finished his part of the picture. Just before he left he asked to have the orchestra assembled so that he could say good-by. He made no speech, spoke no word of praise. Instead, he called every child over and gave him—or her—a picture of himself, autographed to that child; a gift from one artist to another.

Just now I mentioned that seriousness of his approach to music. I have never known a musician with more complete artistic integrity. He will rehearse for hours to prepare for a benefit concert whose audience would be satisfied if he came out and played *Pop Goes the Weasel*. During the shooting of *They Shall Have Music* he wore out even the fatigue-proof studio crews with his patient and tireless "Let's shoot that again." Nor have I ever known a musician with less of the show-off element in his make-up, or less conceit. He knows he is good—why shouldn't he? But he has reached the point, I think, that every great artist, creative or interpretative, must reach; the point where he has achieved such mastery of his craft that he knows he will never completely master it. He plays the violin so well that he knows what a lesser artist will never know: how good violin playing might be. And so, as he nears his forties, he is still learning to play. He has only one rival, one violinist whom he is trying to beat: Jascha Heifetz.

PART THREE

The Hearers

I

The Violent Ward

"THERE may soon be no other place in the world where music can be heard without the intervention of politics, where men can be free in mind and spirit to soar aloft as they feel like soaring. This may be the only country left where that can be done, and it is our responsibility to see that it can be done here. We have got to do in the twentieth century what Germany did for human culture in the nineteenth century, and we have got to prepare ourselves for it."

Those are not my words. They are from an address by George Sokolsky, speaking before the Philharmonic-Symphony League of New York. Let me point his words by another quotation, a letter from a professor of sociology in a Midwestern university:

"My wife's cousins are Swedish. During the Great War one of them took on a German war orphan whose father had been a Communist. He supported and educated the boy, who proceeded to become a one hundred per cent National Socialist—that is, Nazi. Recently he visited his benefactor in Sweden. The victrola was playing a record sung by Taube, the famous Swedish tenor. When it was mentioned that Taube was Jewish, the young man immediately plugged his ears. On another day a similar record was played, and he was allowed to express his appreciation of it. Later he was told that this was also sung by a Jew. Shortly after he was found in the grove near by, on his face, weeping because he had enjoyed the singing of a Jew."

Even as recently as five or six years ago, if I had received that letter I wouldn't have quoted it, though it did come from a man holding a responsible academic position. It would have sounded too fantastic to be taken seriously. But unfortunately we are now living in a fantastic world, a world in which intelligent people seem honestly to believe that they can detect hostile racial and political characteristics in pieces of absolute music; a world in which one of Russia's most brilliant young composers, Shostakovich, undertakes to abandon thematic development and to write music with no two bars alike, because thematic development is a bourgeois theory; a world in which the German government decrees that the music of the Jewish composers Felix Mendelssohn, Jacques Offenbach, and Giacomo Meyerbeer may not be played, forbids the conducting of any German orchestra by a Jewish conductor, and confiscates the works and copyrights of Johann Strauss —because he had a Jewish stepdaughter; a world in which an important Italian newspaper announces that no true Italian can laugh at the Ritz Brothers, the Marx Brothers, or Charlie Chaplin. It is quite possible to say, with a straight face, that the day may come when the political opinions of Mickey Mouse may cause him to be banned by half the governments of Europe. Imagine the most fantastic conclusion at which the human mind is capable of arriving, and you can no longer say that it will not be taken seriously in some quarter of the earth.

Now artistic censorship has always existed in one place or another, even censorship of music. Verdi's opera, *A*

Masked Ball, dealt with the assassination of an Italian state official. The censor, deciding that it might put ideas into people's heads, banned it until Verdi's librettist changed it to a story of the assassination of the governor of Boston. The King, in Verdi's *Rigoletto,* had to be demoted to Duke before the shocked censor would allow it to be produced. In Russia, up to 1918, a folk song called *Dubinushka* could not be sung in public, because it had been the battle song of the attempted revolution of 1905. Notice, however, that in all these instances, what the censor was really after were the stories or the words or the events behind the music. The music was forbidden merely because it was associated with those stories or words or events.

Now I may or may not agree with censorship of that sort, but at least I can understand it. I can perfectly comprehend the purpose of a censorship of ideas, and I can even admit that, for a time at least, it works. But I cannot comprehend the workings of a mind that thinks it can regulate abstract thought and emotion. All of us, in our esthetic criticism, do a certain amount of loose talking. I have heard Arnold Schönberg called an anarchist and a Bolshevik by people who found a certain lack of charm in his music. But it never occurred to me—nor, I think, to them—that because they hated Schönberg's music they honestly thought he was planning to assassinate the President and overthrow the government. Apparently, today, there are people, millions of them, who believe that a composer's race and political opinions can be deduced by listening to his music.

This belief leaves me honestly bewildered. If there is an art in the world that has nothing to do with definite thoughts and images, it is music; and among composers who rise above mediocrity it has very little to do, as well, with race, or even nationality. Pretending to think otherwise does no one any good, in the long run. If a man whom you hate builds a beautiful house, you are doing a very dangerous thing to go about saying that it looks like a dog kennel. In the first place, you are fooling very few people. Most of them know, when you say that you hate the house, that you're merely announcing that you hate the man. In the second place, if you refuse to see any merit in a work of art because someone you dislike created it, in other words, if you let your emotions replace your critical sense, before very long you will have no critical sense left. And that is what is happening today. Vast numbers of persons, for one reason or another, are deliberately destroying their sense of taste, are trying to forget that they ever knew what music is.

And what is it? Let me give you another quotation, this one from Cecil Forsyth's *Music and Nationalism*. He says:

"The painter, the sculptor, and the poet gather in the things which they can see and touch and hear. They pass these sense-impressions through their minds, and bring forth a version of them colored and modified by their own personalities. The musician, wholly self-centred, passes through the same process, but the creative act begins in a quite different manner, in that he looks for his stimulus to nothing outside his own personality. . . . Lock the painter, the poet, and the sculptor up within four bare walls: give them light, paint, canvas, pen, ink, paper, clay —and in ten years they will produce nothing but from memory. Lock the musician up with his pens and paper:

rob him of every external impression possible: take away even sight and hearing—and he will continue his artistic development unchecked by his surroundings."

I believe that. Take a piece of music like the Beethoven Fifth Symphony. What possible connection can you find between those sounds and any person, place, or definite literary or political idea? Or take Stravinsky's *Firebird* suite. It doesn't even pretend to be *absolute* music; yet if you were hearing it for the first time, and knew neither its title nor its story, how sure are you that you could invent the correct story to go with it?

The other arts all possess a degree of definite outline and expressiveness that do make it possible to use them for propaganda of one kind or another. You can easily make a Communist play or a Fascist motion picture, depending on the choice and implications of your story; you can write democratic poetry, or a proletarian novel, or a socialist essay. You can even put up a Communist or democratic or Fascist building, identifiable as such by the swastikas or fasces or liberty caps or hammers and sickles with which you ornament it. But how under the sun are you going to write music expressive of proletarianism, or Fascism, or socialism, or New Dealism, or any other ism? If you could, the evidence would certainly be found in the music of Richard Wagner. In 1849 Wagner took part in a revolutionary uprising in Germany. A revolutionist, in the Germany of those days, was a Democrat—or even a Republican—in other words, the equivalent of what we would call today a Red. The uprising failed, and Wagner had to flee the country. Four years later, in 1853, while he was still a political exile, still a Red, he started composing his great tetralogy, *The Ring of the Nibelungs.* By

1857 he had got as far as the middle of the second act of
Siegfried. Then, despairing of ever getting the cycle produced, he stopped short, halfway through the Forest Scene.
Not until eight years later, in 1865, did he pick up the
work again where he had left off. But by that time he was
back in Germany, under the subsidy and protection of
King Ludwig of Bavaria. And he was a wholehearted royalist, if we are to judge from his letters.

Now if music could be expressive of political and soci-
ological opinions, one ought to be able to listen to the forest music of *Siegfried* and, up to a certain point, say, "Ah,
that's proletarian music"; and after that point, be able to
say, "Ah, there speaks the economic royalist." But one
can do no such thing. I defy anybody, who hasn't been
told, to pick out the place where Wagner stopped work on
his score in 1857. I am not denying that a composer's
political convictions can arouse emotions which he attempts to transmit in music. But you can't read art back-
wards. You can't deduce the cause from the effect. If you
see a woman weeping, you cannot always be sure whether
it is because she has lost her lover or because she has been
peeling onions.

Nor do I believe that race counts for much in writing
music. In the Orient, perhaps, where people hear little
music except that which has sprung up in their particular
corner of the earth, musicians do tend to go on creating
the sort of music they have always heard. But in Europe,
where for centuries people have been hearing music written by all sorts of other people, and in this country, to a
lesser degree, it seems incredible to me that a man should
reveal his blood stream by the music he happens to write.
Suppose, without ever having heard them before, and

without knowing who their composers were, you were to hear three violin concertos in succession: the D major Concerto by Beethoven, the E minor Concerto by Mendelssohn, and the D major Concerto by Tchaikovsky. Search your esthetic soul and tell me, if you can, that you are absolutely positive that you would know, from the music alone, that the first concerto had been written by a German, the second by a Jew, and the third by a Russian.

One of the musical gods of Germany today, as he has been for three generations, is the great Aryan composer, Richard Wagner. Now for half a century there has been a theory, among a certain school of musical scholars, that Wagner's real father was not, as the records have it, Police Actuary Carl Friedrich Wagner, but the actor, Ludwig Geyer. The theory has never been proved correct, but neither has it ever definitely been disproved. It is still a subject of violent controversy. Now Geyer is said to have been a Jew. Suppose that tomorrow documents should be discovered that proved, beyond the possibility of refutation, that Geyer *was* a Jew and *was* Wagner's father. Wagner's music would instantly become anathema in the country of his birth. Yet would one note of his music be changed? Would it sound any different? Would it suddenly convey meanings that had hitherto been obscured? As a matter of fact, if music could reveal its composer's race beyond any doubt, the Wagner-Geyer controversy would have been settled long ago. Wagner's music would sound definitely Aryan or non-Aryan, and that would be the end of it. In fact, I think it is the suspicion that their citizens will *not* detect the difference that causes certain countries to censor the music of certain musicians on racial grounds.

227

Incidentally, when we read of nations that suppress the music of undesirable composers, let us not laugh *too* loudly. Let us cast our eyes—or those of our parents—back to the brave days of 1917 and 1918, when the music of Richard Strauss and the operas of Richard Wagner could not be played, when Beethoven was tolerated only because we discovered that his ancestry was Dutch. We think ourselves broad-minded and tolerant, willing to listen to music for its own sake and for its own, musical, message, unaffected by the bigotry and pathological nationalism of Europe. Perhaps we are. But we have been poisoned by that virus in the past, and we can be poisoned again. If we are to keep our love of music pure, we shall have to do something beyond merely taking that purity for granted.

2

Euterpe and the Gestapo

SUPPOSE we look a little further into this question of sub-versive music. When the preceding chapter appeared in its first incarnation, as a broadcast, its reception was not unanimously uncritical. The following is fairly typical of the point of view of the dissidents:

"May I take the liberty," this particular correspondent writes, "of differing with your conclusion that music can never be proletarian, or royalist, or Nazi, or have any other 'ism'? Can you say that *La Marseillaise* was not a revolutionary piece of music? Is it not almost a cliché now, among writers on the French revolution, to refer to the influence of De Lisle and 'that terrible song'? Can you listen to *Finlandia* and not recognize that, from their point of view, the Russian police were justified, first, in suppressing the title, and then the music itself, as subversive to Tsarist Russia? If music is entirely art, why was the *"Eroica"* dedicated to Napoleon, and why did Beethoven tear up the dedication when Napoleon became emperor? If there is no politics, why, years later, when Beethoven learned of Napoleon's death, did he say that he had already written the funeral march for that tragedy? What is the meaning of the opening of Beethoven's Fifth Symphony, if it is not political? Would you say that the *Internationale* is not proletarian music? In Hemingway's play, *The Fifth Column,* the leading character, hearing the song being sung off stage, says 'the best people I knew have died for that song.' "

I think I can answer that. The words of *La Marseillaise* are certainly revolutionary, but I still think that anyone who had never heard of the song, hearing the music alone, for the first time, would not necessarily find it to be anything more than a stirring march. I believe, too, that if Sibelius had called his composition, not *Finlandia,* but *Orchestral Rhapsody No. 1,* the Russian police would never have dreamed of suppressing it. What they did suppress, as my correspondent points out, was, first, the title. What they suppressed later was the fact that no Finn could hear the music without being *reminded* of the title. In both these cases, what gives the music its supposed political flavor is the set of words with which it is associated. But that's a literary idea, not a musical one. As far as Beethoven's dedication of the *"Eroica"* to Napoleon is concerned, the significant fact about that, as I have said previously, is that Beethoven changed the dedication, but not the music. If the slow movement is really a funeral march for Napoleon the tyrant, did it begin as the funeral march for Napoleon the liberator? Let me say again, that while I don't for a minute deny that a composer's political convictions may arouse in him a set of emotions which he turns into music, I do maintain that all that the music can communicate is the emotion, not the views, that inspired it, and that the music may turn out to be equally appropriate to express an entirely different set of views. That is why, when we do want music to express definite ideas, patriotic, economic, or whatnot, we have either to give it a provocative title, or set words to it. As evidence of that necessity, consider the fact that when an American hears a certain tune, he recognizes it as *My Country, 'tis of Thee*; when an Englishman hears the same tune, he thinks of *God Save the King*; and when a German hears that selfsame tune, he sings *Heil dir im Siegerkranz*.

Take the Fifth Symphony, which, my correspondent is convinced, is political in its intentions. According to Lawrence Gilman, various commentators, at various times, have heard in the Fifth Symphony the summons of fate, the repercussions of one of Beethoven's unhappy love affairs, a martial celebration, and the note of the yellowhammer heard in country walks. As for the *Internationale*, when I first heard that tune, I had no idea what it was; and while I rather liked it, I must confess that it did not in the least make me think of Karl Marx. I was honestly surprised to discover, later, that its words were revolutionary. Not long ago I heard it, embodied in the first-act finale of the musical comedy, *Leave It To Me*—the tune, that is, not the words. The audience neither rushed to the stage to lynch the actors, nor rushed out of the theater to lynch the New York police force. They accepted it as a pretty good marching tune, and let it go at that. I had much the same experience with the *Horst Wessel Song* of Nazi Germany, the music of which strikes me as being dreary and uninspired, and utterly inexpressive of the sentiments conveyed by the words.

One piece of music has always struck me as a superb example of how unsuccessful a tune can be in expressing the words with which it is linked. Find some friend of yours who doesn't know the story of *Tannhäuser*, or, if he does know it, has never seen a performance of it. Then play him, either on the piano or on a phonograph record, the first part of the overture. I think he might recognize the Pilgrims' Chorus as religious in character, and he might even identify, as fantastic, the Bacchanale music that follows. But when he hears the theme that follows, I am almost positive that he will hear it as a stirring military march. I would give odds of a hundred to one that never, in his wildest guess, would he describe it for what it is supposed to be—a hymn to Venus.

Brahms's *Academic Festival Overture* is based upon four German students' songs. The one with which the overture concludes is the famous old Latin song, *Gaudeamus igitur*. As a matter of fact, when I hear that song, I think of it as *Cantemus, Psi Upsilon*, because the first time I heard it, it was one of the songs of my college fraternity. Another of the airs that Brahms uses is called *Was kommt dort von der Höh*, but I can't think of it as that, because I was brought up knowing it as *The Farmer in the Dell*.

One of the commonest mistakes we make, in listening to music, is that of reacting to the *literary* associations of the music, in the belief that we're reacting to the music itself. To me, music has many of the characteristics of textile fabrics. A piece of absolute music, such as a symphony, is like a wonderful Persian rug: meaningless—that is, meaningless in any intellectual sense—and beautiful. Program music is like a richly ornamented cloak. As long as it is being worn by someone, you are aware that it fits its subject. But look at the cloak without knowing the wearer, and you will realize that you cannot, with any positiveness, describe that wearer. You cannot be sure even of his height and weight, to say nothing of the shape of his nose, or the color of his hair and eyes.

When people speak of subversive music, you will almost

always find, as I say, that they are talking about music that has words to go with it. Talk of political music, and you are probably talking of music that quotes familiar airs that possess historical or patriotic associations. But those associations have nothing to do with music. That is why all the well-intentioned attempts to find or write a new American national anthem have failed, and will probably continue to fail. People criticize *The Star-Spangled Banner* on the ground that it is hard to sing—which is true; or that it was originally an English drinking song—which is likewise true. As if that mattered. When we hear *The Star-Spangled Banner,* we're not listening to music. We are listening to ideas and images and recollections and associations that go back a hundred years.

But when we do listen to music, as music, let us not listen to titles, or words, or the spellings of composers' names. A great work of art, if it is truly great, is always bigger, and better, than the artist who made it. Once a piece of music is written, it escapes from its creator. It takes on a life of its own, and is not concerned with his race, or politics, or intentions. It reflects only the intensity and sincerity of his emotions, not their object. And if it speaks to us truly and beautifully, nothing that we can do or say will change it. It remains always true and beautiful, no matter whether its creator be Jew or Gentile, patriot or enemy alien.

Do I seem to labor my point, to worry unnecessarily for fear something should make us lose our musical tolerance? In the last chapter I made passing mention of our attitude toward German music during the World War. Let me allude to it again. Keeping in mind Beethoven's Fifth Symphony, the Brahms Violin Concerto, the Schumann Piano

Concerto, and Wagner's *Siegfried Idyl,* and Strauss's *Death and Transfiguration,* read this:

"Every conductor, musician, or singer who renders German music in public enacts the role of a Prussian spider that attracts musical flies to his weaving way. . . . For Americans to listen to German songs composed before the Franco-Prussian war is, in the present crisis, highly demoralizing to patriotic sentiment. Such music creates sympathy through sentimental channels, while the music composed since 1870 is militant, anti-democratic, and psychologically inimical. . . . The same music that was innocent yesterday can be fraught with the most insidious meaning today. It makes no difference, in this connection, how long a composer has been dead . . . German music is German through and through. It is made in Germany. And at this terrible crisis it cannot be heard in America except when Americans are ready to part with their birthright for a mess of musical pottage cooked in the Kaiser's kitchen and served in helmets stained with the gore of women and children along a frontier of two thousand miles. In extenuation they offer us Beethoven's symphonies!"

That, dearly beloved, is a short extract from a long article, by an otherwise sane American, that appeared in the columns of the *Kansas City Star* a little over two decades ago. In quoting it I intend no disparagement of the *Star.* Dozens of similar articles appeared in dozens of American newspapers twenty-two years ago. Twenty-two years is not a long time. I wonder if it has been long enough for us to have acquired clearheadedness and a sense of proportion as completely and permanently as we like to think we have. I don't know. I can only hope, without much conviction, that we shall never go mad again.

3

Saying It With Music

IN A WAY, composers—and their commentators—are partly to blame for our present-day tendency to look for extramusical meanings in purely musical works. For upwards of a century they have been encouraging us, with increasing urgency, to accept music as a medium for the conveyance of definite images, have been breaking away from the older, abstract forms in an attempt to tell symphonic stories and paint tonal pictures—to write, in short, what we call "program" music.

Now program music is a comparatively late invention. It dates, roughly, from the first quarter of the nineteenth century. Go back of that period, and although you will find Beethoven occasionally breaking down and writing something like *Wellington's Victory* or the "Pastoral," or Haydn undertaking to depict chaos in his oratorio, *The Creation,* generally speaking, the so-called classic masters made almost no attempt to make music say anything outside of itself. One reason for this fact was that the melodic and rhythmic and harmonic vocabulary of music was not as extensive as it was after Beethoven's death. This doesn't mean that Bach and Haydn and Mozart and Beethoven were simple, primitive creatures, uttering simple, uncomplicated things. An artist's stature is not determined by his resources.

Chaucer, using an English vocabulary about one third

the size of Shakespeare's, manages none the less to be a great poet, and the fact that Fra Angelico's grasp of perspective is not that of Michelangelo doesn't keep him from being a great painter. On the other hand, there are certain things that Fra Angelico, and Chaucer, and Mozart simply were not equipped to convey with any precision, and from which they wisely kept away. A man who writes a string quartet or a sonata or a symphony can develop his themes in terms of purely musical logic; but let him start to paint a picture or tell a story, and he finds himself confronted by the necessity of making sudden changes in speed and rhythm, and harmonic excursions into unexpected keys, not for musical, but for dramatic reasons. And in the days of the classic masters, those extramusical considerations didn't enter into their calculations. Their minds didn't work that way. Even in opera, their dramatic devices were still almost purely musical. A friend of mine once remarked, apropos of Gluck's *Armide,* that "the hero enters in the midst of a terrific tonic-and-dominant thunderstorm."

As the vocabulary of music grew in what you might call specific expressiveness, it was natural that composers should experiment with conveying something more than purely abstract musical ideas. I say natural, because one of the oldest forms of music, the folk ballad, is a narrative in musical vocal form; and it is not unreasonable to call a symphonic poem a ballad in *instrumental* form. People generally think of Franz Liszt as the inventor of program music—which of course isn't so. He invented a particular form of dramatic rhapsody, which he called the symphonic poem, but I think that the men who really made the modern tone poem possible were Berlioz and

236

Wagner. The latter not only developed the dramatic expressiveness of music to a point that wasn't even dreamed of fifty years before his birth, but, along with Berlioz, developed the pictorial and dramatic expressiveness of the orchestra to a degree that even Richard Strauss has never exceeded. In addition, Berlioz had taken dramatic music out of the opera house and put it in the concert hall. Since their day, composers, with the exception of Schumann, Brahms, and César Franck, have tended more and more to base their music upon stories and pictures, until—always excepting the classics—program music is the rule, rather than the exception, upon so-called "symphony" programs.

Now a program is a great temptation to any orchestral composer, and properly treated, allows him a range of expressiveness and a freedom of treatment that is rather beyond the limitations of symphonic form. It is a temptation because it gives him a ready-made, nontraditional structure. And just as plan is the architect's hardest problem, and plot the dramatist's, so is structure the most difficult branch of musical composition. Granted that a composer has a group of themes, in what order shall he present them, how elaborately, and how long shall he develop them? If he has a plot, or a scene to describe, half of that question is answered for him. He knows the definite mood he has to express, and what his themes must and must not be.

Such a limitation, far from being a handicap to any artist, is a great stimulus, because, having the form set for him, he can forget form and concentrate upon detail. The great Renaissance and post-Renaissance painters, for example, were extremely limited in their choice of subjects. Their patrons were either churches, or political personages whose tastes were either religious or classical. In consequence, they painted either Bible stories or mythological subjects. When a painter like Raphael stood before a fresh canvas, he didn't have to worry about *what* to paint. That was all decided for him—a Madonna and Child, or a Holy Family, or a Flight into Egypt, or the like. His only preoccupation was to paint as beautiful a Madonna or Holy Family as he could.

Incidentally, did you ever stop to think how curiously painting and music have developed in precisely the reverse order? Our classic paintings are largely illustrations of stories, while modern painting tries to become more and more abstract. Contrariwise, our classic music is all abstract, while modern music turns to illustration. You could almost say that each art is now busily engaged in trying to become the opposite of what its founders thought it was.

But to get back to our Renaissance painter. His limitation of subject really worked greatly to his advantage. In the first place, it not only left him free to paint as well as he could, but it left his public free to judge him solely as a painter, and not as an illustrator. A man looking at Raphael's Dresden Madonna, or Michelangelo's ceiling for the Sistine Chapel wasn't going to ask himself how accurately Raphael had portrayed the Virgin, or whether Michelangelo's Adam and Eve were true to life. He had seen both subjects painted a hundred times before, in a hundred different ways; so the idea of discussing the correctness of this particular illustration never entered his head. He admired or criticized the painter, *as such*— as a master of the art of painting—and not as a candid cameraman. In addition, the painter, having no authentic model, and no authentic tradition as to the appearance of his subjects, was in no danger of wasting time and talent in being too literal. Far from worrying about the correct cut of St. John's cloak, he was just as likely as not to paint him in what was then modern dress, with no one objecting.

Now those dangers do threaten the composer of program music. We who listen to music are all children, in that we adore to listen to a story. I'm afraid that if we're quite honest with ourselves, most of us will have to admit that Respighi, calling his piece *The Fountains of Rome,* creates a little more anticipatory interest in it than if he had called it, simply, "Fantasy in Four Sections." But that very interest that we take in the composer's program is risky—for him. For he does run the danger of having his audience devote all its critical faculties to deciding how accurately he has conveyed his program, instead of how well he has written his music. If you will forgive my being autobiographical for a minute, I once wrote a symphonic poem based on James Branch Cabell's—then—scandalous novel, *Jurgen.* What happened was that everybody who had read the book, or even heard it described, came to hear the music with a preconceived idea about what it ought to sound like, and when I read the reviews of the first performance I discovered that most of the critics had devoted more space to discussing how successfully I had set the book to music than to whether the music was any good or not. I remember that one critic, in particular, went to considerable length to complain that I had utterly failed to convey a certain sense of spiritual malaise that runs through the book. Now if, instead of calling the piece *Jurgen,* I had called it "Rhapsody in D Major"—which is about what the actual form was—the critic would never have noticed the absence of that spiritual malaise. He might even have liked the piece a lot better than he did.

That tendency, while it is deplorable, is natural, and almost inevitable. I, too, when I see a long and detailed program note affixed to a musical composition, find myself reading the notes and trying to spot the episodes instead of paying strict attention to the music. Eighty-five years ago, a writer named George Horatio Derby uttered the all-time comment upon the overelaborate program note in a burlesque description of an imaginary symphony that he wrote for a San Diego, California, newspaper. It runs, in part:

"The symphony opens upon the wide and boundless plains, in longitude 115 west, latitude 35 21' 03" north, and about sixty miles from the west bank of Pitt River. These data are beautifully and clearly expressed by a long note from an E-flat clarinet. The sandy nature of the soil, sparsely dotted with bunches of cactus and artemisia, the extended view, flat and unbroken to the horizon, save by the rising smoke in the extreme verge, denoting the vicinity of a Pi Utah village, are represented by the bass drum. A few notes on the piccolo call attention to a solitary antelope, picking up mescal beans in the foreground."

It's dangerous for an artist to be too specific in labeling his work. I have a great deal of trouble, for instance, with a lot of modern painting and sculpture, for that very reason. When I see a canvas covered with an abstract pattern of rectangles, interspersed with a guitar, a shoehorn, and a copy of *The New York Times,* I am perfectly willing to admire it as a feat of pure painting. But when I find that the artist calls it *Portrait of My Uncle George* —well, it worries me. It's just not my idea of Uncle George. Or I go to an exhibition of sculpture, and see a dropsical young woman biting her left foot, I start enjoying its contours and masses, and then discover that it's called *The Brotherhood of Man,* or *Spring's Awakening.*

In other words, if a composer is wise, he will either not choose too elaborate a program, or, if he does take one, he'll accept it as a stimulus to his musical imagination and keep the details to himself. For as a piece of program music grows older, people tend to forget or ignore the program that its composer thought was so important, and to estimate the music at its own abstract value. How many of you, for instance, know the program of the most incorrigibly popular of all symphonic poems, Liszt's *Les Préludes?* Could you give a detailed account of the program of Strauss's *Don Juan,* to take a more nearly contemporary example? I have an idea that if you like *Don Juan,* it is not because of the accuracy with which it describes the hero's adventures.

In that fact lies the greatest risk the program composer faces, the risk to himself as a musician. There is always the danger that he may become so interested in conveying the fine points of his story, or the details of his picture, that his piece becomes incoherent or too literally imitative. And music, if it is to survive, *must* possess some vestige of musical form and balance, and must paint its pictures in terms of music, and not of natural sounds. Richard Strauss is a striking example of the fatal results of being too programmatic. Of all his tone poems, the three that remain universally popular are *Don Juan, Death and Transfiguration,* and *Til Eulenspiegel.* The first two express their program in only the broadest and most general terms. *Till Eulenspiegel* is a bit more literal, but is saved by being written in a strict rondo form that allows us to follow it as pure music. We have no need to read program notes to enjoy these three works. But what is going to happen to *Also sprach Zarathustra, Don Quixote,* and the *Domestic Symphony* when their program notes are not available or are forgotten? *Zarathustra* is an attempt to express a philosophy in terms of music, and is so laden with elaborate symbols and literary figures of speech that at times it means nothing without its libretto. In *Don Quixote* there are at least two passages, the episode of the wind machine and the famous "sheep" episode, that are not music at all. They are imitations of natural noises, and mean absolutely nothing without the accompanying text. The *Domestic Symphony* is an example of music that is too ambitious for its program. Heard without its program it sounds rather like a description of the home life of the dinosaurs. Better to hear it that way than to read the note and make the disconcerting discovery that it is supposed to represent the composer in the bosom of his family.

The difference between the descriptive painter and the descriptive composer is that the former paints his program note, as well as his images. His story is painted on the canvas, and is an inseparable part of what you see. The descriptive composer, on the other hand, has his program only in the form of words printed upon a slip of paper. All that he can hope to convey, in music, are the moods and sentiments that lie behind those words. If he wants his music to survive, therefore, he will do well to write something that conveys its own, musical meaning to the listener who arrived late and didn't get his copy of the notes.

4

Landmark

JUST NOW I mentioned Hector Berlioz as a man who, with Wagner, did most to open the way to the development of the modern orchestral tone poem. In actual graphic and dramatic expressiveness his music lags far behind Wagner's; none the less his contribution is a very real one, in that he made a partially successful attempt to tell a dramatic story in terms, not of the theater, but of the concert hall. That attempt was—and is—his *Fantastic Symphony*. Suppose we examine it somewhat in detail.

The *Fantastic Symphony* is a phenomenon, first, by reason of its instrumentation. Besides the instruments of the customary symphony orchestra, the score calls for an E-flat clarinet, four bassoons (instead of the ordinary two), two cornets (as well as two trumpets), two tubas, four kettledrums, two harps, and church bells. Berlioz also stipulates that there be at least sixty players in the string section, and, if possible, four harp players. This means an orchestra of not less than ninety men. Reasonable enough, to our modern ears; but if you will remember that the first performance of Beethoven's Ninth Symphony, only six years before the *première* of the Berlioz work, was given by what was then considered a gigantic orchestra of about seventy-five players, you can imagine what a sensation this *Fantastic Symphony* must have caused when Paris first heard it in December of the year 1830.

Not only did the piece make unheard-of demands as to the size of the orchestra that was to play it, but it was equally revolutionary in its treatment of the instruments. Cast your mind back to the symphonies of Haydn and Mozart, and the way they are scored for the orchestra, and you will notice that they remain pretty faithful to the tradition of seventeenth- and early eighteenth-century orchestration. According to this tradition, reduced to its simplest terms, the woodwind, brass, and string sections of the orchestra were regarded as separate choirs. That is, broadly speaking, when the woodwinds played together, the strings remained silent; when the strings were playing, the wind instruments rested. There was little attempt to mix and blend the tone colors of the various sections of the orchestra, in the manner with which we are now familiar.

Of course there were always instrumental solos, accompanied by strings, and the so-called tutti passages, in which everybody joined. But ordinarily even Beethoven, although he experimented in tone coloring much more boldly than his predecessors, accepted this splitting up of the orchestra as a sort of standard practice. Meyerbeer, in turn, went a little further than Beethoven. But it is Berlioz who dared, more completely than any of them, to look the orchestra in the face as a single gigantic instrument, a variety of human pipe organ upon which the composer could play as he chose, pulling out any combination of stops that his imagination could conceive. Since his time there have been only six composers, I should say, who can stand beside him as masters of the art of orchestration: Wagner, Rimsky-Korsakoff, Strauss, Debussy, Ravel, and Stravinsky. That's a rather impressive achievement for a man who has been dead nearly seventy years. His treatise on orchestration is still a standard work of its class, one that can still be studied with profit by any composer. This *Fantastic Symphony* of his is still remarkable for the extremely *modern* sound—not of the music, but of the orchestra. It is hard to realize that its instrumentation was finished only two years after that of Schubert's C major Symphony.

But there is another, equally important, way in which the Berlioz *Fantastic Symphony* is a landmark. It is one of the earliest true symphonic poems. Liszt, of course, is generally credited with the invention of the symphonic poem, or tone poem, for orchestra—that is, a composition, very free in structure and style, that attempts to convey a literary or dramatic program. It is a musical form that has since been developed to the utmost by Strauss, in *Till Eulenspiegel, Don Quixote,* and the rest of that great series. But it has always seemed to me that Strauss learned much more from Berlioz about this sort of writing than he did from Liszt. The Berlioz work, while it is, technically speaking, a symphony (in five movements, to be sure, but so is Beethoven's "Pastoral" Symphony), and develops its themes in the symphonic manner, it is essentially descriptive music, and follows a specific and elaborate dramatic program.

There is no difference in the composer's *intent* between this work and Liszt's *Les Préludes,* for example. The only difference in form is that Liszt writes his tone poem in one movement, while Berlioz writes his in five, and calls it a symphony. As a matter of fact, he calls it that only in the subtitle. The full title is *Episode from the Life of an Artist; Fantastic Symphony in Five Parts, by Hector Berlioz.* On the programs for the first performance appeared this foreword, written by Berlioz himself:

"The aim of the composer has been to develop, so far as they are musical, different situations in an artist's life. The plot of the instrumental drama, deprived of the aid of the spoken word, must necessarily be explained in advance. The following program, therefore, should be considered as similar to the spoken dialogue of an opera, serving to lead into the musical sections whose character and form of expression it motivates." In a later edition of the orchestral score he modifies this somewhat, and writes:

"The following program should be distributed in the auditorium every time the fantastic symphony is played dramatically [he means, in a theater] and is consequently followed by the monodrama of Lelio which terminates and completes the episode from an artist's life. However, if the symphony is played separately, at a concert, this is not absolutely necessary. One could even omit distributing the detailed program, retaining only the titles of the five pieces, as the author hopes that his symphony possesses musical interest independently of its dramatic intentions."

Then Berlioz writes what you might call his five-star final introduction, his general program note for the work as a whole: "Program of the symphony. A young musician, morbidly sensitive and endowed with a vivid imagination, drugs himself with opium, during an access of lovesick despair. The dose of narcotic, too weak to prove fatal, plunges him into a heavy sleep, accompanied by the most fantastic visions, during which his sensations, his feelings, and his memories, translate themselves, in his sick brain, into musical thoughts and images. Even the woman whom he loves has been transformed into a melody, has become, as it were, an *idée fixe*—a fixed idea that keeps recurring and which he hears throughout the music."

Now this, of course, is not only the general program, but a general apology for *having* a program. Where a modern composer would simply say, "a young man drugs himself and sees strange visions, and here they are," Berlioz is quick to explain that the visions have accommodatingly turned themselves into music—a concession, I should say, to the prejudices of his generation, which wasn't used to such outlandish things as tone poems.

The first movement is called "Dreams—Passions." Berlioz's note is as follows: "He recalls at first the soul-sickness, the waves of passion and of melancholy, of reasonless happiness, that used to sweep over him before he first saw the Beloved One; then he recalls the volcanic love that she inspired in him, his moments of delirious anguish, his jealous rages, his moments of returning tenderness, and of religious consolation."

Now this, as you see, is not particularly definite, and the music for it has none of the detailed, literal pictorial quality of the score of one of Richard Strauss's tone poems. Its most noteworthy feature is that the melody representing the Beloved One, who is the cause of all the trouble, occurs right at the outset, played very slowly and softly by the muted violins. This is the Fixed Idea the artist cannot escape: one can find it somewhere, easily identifiable, in every movement of the symphony.

The second movement is entitled, "A Ball." In it the artist, in the words of the composer, "finds his Beloved at a ball, in the midst of the tumult of a brilliant fête." Nothing complicated here, simply a brilliant dance movement, interrupted by quieter sections wherein one hears again, in unmistakable terms, the theme of the Fixed Idea.

Third movement: "A Scene in the Fields." Berlioz describes it as follows: "A summer evening in the country. He hears two shepherds who play, back and forth, a pastoral tune, the *ranz des vaches*. This rural duet, the setting, the soft murmuring of the trees, lightly swayed by the breeze, some glimmerings of hope that he has lately perceived, all unite to bring an unaccustomed peace to his heart, and to lend a more smiling tint to his thoughts. But She appears again; his heart contracts, painful forebodings oppress him; What if She should be false! One of the shepherds resumes his naïve tune. The other fails to answer. The sun slowly sets . . . distant thunder . . . solitude . . . silence."

Next, the fourth movement: "The March to the Scaffold." This is perhaps the most famous single movement of the entire symphony. Berlioz describes it as follows: "He dreams that he has killed the one he loves, that he has been condemned to death, and is on his way to the gallows. The procession advances to the sound of a march, sometimes sombre and threatening, sometimes brilliant and yet solemn, in which the heavy sound of slow footsteps succeeds, without transition, the wildest outbursts. At the end, the Fixed Idea reappears for an instant, a last thought of love, as it were, cut short by the deathblow."

Now comes the finale. It is called "Dream of a Witches'

Sabbath." Berlioz's note reads: "He sees himself at the Witches' Sabbath, in the midst of a company of fearful ghosts, sorcerers, monsters of all sorts, united for his funeral. Strange sounds, groans, bursts of laughter, distant cries, to which other cries seem to answer. The melody of the Beloved reappears, but it has lost its characteristic nobility and timidity. It is nothing but a vulgar, trivial, grotesque dance tune. She, too, has come to the revel. Yells of joy greet her arrival; she plunges into the diabolic orgy. Funeral bells . . . burlesque of the *Dies Irae* . . . round dance of the witches. The round dance and the *Dies Irae* are heard together." Now this movement is in several distinct sections. First come the "ghosts and monsters," then a sort of jig version of the Fixed Idea theme, played shrilly on the E-flat clarinet. Next we hear the sound of chimes, followed by the medieval hymn, *Dies Irae*, played first by the tubas. When the bells stop tolling, we find ourselves at the round dance of the witches, the fourth section. The revelry grows wilder and wilder, the *Dies Irae* re-enters, in combination with the witches' dance, and the symphony comes to its end on a terrific sustained C major chord.

It would be too much to say that the *Fantastic Symphony* is an unqualified success. Parts of it are naïve, parts of it are bombastic, and some passages are too trivial for the ambitious sentiments they are supposed to express. Nevertheless it is a brave try. Berlioz ventured into a virtually unexplored wilderness, cutting a path down which a host of composers, from Liszt and Tchaikovsky to Strauss, Debussy, and Ravel, have since traveled. They—and we—owe him much.

5

All Things to All Men

How far can program music go? That is, granted that music such as *The Afternoon of a Faun* sounds vividly expressive of its program when we know that program, exactly how definitely does it suggest a program that we do *not* know—when the music is, so to speak, on its own? So far as I am concerned, that is a more or less rhetorical question; for, as I have already said, I don't believe that music conveys precisely the same message to any two persons. But does it convey any definite message at all? Has anyone ever tried to find out?

Someone has. I have a report, from the *Journal of Experimental Psychology* in which Professor Melvin Rigg, of Kenyon College, Ohio, describes an experiment that he made in what one might call musical identification. In a brief foreword he explains what he was trying to determine. "Is the best of our operatic and program music," he writes, "really descriptive of the action it is supposed to convey? Or could the music of a song of farewell have been set, just as appropriately, to the words of a love-lyric or a prayer? Music enters readily into associative bonds. It is true, consequently, that when we know the traditional meaning of a selection, the appropriateness of the musical setting seems natural to us. Mendelssohn's Wedding March will make us think of orange blossoms, and *The Star-Spangled Banner* of patriotism."

What Professor Rigg did was this: first he selected eighteen recordings of works that come under the general description of "standard classics." But they included Siegfried's Funeral March, the death scene from *Madame Butterfly*, the "dawn" portion of the overture to *William Tell*, the King's prayer from *Lohengrin*, the garden music from *Faust*, Mimi's farewell, from *La Bohème*, Debussy's *Moonlight*, the Good Friday music from *Parsifal*, and Strauss's *Death and Transfiguration*.

Next he made up an outline, enumerating the general characteristics of the music that he had selected. He divided it into two general groups. Number one, music that was sorrowful, serious, or religious in mood. Number two, music that was energetic and joyful. Then he made subdivisions of the two main categories. The serious music he classified under Death, Sorrow—including Farewells, and Religion. The last-named he subdivided again as Good Friday Music and Prayer in general. The music supposed to be expressive of joy he subdivided into Love Music, including Serenades, Active Music, further subdivided as Spinning Songs, Cradle Songs, and Dances; and Nature Music, subdivided as Morning and Moonlight. The complete outline looked something like this:

SERIOUS	JOYFUL
I. *Death*	I. *Love, Serenades*
II. *Sorrow, Farewell*	II. *Active*
III. *Religion*	1. Spring
1. Good Friday	2. Cradle
2. Prayer	3. Dances
	4. Nature
	(*a*) Morning
	(*b*) Moonlight

He then selected a group of about seventy first-year psychology students, gave each one a copy of the outline and a blank form, played the music for them, and asked them to classify it. Obviously, as you can see by glancing at the outline, every listener had a detailed guide that was also a strong hint as to the character of the music he was about to hear.

Incidentally, the listeners were young men of various degrees of musical training and experience. As the music was played, everyone was asked, first, to put down, on his answer blank, whether the selection he was hearing was predominantly serious or joyful. Next, he was asked to classify a little more in detail, to say whether the music was expressive of death, sorrow, religion, love, activity, or nature. Then he was asked to go into even greater detail, and indicate, under the head of Death, for example, whether the music was a death scene, a funeral march, or an elegy; or, under Love, whether it was a love song or a serenade—and so forth. Last of all, he was asked whether he had heard the composition before, and what it was called. If he did recognize it, his answer was not counted. This last question evoked rather surprising answers. You can see by the preceding partial list that the works played were classics that almost anyone might be assumed to have heard. Yet most of the listeners failed to recognize any of the music, and among those who did, only one per cent of them knew the correct title of the piece that they recognized.

Now I think that offhand, you would say that anybody could determine whether a given piece of music is sad or joyful; and a good many of these listeners could—that is, seventy-three per cent of them could. But isn't it astonishing that out of a group of seventy average, intelligent American college students, only fifty-one could determine even the prevailing *mood* of a musical selection?

Forty-one per cent, that is, about thirty of the seventy, succeeded in classifying the music correctly into the narrower categories of death, sorrow, religion, love, activity, and nature. As for going further into detail, only twenty-five per cent, that is, eighteen of the seventy, had any success at all.

The successes and failures were rather interesting, and in some cases amusing. More than half of the listeners were able to classify correctly the garden scene from *Faust,* a Swedish cradle song, and *Omphale's Spinning-Wheel,* by Saint-Saëns. They did fairly well, too, with *Death and Transfiguration.* Twenty-five of them got that right. Most of them thought that Madame Butterfly's death scene was a song of farewell. That's interesting, because while it is technically wrong, I think it is emotionally correct. We can say that Puccini did succeed in conveying the mood he was trying to express. The "morning" section—you know, that English-horn solo—from the *William Tell* overture, was interpreted by more than half the class as expressing the wrong kind of mourning— that is, instead of dawn, they thought it represented sorrow. Twenty of them correctly identified the King's prayer, from *Lohengrin,* as a prayer, but almost as many thought it was a serenade. Mimi's farewell was generally classified as a love song. The worst guess was the Good Friday music from *Parsifal.* Twenty-three of the listeners thought it was sorrowful, but not religious, and thirteen of them thought it was a serenade.

One curious feature of the test was the fact that the amount of musical training any given listener had had seemed to have very little to do with his ability to classify the music correctly. The correct answers and the mistakes were almost equally divided among those that had some musical experience and those who had none. Professor Rigg's summary of the results of the experiment is the rather gloomy one that "College students listening to recorded music can tell whether the music is intended to be sad or joyful, but when progressively finer discriminations are attempted, they are progressively less successful. There is little justification for the assertion that any certain composition is exactly right to express farewell, or the early morning, or the like. Such feelings, when they do occur, would seem to be the result of association, and are more or less individual." "Symphonic program notes," he writes, "in so far as they attempt to give to the music any such inner appropriateness to particular moods or events, are without validity, although these notes may be instrumental in establishing widespread associations."

Now of course it is perfectly reasonable to argue that this particular experiment doesn't necessarily prove anything more universal than itself: that a group of seventy students in a Midwestern college had great difficulty in deciding the meaning of certain pieces of program music, outside of the fact that they were serious or cheerful. You could even argue that those particular students may have been exceptionally insensitive to music; that listeners more musically inclined might penetrate the meaning of the music much more deeply. Even so, discounting everything, I think the results of that test were interesting and rather significant. I find the failures particularly so.

Take, for example, the mistake that so many of the listeners made in thinking that the "dawn" passage from the *William Tell* overture was expressive of sorrow. That passage is played by the alto oboe, the English horn, an instrument whose tone undeniably is a melancholy one. What other music, for instance, could so successfully convey the mournful mood of the opening of the third act of *Tristan and Isolde*? In the *William Tell* overture, of course, the English horn is playing a sort of slow bugle-call passage, of a kind that is always associated with the *ranz des vaches* that is played by Swiss shepherds. But if you don't happen to know that, all that you actually hear is some very slow and quiet music, played by an instrument with a somber and melancholy tone. It is not at all impossible that the student, and not Rossini, is right; that Rossini is cheating a little, relying on our historical and literary associations to establish the pastoral mood of the scene, rather than on the actual mood of the music itself.

Again, thinking that the Good Friday music from *Parsifal* is a serenade is not so absurd as it seems, if you think about it. It is a lovely, eloquent theme, beginning in a mood that fairly smells of spring, and warmth, and serene happiness, developing to a triumphant climax that is throbbing with an emotion that may be religious, but is certainly not to be associated readily with the day of grief and mourning that Good Friday is supposed to be. Forget the scene. Forget Kundry's cave, and the mountains, and the green meadows beyond; forget Gurnemanz, and Parsifal, forget all that you know concerning the significance of their meeting; listen to the Good Friday Spell as an anonymous orchestral work that you have never heard before, and I, for one, would hardly be thunderstruck if you thought it was the voice of a lover singing the praises of his beloved.

I can cite you an analogous experience of my own. I have heard the Ride of the Valkyries countless times at the opera, and find it a perfect accompaniment and enhancement of the scene. But at various times, viewing various motion pictures, I have also heard the Ride of the Valkyries used to accompany a buffalo hunt, a fight on an ocean liner, a tornado, and an automobile race; and the music fitted perfectly, in every instance. In other words, the Ride of the Valkyries is superb music to accompany *any* scene of violent action. If, hearing it, we see in our mind's eye a group of warrior maidens riding their plunging steeds through the sky, that is because of something we already know, or are seeing on the stage, rather than of something that the music itself has to say.

About the best, in short, that program music can do is to be *appropriate* to its story or picture, to be a cloak that fits many wearers without belonging exclusively to any one of them. The minute the composer tries to tailor his music, so to speak, to make it fit his program too literally, he pays the penalty, like Strauss with his sheep, of rendering his music meaningless, *as music,* once the explanatory notes are not available. To change the metaphor, the wise composer tries to paint a portrait rather than take a photograph; for the interest of a photograph lies only in the accuracy with which it depicts the sitter, while a great portrait long outlives its otherwise forgotten subject.

6

Culture the Hard Way

IF FRANK MOORE COLBY had been born an Englishman he would have been as famous as Gilbert Chesterton, for his essays are as brilliant as Chesterton's and twice as sound. But as the author of *Imaginary Obligations, Constrained Attitudes,* and *The Margin of Hesitation* was only an American, and an encyclopedia editor at that, he was never invited even to make a lecture tour. Rereading the last-named book, I was particularly struck by the following—Colby is commenting upon sociologists, but he might just as well be discussing some of our more lethal musical modernists:

"A 'new thinker,' when studied closely, is merely a man who does not know what other people have thought. The 'new thinker,' if I may attempt a definition . . . is a person who aspires to an eccentricity far beyond the limits of his nature. He is a fugitive from the commonplace, but without the means of effecting his escape."

That quotation from Colby, by the way, is all I have to show for a two-hour attempt to dip into *Music and the Superconscious* by J. F. G. Drybones. I had made a high-souled resolve to buckle down and do some intensive reading among the new books on music that have accumulated since last spring, and selected Dr. Drybones's volume as the first. And somehow, before I had finished twenty pages, I was reminded of something Wells had said about a pianola, and so had to get out *Tono-Bungay* to look it up. Then, of course, as long as I had the book there, I decided that I might as well read again the description of the flight over the Channel in an airship, and Uncle Ponderevo's death, and did; and then put *Tono-Bungay* back, and found the Colby book next to it, and read some of that, and then wondered whether Roland Young had ever returned my father's copy of *Happy Thoughts*, and had to look for it; and he had, and so some of that had to be read, and a chapter from *Hope of Heaven*, and part of a back number of *The New Yorker*; and one thing led to another until, by some mysterious chain of circumstances, I had answered four letters and was filling out an application blank for a driver's license, with the unfortunate Dr. Drybones lying lonely and neglected, just where he had been laid down, and just as unread as he had ever been.

Do other people, I wonder, have the hard time reading musical books that I do? There is nothing fundamentally wrong with Dr. Drybones. He is an indubitably learned man, and his book looks like a worthy contribution to musical esthetics. But somehow the sight of it, something about those neat pages, embellished with little heaps of consecutive fifths, and marked passages from Beethoven sonatas indicating Dr. Ebenezer Prout's conception of where the strong accents should fall—something about a book like that intimidates me. I know that it contains a great deal that I don't know, and I am always assailed by a gloomy conviction that I never shall know it, and probably would get no good out of it if I did. Years ago, thirsting for culture, I bought a book called *The Thought in Music*, by MacEwen. If I have tried once to read that book I have tried forty times, and I never get past the middle of the second chapter. Every time I find myself thinking that I know a thing or two about music I hunt up that book, and tackle Chapter One, and in ten minutes I am humbled to the dust. I simply cannot make head or tail of it. There must be a thought in music and I ought to try to find out what it is; but I doubt if I shall ever know. One of us, I fear, is dull.

7

A Share of the Air

DEAR MR. TAYLOR:

Perhaps what I am going to write in this letter won't be of any interest to you, but I can't think of anyone else to write it to, so you might as well be the victim. About five months ago I conceived the idea that it might prove interesting to keep a record of all the symphonic music that I heard on the radio. And so, ever since that day, I have written down in a little black book the name and composer of every number I have heard, and also the orchestra performing it, and the date it was played. As I am attending high school, practicing the oboe, and of course occasionally have to miss programs, I haven't by any means heard all of the good music available on the radio. However, I have listened to everything I could, and I think the result is rather an accurate account of what an average listener who is really interested in good music can hear. I have not included in my list any of the operas, performances by chamber ensembles, or recitals by concert artists that I have also heard —nothing but strictly symphonic music. Also, nothing that I have included was a recorded performance. Here are a few of the results of my five months of radio listening.

I have heard fifty-two complete symphonies, including all of Beethoven's, Brahms's, and Sibelius's, and others by Franck, Mozart, Tchaikovsky, Borodin, and Shostakovich—to name only a few. I have heard a total of 582 overtures, suites, symphonic poems, and ballets, played by practically all of the important orchestras of the country. Needless to say, I have heard as many fine conductors as I have orchestras. I listened to six all-Wagner concerts, two all-Strauss, and two all-Ravel. As played on the radio, the composers ranked, I find, as follows: first place goes to Wagner. Following him, grouped closely in point of popularity, come Tchaikovsky, Mozart, Johann Strauss, Sibelius, and Ravel. Next, almost equally popular, come Brahms, Beethoven, and Bach. Following next, with not so great an amount of their music played as the above nine, but still standing very well, (and all about equal), were Schubert, Mendelssohn, Rimsky-Korsakoff, Von Weber, Debussy, Saint-Saëns, Haydn, Dvořák, Schumann, Richard Strauss, Bizet, Handel, and Rossini. The following also showed a number of performances: Liszt, Franck, Smetana, MacDowell, Berlioz, and Grieg, to say nothing of many others whom I have not listed. I hope I have not bored you too much, and I hope you will not think that my purpose is merely to collect uninteresting statistics. All this has been incidental to the real enjoyment that I have received from these radio concerts.

This, from a young woman in Santa Barbara, California. I reprint it because it has a bearing upon a controversy that has been raging ever since the earliest days of broadcasting. It still rages. Hardly a day goes by that I— and you, too, probably—don't have to listen to some self-appointed custodian of American culture bewailing the cheapness, the dullness, and the vulgarity of American radio entertainment. He will tell you, if you listen—or, rather, whether you listen or not—that all you can get on the radio is cheap jokes, cookery talks, melodramas, and jazz, jazz, jazz. He wishes we could have a licensed and government-controlled radio, as they do in Europe, so that the public could have a chance to hear really good things, and *only* good things, with no propaganda and no commercial plugs.

A SHARE OF THE AIR

I think he overlooks a number of factors. The first is, that if I must choose between radio entertainment furnished by people who use it as a means of advertising something that they have to sell, and radio entertainment furnished by a government—any government—that uses it as a means of shaping and controlling public opinion, I choose the commercial plugs, thank you. And these are the only alternatives in the world today. However, that is beside my present point, which is that those who disapprove of the level of radio entertainment in this country always assume that the level is higher abroad. I wonder how many of you ever heard many peacetime European broadcasts—aside, that is, from special short-wave broadcasts designed for your consumption. If you did, you will have noticed several things. One is that they contain an enormous percentage of talk; another is that the average European station goes off the air for as long as two hours at a time, several times a day; another is that there are almost no network broadcasts; still another is that of all the music they broadcast, at least half of it is merely the playing of phonograph records. It is quite true that the average European station doesn't broadcast nearly as much popular music as ours do. Instead, it simply goes off the air.

The stations of the four large American networks are on the air eighteen hours a day. The smaller stations average eight to twelve hours a day. They broadcast to an audience estimated at about eighty million persons, the largest radio audience, by a huge margin, in the world. Now I don't think it's treason to venture the opinion that the *average* standard of taste and intelligence of eighty million people is not likely to be exactly alpine in height.

To me, the marvel is, not that so much cheap stuff is broadcast, but that there is such an enormous audience for good stuff. I remember hearing Dr. Walter Damrosch estimate that in New York City about 125,000 persons, that is, about 1.8 per cent of its seven million population, actively support serious music, to the extent of attending concerts, recitals, and opera performances. It is fair, I think to accept these figures as applicable to our other large cities. On the other hand, the radio audience of the Philharmonic-Symphony broadcasts and the NBC Saturday-night symphony concerts is estimated as between *five* and *seven* per cent of the total number of listeners—under the circumstances, a rather impressive proportion.

Now comes a radio listener who has taken the trouble to tabulate, in black and white, the amount of music that she heard in a given season. Naturally, if it was available to her, it was available to all of us. She says that she has heard fifty-two symphonies and 582 miscellaneous works in the course of five months. Since the average symphony program contains five selections, this means that she has heard the equivalent of one full-length symphony concert every day in the week for five months. That, I think, is a record of which radio may be reasonably proud.

Suppose we examine that record a little more in detail. Granted that the American radio audience for serious music is about six million—that is, something over seven per cent of the eighty million total—is it receiving attention from the broadcasters *in proportion* to its numbers? In order to arrive at an approximate answer, let us take the actual record. Let us take a typical week of broadcasting. Here is a condensed list of the programs of serious music, originating in New York, that were offered by

264

the four major networks (NBC, red and blue, CBS, and Mutual) during the week of April 23, 1939:

	Morning	*Afternoon*	*Evening*
SUNDAY:	Organ recital Recorded symphony concert	Organ recital Opera broadcast Song recital Symphony concert Music festival	Bach cantata Symphony concert
MONDAY:		Two symphony concerts with soloists	Two symphony concerts with soloists
TUESDAY:		Lecture-recital Song recital Chamber orchestra	Song recital Two symphony concerts
WEDNESDAY:			Symphony concert Pop concert
THURSDAY:	Organ recital	Light-opera con- cert Band concert	Symphony concert Chamber orchestra
FRIDAY:		Music-appreciation hour Two band concerts Chamber orchestra	Two symphony concerts
SATURDAY:	Organ recital Symphony concert		Symphony concert with soloists Symphony concert String orchestra

Notice, please, that I have included in this list only the *networks,* whose stations extend, not only over the New York district, but over the entire country. There are numerous local, unattached stations, from coast to coast, that broadcast more or less elaborate programs of recorded symphonic and operatic music for several hours every day. For the moment, however, let us confine our analysis to the official network list. You will notice that except on Saturdays and Sundays there is very little serious music available before one or two o'clock in the afternoon (EST). That is not a sign of carelessness or indifference on the part of the broadcasters; quite the contrary. The radio audience, up to lunchtime, consists overwhelmingly of women, a large proportion of whom do their own housework. They haven't the leisure to sit down to listen to a radio program. That being so, they would much prefer to hear a dramatic sketch, or a talk about domestic science, than a symphony concert. If they don't get much serious music, it is because most of them don't want it—then. You will notice, too, that there is an overtendency to concentrating the serious programs on Saturday and Sunday, at the expense of the other days in the week (the serious programs also overlap sometimes, although the overlapping does not show on the list). That is because time on the other days of the week is in great demand by the commercial broadcasters; and the stations simply must sell a certain amount of commercial time if they are to be self-supporting. Incidentally, the problem of over-concentration and overlapping is one that worries the broadcasters as much as it exasperates the listeners. It has yet to be solved.

Just what *is* the proportion of serious music to other entertainment on the four networks, as shown on that list? Here are the figures and the percentages: the four stations broadcast for sixteen hours a day, six days in the week, and fifteen hours on Sunday. That comes to 111 radio hours for every station, or a total of 444 hours. The ranking of the various kinds of programs is as follows:

Sermons, Talks, and Interviews: 115 hours, or about 26 per cent. Popular Music, including Dance

Bands:	108 hours, or about 24 per cent.
Sketches and Radio Dramas:	84 hours, or about 19 per cent.
Variety Shows:	72.hours, or about 16 per cent.
Serious Music:	24 hours, or about 5 per cent.
Children's Programs:	19 hours, or about 4 per cent.
Sporting Events:	14 hours, or about 3 per cent.
Unclassified:	8 hours, or about 2 per cent.

Now is serious music getting its proper representation on the air? How does its five per cent compare with what it gets in the world of entertainment that is *not* broadcast? Suppose we take New York as a criterion. It is supposed to be a "musical" city. In New York we have 1,343 motion-picture houses, 30 legitimate theaters open at the moment, 4 concert halls, and 1 opera house. In other words, judging by the accommodations we provide for the various branches of entertainment, our audience for serious music is as 5 to 1373, or just about four tenths of one per cent of our entertainment-seeking population. So radio's five per cent doesn't look so bad.

Furthermore, remember that there are not a dozen programs of serious music on the air that are commercially sponsored. People who buy time on the air to advertise their goods naturally want to reach the largest possible audience; and the largest possible audience is inevitably attracted only by programs that include comedy and popular music. Only one third of the time on the air is sold to commercial sponsors, but that third is almost entirely devoted to popular entertainment. The other two thirds of the time must be filled with programs created and broadcast at the expense of the broadcasting stations—the so-called sustaining programs. Since the stations, too, need to attract a large audience, in order to make their services commercially desirable, a large number of their programs must also be light in character. If they are giving their serious listeners their due proportion of time, they are serving the public properly. Are they?

Let us see. It is estimated that there are about thirty-seven million radio sets in use in this country, over which an audience of approximately eighty million persons listen in. The average audience for good music is about six million. Well, six is seven and one half per cent of eighty. That percentage, consequently, should be devoted to serious music. To repeat in another way what I said before, one third, or 148 of the 444 weekly hours, of the networks are sold commercially for what are largely popular programs. That leaves 296 hours for the stations to care for at their own expense. Since it is almost entirely up to them to provide our better music, they should give seven and one half per cent of their available time, or twenty-two hours a week, to serious music. Actually, they give us twenty-four—which means that we who listen on the four networks have available an *average* of three hours and twenty-five minutes a day of serious music. It may not come to us when and as we would like, but at least we get it; and if the proportion allotted to us is not generous, it is at least fair. The networks may not be doing as well as some of us would wish, or as well as they may do in the future; but they are giving us music lovers a well-intentioned and fairly adequate service, in proportion to our numbers. We should, on the whole, be grateful.

8

Other People's Poison

MUCH as I hate to admit it, I think it is rather a good thing that we do hear a certain amount of bad music on the radio. Mind you, I think it would be an even better thing if we heard nothing but good music on the radio—provided everyone wanted to hear it. Since everyone doesn't, since there are vast numbers of people who want bad stuff, they should be allowed to have it, simply because if they are *not* allowed to have it, they will not listen to anything at all. Which is bad for us missionaries; for so long as his radio set is working, there is always the hope of luring the Philistine listener into hearing, and learning to like, something better than what he thinks he likes. But you cannot elevate anybody's taste over a dead radio set.

I am aware that this belief of mine is not universally shared, that in some other countries broadcasting is controlled by certain persons who are so confident of the infallibility of their own taste that they undertake to decide what is and is not good for the public to hear, who allow the public to hear only such music as is, in their opinion, "good." I have often wondered whether they were equally confident that the public was obediently listening to the "good" music, and upon what grounds their confidence was based.

Of late I have wondered less, particularly after reading

a report that was published in the *Printer's Ink Monthly* for June, 1938. It runs, in part:

Critics of American radio who point with envy to the system in Great Britain . . . may be interested in the results of a poll taken by the Philco Radio & Television Corporation of Great Britain. . . . The Philco poll was taken in order to determine the British listeners' favorite station. It covered 5000 radio dealers and their customers in all parts of Great Britain, as well as the general public, with an approximate number reached of more than 500,000. The station which placed first, drawing 95.6 per cent of all the votes, was Luxembourg, which is not in Britain, or affiliated with the B.B.C., but is located on the Continent, across the English Channel, and broadcasts sponsored programs, in the American style. Second was Athlone, in the Irish Free State, and also a broadcaster of commercially sponsored programs. Britain's premier station, Droitwich, stood only third, with other Continental commercial stations capturing the great majority of places among the first ten in popularity. The poll seems to indicate that the British radio public prefers entertainment to education, and would accept a commercial in return for that entertainment.

All of which gives rise to the following grim reflections: that you can lead a horse to water, but you can't make him drink; that you catch more flies with molasses than with vinegar; and that if you are absolutely determined to improve people's minds, you had better do it in easy stages, and make sure that they're having a good time while you are doing it.

9

The Latecomers

ONE thing about the radio audience that rather puzzled me for a while is its extreme conservatism, compared with the audience in the concert halls. A certain number of radio listeners do want to hear new music, or less-new music that is seldom played. They write to the broadcasters in violent terms, demanding to know why they must listen to the same old round of Mozart, Beethoven, Brahms, Wagner, Tchaikovsky, etc., instead of more Stravinsky and Shostakovich and Hindemith and Bartók. But they are very much in the minority. Most of them want the classics first, last, and all the time, and are inclined to be suspicious of even so harmless a piece as Stravinsky's *Firebird* suite. As I say, I wondered about this for a long time; but I think I know the answer now. Many of us forget, and certainly we in the larger cities, who are soaked in music, tend to forget, that the radio is carrying symphonic music to a vast new audience that is not only eager, but incredibly young—young, not in years, but in experience. A symphony orchestra, broadcasting, plays for literally millions of people who never before in their lives have heard symphonic music, people to whom the symphonies of Mozart and Beethoven and Brahms and Tchaikovsky are a new and thrilling discovery.

I envy those people. Think of suddenly realizing, after half a lifetime, that the *"Eroica"* Symphony has something important to say to you, personally! No wonder such people don't want to go too fast. How can they? Think of trying to make sense of *The Rite of Spring* when you haven't yet digested Brahms's Fourth Symphony. A considerable part of this audience is trying to cover three generations of symphonic music in part of a lifetime. So think of that, sometimes, you of the listeners who are lucky enough to be more informed and experienced. When the orchestra plays those tremendous opening bars of the Brahms First, don't shrug your shoulders and say, "Oh, that again." Think, instead, back to the first performance of that symphony that you ever heard, and try to remember how you felt. And so remembering, resign yourself to hearing one more performance of a masterpiece.

10

Making the Most of It

THERE is—or was—a certain singer on the air for whose excessive popularity I could not, for the life of me, account. Her voice was true enough, and of adequate range, but beyond that there wasn't much that could be said for it. It was monotonous in range of expression, and as nearly colorless as a voice can be and still *be* a voice. There were a dozen singers on the air whose voices were infinitely superior to hers in color and expressiveness, but who seemed to mean little to the average radio listener. One day it occurred to me to ask a radio engineer whether he could explain the mystery of her nation-wide popularity.

"That's easy," he replied. "She sounds good on a ten-dollar set." He went on to explain that the very poverty of her voice, its very lack of the overtones that give more interesting voices their individuality, made it possible for the very simplest receiving set to pick it up exactly as it was transmitted. On such a set the other voices sounded no better, if as well.

In other words, if you want to get the most pleasure from the music that comes to you over the radio, you must, first of all, see that your radio set is the best you can afford. The small, three- or four-tube, low-priced sets serve fairly well to transmit speaking voices; but the cheap set cannot pick up (and if it could, its loudspeaker could not transmit) the enormous range of overtones that give vocal, instrumental, and orchestral music its characteristic quality. A ten-dollar set is certainly better than no set at all. But don't delude yourself that you are getting the full quality of the music that it brings you, and don't ever abandon the hope and intention of getting a better one.

Having conditioned your set, you must next find out what music is available. If you live in a city or large town, your daily paper probably prints the daily programs of most of the better stations and networks. But suppose you live in a village that supports only a weekly paper, or out in the country, with no paper at all? In that case, find out, by experimental listening-in, at what hour of the day your local stations announce their forthcoming programs. Most stations do so either around seven-thirty in the morning or at night, just before signing off. Whatever the hour is, listen in at that time for about a week, and copy down all the musical programs that sound promising, together with the time they are broadcast.

Since musical programs are generally put on in series of thirteen weeks, your list will give you very definite information as to what to expect at a given hour on any day of the week. Keep this list near your radio set, and make a point of listening regularly to the programs it offers. Take a broadcast concert as seriously as you would one for which you had bought tickets. You needn't go quite so far as to dress for it, but at least go to a little pains to listen. Get yourself a comfortable chair, adjust your set so that it neither blasts nor whispers, relax, and give the music your undivided attention. Don't sit down to a symphony broadcast with a book or newspaper in your hand, and expect to get much out of the music.

And don't make good music a background for conversation. If you and your friends and family find that you simply *must* talk, tune in to a night club—or, better yet, turn the radio off. Incidentally, don't listen to more music than you can assimilate. In order to qualify as a music lover, you need not, necessarily, put in most of your waking hours listening to it, any more than you need keep your nose buried in a book all day, to be a book lover. If you find your attention wandering, reduce the dose. Hear just as much music as you can hear with real, concentrated attention, and no more.

If serious music is a comparatively new thing in your life, don't have a guilty conscience if you find that you still like light music. The music of Herbert and Kern and Berlin and Gershwin is just as good, *of its kind,* as that of Schubert and Brahms and Tchaikovsky, and there is no more necessity for omitting it from your musical bill of fare than there is for banishing pancakes and ice cream from your household menus. Only—well, remember what happens when you have too much pancakes and ice cream!

Last of all, when you find a musical program of exceptional merit offered by any station, write to the station and say so. Programs of serious music, as a rule, are "sustaining" programs, that is, programs offered at the station's own expense, with no commercial sponsor to back them. The sponsor of a commercial program can get a pretty good idea of the popularity of his entertainment by looking at his sales reports. But the humble fan letter is about the only means any station has of finding out what the listeners think of the sustaining programs. So if you hear something you like, and would like to have continued, *always* say so.

II

The Lighter Side

THERE is a type of music lover, and a fairly prevalent one at that, who becomes instantly suspicious of any piece of new music that is comprehensible at a first hearing. His attitude seems to be that a composer should write exclusively for posterity; that if a new work can be understood and liked by the average listener at its first performance, it can't possibly be any good. It is lucky for us—and music—that this attitude was not particularly widespread in the past. If it had been, many a work by the classic masters would never have survived.

For the great composers of earlier days were generally popular composers. Not only were they popular, but they actually wanted to be. What they hoped for their music was that it make an immediate appeal to the average listener. Handel, in his day, was as popular as Jerome Kern is, in ours. His *Water Music*, for instance, written for a sort of nautical parade on the Thames in honor of George I of England, delighted the monarch so much that he insisted on having the whole thing played through twice, notwithstanding the fact that the piece is an hour long— and that George I was no music critic. Verdi, at the rehearsals of *Rigoletto*, refused to allow the Duke's song, *"La donna è mobile,"* to be sung *at all*, for fear it might leak out and be sung to death before the opening night. Verdi is perhaps not a wholly fair example, because he has not yet achieved any musical social standing, except in opera houses and similar places of low repute. But Handel is respectable enough. His *Water Music* now frequently appears as one of the prize exhibits on some of of our heaviest symphonic programs, despite the fact that it began by being popular. But along comes a contemporary piece—the Poulenc Two-Piano Concerto, for instance—and a battalion of listeners jump all over the poor thing with hobnailed boots because it doesn't pretend to be serious.

But the serious intent of a musical composition has nothing, necessarily, to do with its merit as music. Take, for example, Mozart's 34th symphony. Can you honestly maintain that Mozart was trying to express any tremendously profound musical message in that delightful, lyric, lighthearted little work? And does the fact that it is not particularly serious in intent keep it from being a masterpiece? I attended Josef Hofmann's fiftieth-anniversary concert, and one of his encore numbers was Mozart's "Turkish March." Now I can't believe that even the most fanatical Mozart worshiper would say that the "Turkish March" was meant to be anything more earth-shaking than a Turkish march; nevertheless, it is good music, and Mr. Hofmann was quite right in playing it. There are dozens of similar pieces, gay, melodious things, that are about as innocent of double meaning as a kitten, which, nevertheless, we admit without question to the programs of our greatest orchestras, and admire and enjoy.

But when a contemporary composer writes a piece of music which makes no pretense at delivering a profound message, a certain number of his hearers make up their minds beforehand that his music isn't worth hearing.

Now I'm not arguing that our symphony programs should degenerate into pop concerts, or that music that makes an immediate appeal is *necessarily* good music; but I do think we ought to maintain a single standard in our listening. Unfortunately, it is fair to say that, generally speaking, when we hear a piece of old music we listen to its composer; but that when we hear a piece of new music we're too likely to listen to its title.

Brahms's *Academic Festival Overture* is good music, and it has been taken seriously, as good music, ever since its first performance; and the merits of that overture are not impaired by the fact that all of its principle themes are based on German student songs. I sometimes wonder what sort of reception an American composer would get if he wrote an overture based on American college songs —granted that he did as good a job as Brahms did. I don't know, but I have my suspicions. I do know that Roy Harris has written an orchestral piece based on the old tune, *When Johnny Comes Marching Home*. It is good music; but it isn't played as often as Charles Griffes's *The Pleasure Dome of Kublai Khan*, which is also good music, and which enjoys the advantage, so far as audiences are concerned, of having a more exotic and serious program.

I think it is not possible to stress too heavily the point that the pretensions of a piece of music are not necessarily any index of its merit. Not long ago I heard an all-Russian program. Next to each other on that program were two works: Liadoff's *From the Apocalypse*, in which the composer undertook to convey the spiritual content of a tremendous passage from the Book of Revelations, and a suite from Rimsky-Korsakoff's *The Golden Cock-*

erel, in which the composer attempted little more than to give his hearers a thoroughly pleasant time. I venture the opinion that the Liadoff work is a failure, and the Rimsky-Korsakoff one a complete success; and that the latter is five times as good music as the former.

When you go to a cocktail party or an afternoon tea, you talk to various people whose conversation may be serious or trivial. When you come away you will probably remember some particular chat as the most interesting one of the occasion. The interest of that conversation lay, not in its lightness or heaviness, but in the quality of the speaker's mind. Of two persons, conversing in equally casual and superficial terms, the first may have given you something to remember for the rest of your life, while the second merely bored you. In both cases, what mattered was not *how* things were being said, but who said them.

I remember a passage from Shaw's *Man and Superman,* the scene in which Tanner is warning Octavius that his bride-to-be is not an angel, but a woman. "Marry Ann"; he says, "and at the end of a week you'll find no more inspiration in her than in a plate of muffins."

"You think I shall tire of her!" exclaims the shocked Octavius.

"Not at all: you don't get tired of muffins."

That is a light comedy scene, obviously written for a laugh. Nevertheless, it manages to convey the profound truth that it is possible to become habituated without being bored. A duller playwright might have expressed it in just those words. Shaw, not being a dull playwright, says it in terms of comedy.

Music can be like that. Whether or not a composer's music is important, and permanent, is a matter, not of what the music claims or does not claim to say, but of what sort of person the man is who writes it. Rimsky-Korsakoff and Mozart and Handel and a host of others manage somehow to say more, in their lightest and most tuneful and apparently superficial moments, than a whole roomful of Liadoffs and a wagonload of *Apocalypse*s. I hope I don't give the impression of arguing that music that makes great pretensions is *ipso facto* dull, and that all light and tuneful music is necessarily good. That would be nonsense, of course. But I do believe that, in listening to any new music, it is wise to try to hear what the composer has to say, without being too much influenced by the manner in which he says it. A work may be light, and gay, and amusing, and still possess greatness if its composer happens to be—as, for instance, Mozart was—a great man. Don't scowl too fiercely at a new piece of music, just because the poor thing manages to be attractive.

12

Never Mind the Three B's

INCIDENTALLY, this solemn insistence on weight and pretentiousness in new music is one of the heaviest handicaps under which the American composer labors today. We all still tend to think of an art like music as being a competitive business. We still think in terms of championships. If four or five first-rank men happen to be conducting orchestras in this country, we're not entirely happy unless we can convince everybody that one of them is the champion, another the runner-up, another number three player, and so on. And the same tendency holds good in our judgment of music itself. We're still looking for *the* great American symphony, for *the* great American opera. When we hear a work by an American composer, we're not satisfied to dislike or enjoy the music. We start worrying as to whether it's better or worse than some work by one of the masters, as to whether its creator can really be called a great composer.

I think that attitude is rather childish. There is no yardstick for judging art. There is no provable greatest symphony in the world, no masterpiece of masterpieces of music. . . . Yes, I know. You are dying to tell me that you do know one, and can prove it. But what you do not know is that somebody else is equally sure that he knows one, and is equally able to prove it, and that his choice is not yours.

There was an extraordinarily fine play produced in New York not long ago, a play called *Abe Lincoln in Illinois*, by Robert E. Sherwood. Another extraordinarily fine play was also running there. It was called *Hamlet*, by William Shakespeare. I heard both plays and their performances discussed at length by a number of persons; and in all those discussions I never heard anyone draw any comparison between Sherwood and Shakespeare, never heard anyone express any opinion as to whether one was better than the other. Now this may mean that everyone, Mr. Sherwood included, took it for granted that Shakespeare was the better playwright. On the other hand, what I think it really means is that nobody was bothering his head about the ranking of Shakespeare and Sherwood. The question simply didn't occur to people. They enjoyed each play for its own sake, without worrying about which one held the world's record.

In this respect our attitude toward the theater is much more grown up than our attitude toward music. Every time an American composer has some work of his performed by one of our orchestras, some critic, or some section of the audience, promptly stands him up back to back with Beethoven, or Bach, or Brahms, to see which is the taller. Only the other day I read an article reminding us that most of the giants of music lived in other times than ours. That is sad, but it's not tragic; because at least we can still hear what they wrote. But we can also hear, and enjoy, what the comparative small fry of our own day are writing, if we'll just relax and listen to it.

I took a trip to the West Coast last fall, and riding on the train through Arizona I spent a good half day passing through a vast expanse of desert and mountains.

NEVER MIND THE THREE B'S

Now if you've ever crossed that Arizona desert you don't have to be told that, seen from a car window, one part of it looks pretty much like another. Speaking for myself, after I have spent an hour looking at sand and sagebrush and tumbleweed, I've had enough. In short, having grasped the general idea, I don't have to see any more. So I looked at the mountains, instead. And they were magnificent— gigantic heaps of brown and red and purple, many of them capped with snow. Against that intense blue Western sky they were a wonderful sight. But after a while I found my eyes growing tired of looking at even that amazing panorama. I returned to the desert—and it was still a desert. So then I had to look again at the mountains. And after a few hours I had to confess that I was tired even of mountains, and returned ignominiously to my detective story.

I think that experience applies to music as well as to geography, the moral being that we cannot indefinitely gaze at the peaks. If we are not to weary of them we must have some foreground, too. And I am not so sure that an unmixed diet of musical masterpieces is as digestible as some members of the fundamentalist group of music lovers seem to believe. There is room, also, for music that doesn't keep us perpetually on the snow-capped heights, that shows us green grass, and trees, and running water.

Not that I'm inferring that American music is second-rate. In fact, I have already expressed my opinion that Charles Griffes, for one, was potentially one of the great modern composers. I am trying only to say that the highest service we can render to American composers is to listen to their music as music, and not as an examination paper to be graded in comparison with the other members of the class. The standard of American playwriting today is as high as that of any country in the world. I'm not sure that it isn't higher. It has reached its present point of excellence largely because the critics and the public have been content to enjoy and appraise American plays for what they are, seeing and hearing them with the eyes and ears of their own times, rather than those of history. And as public taste has improved, the quality of our plays has improved accordingly—because it had to, if the plays were to find a public.

We must learn to do the same with our native music, to think of it in positive, rather than comparative, terms, to ask of an American composer only that it be good music, without trying to decide whether it is ten points above or below some masterpiece of the *past*. The history of American music a hundred years from now is going to be determined largely by what you thought of American music today, not in terms of the music of other days and other countries, but in terms of itself, here and now.

13

The Swish of the Bow

Do you remember the English Singers, the group of vocalists whose first tour of this country, something over a decade ago, for once deserved the adjective "sensational"? During their first American season they made twenty appearances in the New York district alone, and after every one the air was thick with lay and professional murmurs of "remarkable," "divine," "swell," "delicacy," and "revival of the lost art of madrigal singing."

To me, what gave the concerts of the English Singers their peculiar charm, and gave their work its particular significance, was the extent to which they managed to debunk music, to strip concert-giving of the ritual that makes the acquirement of musical culture such a dreary business. The English Singers did almost none of the things that are supposed to induce a proper spirit of reverence for the art of *bel canto*. They did not file solemnly out upon the platform with the general air of being members of the College of Cardinals about to elect a new pope. They did not stand in a row, like a firing squad. They did not hold their music waist-high, in the genteel pretense that they did not need it. They had no leader to give studies in plastic self-expression while the singing was going on.

Not at all. They emerged, six people who were on the point of having a good time and who produced the illusion of being astonished and delighted to find so many of their friends assembled to share it with them. They sat cozily around a table, their music laid before them, while their chief, Mr. Cuthbert Kelly, made a few apologetically in- formative remarks about the music, or read aloud the words of a song. Then he, too, seated himself, gave an almost imperceptible signal with a lifted forefinger—and they were off. Incidentally, once they *were* off, they sang like a more or less celestial choir. They could have sung considerably less celestially and still have been a success; for they restored at least one branch of chamber music to the realm of mundane enjoyment.

To realize how nearly a lost art that is, one has only to consider the conditions under which most classic chamber music was written and performed. It is, as its name im- plies, "room music," and was no more intended to be played or sung in public halls than the warming pans of our ancestors were intended to be hung on the walls of our living rooms. The madrigals that the English Singers interpreted so beautifully were written originally at the behest of certain English gentlemen, for their private pleasure, to be sung by the host and his assembled guests after dinner—a sort of Elizabethan equivalent of bridge or backgammon. When you hear the huge string section of a modern symphony orchestra thundering through a *con- certo grosso* by Johann Sebastian Bach, try to remember that Bach wrote it for the friends and private orchestra of a Saxon Elector, the passages for solo instruments being played by the professionals, with the amateur fiddlers joining in the tuttis; the audience, if any, being composed principally of the Elector and his entourage.

The modern chamber-music concert, like the modern

song or instrumental recital, is a wholly artificial form of musical entertainment, with origins that are economic rather than esthetic. In the eighteenth and early nineteenth centuries nearly every duke or count of any importance, particularly in Germany and Austria, kept a private orchestra and a private composer or two, to say nothing of a staff of vocal and instrumental soloists. Unfortunately the dukes and counts have almost wholly disappeared, and their social successors incline to airplanes and racing stables rather than musicians. The last-named, consequently, were finally forced to discover that it was easier to make a thousand people pay two dollars apiece to hear them perform than to make one person pay two thousand dollars. Hence the modern recitals and chamber-music concerts, which, however estimable as democratic compromises, are esthetically unfortunate and physically uncomfortable.

For operas and orchestral concerts the large auditorium and the remote performers are not inappropriate, for the large scale of these musical forms, and their comparative impersonality, are part of their impressiveness. But chamber music and solo music are a different matter. To hear a string quartet as it should be heard, one should be close enough to the players, as Cecil Forsyth puts it, "to hear the swish of the bow on the strings." Similarly, if you can be near enough to a singer or instrumentalist to establish some sort of personal contact, your pleasure in his performance is exactly doubled. During the years that I was serving my sentence as a New York music critic I must have heard easily half a thousand recitals. Three of them I still remember with peculiar pleasure, and none of the three was public. The first was the studio party to which

I have referred in a previous chapter, when Jascha Heifetz played for twelve people at four in the morning. The second was another party, at which Arthur Rubinstein and Paul Kochanski played such piano and violin music as it pleased them to play, for as long as they chose to play it—which was hours. The third was an evening in John McCormack's New York apartment, when the great tenor sang straight through two volumes of Hugo Wolf, with Sergei Rachmaninoff to play his accompaniments—and Ernest Newman to turn the pages.

The sheer discomfort of the modern recital is something to daunt any but the most incorrigible of music lovers. To sit in an unpleasantly decorated, vilely ventilated auditorium, twenty yards from the platform, on a seat that was designed with no particular reference to the human frame, holding one's overcoat in one's lap, hoping that one's hat is not hopelessly lost under the seat, wedged in between anonymous and faintly hostile neighbors, friendless, comfortless, tobaccoless—this is a high price to pay even for one cf the "Razumovsky" Quartets.

Someday a genius among concert managers will present the ideal chamber-music series. He will offer it in a room not more than forty feet square. The chairs will be low, roomy, and heavily overstuffed, and not less than two feet apart. The floor will be strewn with rugs, the walls will be hung with pictures, and the lights will come from the sides. The first program will consist of Warwick-William's arrangement of *The Flowers of the Forest,* the Mozart C major Quartet (the one with the introduction to which the critics object so violently), and the Quartet of Claude Debussy. Every hearer, upon arrival, will have his coat, hat, rubbers, and other baggage politely taken away from him and checked—free—and will be introduced to the other hearers. Upon reaching his chair he will find beside it a small, low table, upon which have been placed the following articles: 1 cigarette box, fitted; 1 ash tray; 1 bottle Perrier; 1 bottle White Rock; 1 decanter, fitted; one bowl of ice; 1 tall glass. The price of the tickets would have to be, I imagine, about thirty-five dollars apiece. I, for one, would gladly start saving up for a pair tomorrow.

14

Richard and Joseph—and You

SOMEDAY, someone—possibly myself—is going to write a handbook upon applause, calling it *Audiences and What Makes Them Work*, or something of the sort. Whoever the author may be, he will need no source material other than the works of Richard Wagner and Giuseppe Verdi. Both composers instinctively knew all about the human animal's nervous reactions, how to make him applaud, and—equally important—how to make him stop. Almost any skillful composer has some intuitive knowledge of the subject, but Wagner and Verdi apply their knowledge deliberately. Both are masters of Stop and Go writing.

Take first the case of Wagner, supreme in the field of Stop writing. His most striking innovation in opera, aside from the leitmotiv system, was his abolition of the formal scene and aria—to hear him and his disciples tell it. As a matter of fact, he did nothing of the sort. Search his scores, and you will find dozens of set numbers that, so far as form is concerned, might have been written by Bellini. They may be heavily disguised, but there they are. If Siegmund's Love Song, in the first act of *Die Walküre*, isn't a tenor aria, what is it? If much of the second act of *Tristan and Isolde* isn't a series of tenor and soprano duets, if the quintet from *Die Meistersinger* isn't a formal ensemble number—what are they?

290

The main reason, I think, why we don't recognize these numbers for what they are, is that we don't applaud them. The action doesn't stop obligingly while we cheer and beat our hands together and the singers take a bow. That, of course, would be sacrilege. We are too absorbed in the action, too immersed in the mood of the scene, to wish to break that mood with applause. We believe this, sincerely, and for most of us it is probably true. But just in case there should be some among us who are not properly absorbed in the stage action, the canny Wagner takes jolly good care to make it impossible for us to applaud.

He does it by employing the old and infallible device of the "false" or "surprise" cadence. Ordinarily, a given piece of music comes to a full stop upon the tonic chord of the key in which it started out; even when it does not close in its original key, it comes to a halt upon the tonic of a key that has been definitely established. In either case we take this so-called "perfect" cadence as a signal that the piece is over, and that we may relax, and, if we wish, applaud. In an opera like *Carmen* or *Rigoletto*, for instance, the various numbers that go to make up the score are definitely separated from one another by these stoppages. Wagner, on the other hand, rarely comes to a full stop except at the end of an act. Instead of closing a section of the score in the orthodox manner he ends it, either on a chord that is a preparation for another key, or on a chord that is an actual modulation into a new and totally unexpected key. Our strong impulse to applaud is suddenly checked by our even stronger curiosity to hear what is coming next.

This sounds a bit involved, but it really is not. Let us take a specific example, the closing of Walter's Prize Song in the last scene of *Die Meistersinger*. Walter begins in the key of C, to sing what is, if ever there was one, a tenor aria. In the second verse he makes a brief, slightly complicated excursion into the key of B major, but returns to the original key so unmistakably that we have it firmly fixed in our ears. The music grows more and more impassioned; the chorus enters under the soloist, softly, but wonderfully effective in enhancing the—musical—excitement. Now a quiet coda, with Eva's voice dominating it, one of the loveliest things that even Wagner ever wrote. Orchestra and singer come to a slow close. One more bar, and we shall be back on that terminal tonic chord of C, and some of our less spellbound neighbors are going to break in with ill-timed applause. But that C chord is never sounded; instead, a sudden shift into the key of E minor, as we hear the long, grave phrase that, throughout, has been associated with Hans Sachs. Our nervous tension relaxes abruptly. Even if we wished to applaud, we cannot. It is too late. The master has tricked us. He has made his transition without interruption, and we are off on something new.

Not so Verdi, who, particularly in his old, unregenerate days, positively *asks* for applause—and gets it. Barring accidents or exceptionally bad singing, applause at a Verdi opera, especially in the earlier ones, before Giuseppe began to have esthetic scruples, has been more or less predetermined by the composer.

A high note, of course, is always sure to put an audience into an applauding mood. The rapid vibrations tickle our eardrums and stimulate the nerve centers, and start the blood circulating faster. We accumulate some surplus nervous energy and want to expend it. We have, besides, the added excitement of being present at the performance of a difficult physical feat. Opera audiences like to hear a coloratura soprano leap over a couple of octaves, just as spectators at a track meet like to see a pole vaulter leap over a twelve-foot bar. But the high note alone may not turn the trick. The actual volume of sound is small, whatever its intensity. So the orchestra comes in and goads the nerve centers with its added bulk. Then the noise stops, abruptly, the pressure is removed, and the edified listeners beat their hands and yell in order to work off their surplus energy. It isn't appreciation at all. It is sheer automatism.

Such is the ABC of the art of applause extraction. But the early Verdi is even cleverer than that. He drives his hearers into a frenzy by a further refinement of the art, suspense, and by helping his singers to be at their most effective best. The simplest way to explain how he does it is to illustrate. Let us take the climax of the third act of *Il Trovatore*.

Here is a tenor. Owing to the exigencies of the plot he is not going to have a great deal to do, pyrotechnically, in the act that follows. This is his last chance to shine, and the problem is to help him to get the most out of what he has to do. Verdi begins by smoothing down the nerves of his audience, and the vocal cords of his tenor. He gives Manrico a placid, easygoing scene with Leonora, which pleases the listeners without exciting them and gives Manrico a preliminary canter around the upper middle section of his voice. His little lyric aria, *"Amor, sublime amor,"* gives him just enough work to keep the vocal cords

293

warm without putting any strain upon them. Then an organ plays. The tenor has a moment of complete rest, and the audience is still further soothed. This is the extreme low point of the scene, from a nerve specialist's point of view.

Suddenly Ruiz enters, so excited that the audience, however sketchy its knowledge of Italian may be, knows that something is wrong. The orchestra, too, begins to show signs of worry. From this point on, the process of egging on the audience proceeds remorselessly. The tempo of the music grows faster and faster, and the voices of the singers wax louder and louder. The tenor, well rested, is in the pink of condition and fairly champing at the bit. Ruiz rushes out, and Manrico begins *"Di quella pira."* The audience knows that this must be his big aria—all signs, to say nothing of the argument printed in the program, pointing to it.

But the hearers miss something, they hardly know what. That something is a genuinely high note. Despite a few G's and a brace of A's, the *tessitura,* that is, the general "lay" of the voice in this aria, is comfortably low for a tenor. They wait and wait for that high note. Will it never come? Finally it does come—a high C on *"O teco."* It isn't Verdi's (an enterprising tenor stuck it in, and no tenor since his time has dared not to sing it), but it's effective. To the audience the scene is over, and it prepares to relieve its taut nerves by applauding. But no. Leonora sings a line or two, and the audience, baffled, remains tense. Whereupon Manrico, drawing a sword—always an inspiring object—braces his legs, throws back his shoulders, and emits a terrific high C on *"morir,"* one of the easiest of vowel combinations for a tenor, and rushes out. Verdi unleashes the orchestra—steps on the brass, so to speak—the stage manager gives the cue for a quick curtain, and nature takes its course. Of course the audience howls. How could the poor thing help it?

15

The Judgment Seat

PEOPLE who want to become music critics have my sympathy and commiseration. Sympathy, because it is not hard to understand why the trade sounds like an alluring one: the privilege of hearing all the great music and all the great performers, and being paid for doing it; the sense of power that comes of having one's opinions printed and taken seriously. Commiseration, because these aspiring Solomons don't know what awaits them. The fact remains that anyone who is or ever has been a music critic is besieged with questions and requests for advice from all sorts and conditions of persons who think it would be fun to sit in judgment upon the creators and interpreters of the most intangible of all the arts.

They all ask the same three questions: how can I become a music critic? What qualifications must I possess? What use is a music critic, anyhow? The answer to the first is short and simple. If someone asked you, "How can I become president of Sears, Roebuck & Company?" what would your answer be? My guess is that it would be the obvious one, "Get a job with Sears, Roebuck & Company." And to anyone who asks, "How do I get to be a music critic on a magazine or newspaper?" the answer is precisely the same: "Get a job on a magazine or newspaper." Any paper, any job—advertising, circulation, general news, sports, rewrite. The kind of job doesn't matter in the least. What does matter is having your foot in the door, in being in a position to see your chance when it arrives, to seize it—and to make good with it.

And that brings us to the second question. What makes a music critic? What does he have to know, and how does he learn it? Let me try to define the ideal music critic. In the first place, like the dramatic critic, he has a double responsibility. He must be able to appraise not only the merits of a new work of art, but the merits of its *performance*. A literary critic, or a critic of painting, needs only to say, "Soandso has written a good book," or, "painted a bad picture." The music critic must be able to judge, not only the quality of the music, but how well or ill it was sung or played. His technical background, therefore, must be extensive.

To begin with, he must know a lot of history—the history of the art itself, the history of the instruments, of the orchestra, and the lives of the great composers and interpreters. Naturally, no ordinary human being could retain all these facts in his memory, but he must at least have studied them with sufficient thoroughness to be able to know where to lay his finger on them when he needs them. I have known only one critic who, apparently, never needed to consult a book. That was the late Henry E. Krehbiel, of the *New York Herald Tribune*. A famous colleague of his once remarked that the only library a music critic needed was a set of *Grove's Dictionary of Music* and Pop Krehbiel's telephone number.

Our ideal critic must know a good many things besides history. He should be familiar with the works of the standard orchestral repertoire; roughly speaking, that means upwards of two hundred compositions that he should have heard, either in actual performance or on records, or, if that is impossible, that he should have studied and attempted to play over for himself. That also means that he must know enough about musical notation to be able to follow an orchestral score with some degree of ease. Besides that he must, of course, have a thorough knowledge of the various musical forms, including some acquaintance with harmony and counterpoint. Besides being familiar with the orchestral repertoire, he must know the famous piano and violin concertos, and a vast number of the smaller works that make up the literature of these instruments. He must be on speaking terms with the great string quartets, and other familiar chamber-music works. He must be acquainted with the stories and the scores of the standard operas, as well as the better-known songs of Schubert, Schumann, Brahms, Debussy, Fauré, and a host of other song composers.

He ought to be enough of a pianist to be able at least to thumb his way through a song accompaniment or a piano arrangement of an orchestral work. While he need not actually play the violin, he should know enough of its technique to be able to tell good playing from bad. The same holds true of singing. Most of the critics I have known could not by any stretch of the imagination be called singers, but they have known enough of the technique of the art to be able to diagnose correct and faulty vocal production.

So much for his technical equipment. But we cannot stop with discussing what he should *know*. We must also discuss what he should *be*. And here we enter a field of which the average would-be critic never thinks at all—and which is the most important of all. While anyone who is willing to study hard enough and listen faithfully enough can acquire all of the knowledge that I have just outlined, he may, nevertheless, never manage to become a good critic. For critics, like poets, are born.

The primary and the indispensable qualification of a good critic of any of the arts is the possession of a critical mind. Now that sounds like defining a thing in terms of itself; but let me explain. William James once divided human beings into two categories: the tender-minded, and the tough-minded The former, he said, is the person whose mind is dominated by his emotions, the person who believes something because he wants it to be true; the blind partisan, the person who embraces an artistic or political faith and is, by that act, automatically rendered incapable of seeing any flaws in it.

The tough-minded person, on the other hand, is the one whose mind insists on functioning without regard to the wishes of its unfortunate possessor; the person who, upon being confronted with an irrefutable fact, is able to admit that fact, even though it runs contrary to his secret hopes and convictions. If you can listen to the playing of a string quartet composed of your mother, your sweetheart, your elder brother, and your best friend, and say—if not to them, at least to yourself—"That was terrible!" If you are able to do that, if your judgment functions without regard to your prejudices, then you can hope to be a real critic.

Notice that I say, "if not to them, at least to yourself." For there is another qualification of a real critic. A good critic has a sense of proportion; which means, first, that he doesn't take himself too seriously, is willing to admit that his own opinions are not necessarily the last word on the subject. It means, second, that he is merciful. He tempers his verdict according to the pretensions of the culprit. He doesn't blame a waltz for not being a symphony, and he doesn't abuse a street fiddler for not being Mischa Elman. It is only the very young who think that it is hypocrisy to keep silent, sometimes, when the raw truth would only hurt without curing. A true sportsman doesn't shoot sparrows with an elephant gun.

Which brings me to another point. "Criticism" is not synonymous with faultfinding. A good critic is on the alert, not only for faults, but for merits. He must be capable, not only of disapproval, but of enthusiasm. He must be capable, not only of saying that something is worthless, but that it is wonderful—if it is. That sounds so self-evident that it's hardly worth saying, but it is, nevertheless, one of the hardest parts of a critic's job. In my own brief experience of five years at music criticism I found that one of the easiest things to do was to dissect a bad performance or a bad piece of music, because that required little more than an exercise of one's analytical faculties. The difficult thing was to explain a great piece of music or a great performance; for when you have to do that, you have to communicate an emotion from yourself to a reader. And right there is where you must be, not only an appraiser, but a writer.

And there is the last, and by no means the least, of the qualifications of an ideal music critic. He must be able to write, and write well. He must be able to re-create emotions through the power of words. He must be an enthusiast about music who can contrive to make his *subject* always interesting, regardless of what his topic of the moment may happen to be. If he is bored at a concert, he must be able to make even his boredom interesting. Otherwise he will not be read; and a critic without readers is an actor without an audience. He must know how to structure a criticism, arranging his details so that the general impression of what he writes is the one he wanted to convey. I once wrote a review of Gilbert Seldes' book, *The Seven Lively Arts*. About a week after it had appeared I had a note from Mr. Seldes, in which he said, "Thanks for the review. The others all said the book was fifteen per cent bad. You said it was eighty-five per cent good." I never forgot that note. It is fatally easy, in criticism, to devote so much space to minor flaws that there is no room left for the major merits.

Now needless to say, there is no such thing as the ideal critic I have just outlined. When he does appear, he will probably be drawn instantly to heaven in a chariot of fire. Nevertheless, he does exist as an ideal, and an astonishing number of critics come nearer to approximating his qualifications than you would think. Especially in this country. I have been on both sides of the fence, knowing the critics, first, as colleagues, and latterly, as prosecuting attorneys; and I have read oceans of criticism, here and abroad. And I honestly believe that, *on their average,* the American and English music critics, for general knowledge and experience, for fairness, conscientiousness, and writing ability, are the best in the world. One reason for their pre-eminence, I think, is that, whereas the average Continental critic spends three fourths of his time hearing only music and performers from his own country, we hear music, and interpreters, from every country on the face of the globe—with the possible exception, of course, of our own.

It is all the more to the credit of American music critics that they work under two handicaps that hardly exist on the other side of the water. One is the heartbreaking necessity for speed. The conditions under which a New York critic works are rather typical of the rest of the country. If you are working for a New York morning paper, your review of a given musical event must reach the composing room on the average about midnight. If you leave the concert hall or the opera house, say, about ten-fifteen, you have until quarter of twelve to finish your copy. In other words, you have just one hour and a half in which to sort out your impressions of what may be a new work or a new performer, plan what you're going to say, and write a critical article that—presumably—is going to influence the opinions of several thousand people. The marvel is that our critics can do it at all, let alone that they do it so well. Even the critic who is lucky enough to work for an evening paper is not really much better off. His copy must be in before nine the following morning, which means that he must either sit up half the night or get up when he hears the milkman.

His other handicap is the vast quantity of music that he must hear. People who have never done musical criticism, and who are fond of music, often say, wistfully, 'How I envy you, being able to hear so much music!'' What they don't realize, what nobody who has not tried it *can* realize, is that the one luxury forever denied to a music critic is that of being able to *hear* music. He must listen, with his mind, every second of every minute that he spends at a performance, if he is to do his job well. If a new piece of music is dull, or one of the performers is incompetent, he can't just doze, or let his mind wander until something interesting commands his attention again. He must listen attentively to the bad as well as to the good. He cannot sink back and be carried away by a beautiful passage or a wonderful bit of singing or playing. He must analyze it—and worse than that, analyze himself. "Why do I like that? What is that violinist's particular quality? What is that pianist doing with that Beethoven sonata that Soandso didn't do last week?"

He must do this, night after night, week after week. Here, he gets no respite. In Europe, he does, for musical events don't tread on one another's heels so thickly as they do here. A foolishly conscientious critic in a musical center like New York or Chicago can attend and criticize two hundred musical events in the course of a single season of eight months, and still leave two or three hundred to be covered by his assistants. The nervous strain is something that you wouldn't believe if you have not experienced it. And so, around about the middle of January, with the season nearing its third quarter, if your favorite music critic is a trifle less readable, a little more savage than he was last fall, don't judge him too harshly. Be a little sympathetic. He is merely on the way to his annual nervous breakdown, all in the cause of your information and entertainment.

The Useful Pest

THERE remains now to answer the last of the three questions: of just what use is a music critic? Does he perform any useful function, beyond providing a column of more or less interesting reading matter in a morning newspaper, to be glanced over casually by the average reader, and to awaken the jungle instincts in the breasts of the unhappy composers or performers who happen to be his victims?

I think that he performs several functions, and that if he performs them well and conscientiously he is a highly useful and valuable citizen in the world of music. First of all, he serves as a contemporary historian, a chronicler of the musical life of his times. Long after the critic and his first readers have disappeared, his reviews, filed away in the dusty recesses of the newspaper shelves of a public library, may be invaluable source material for some future historian. One of my most cherished works of reference is a set of three small volumes that Henry E. Krehbiel once gave me, containing his reviews of the musical events in New York from 1885 to 1890. They constitute a history of that period in our musical development far more interesting and comprehensive than any that I have ever encountered in any formal textbook. The same is true of George Bernard Shaw's *London Music in 1888–89*. It is simply a collection of music criticisms, written long be-

fore a good many of us were born. Nevertheless, no matter how old or young you are, you will find it fascinating
reading, not only as criticism, but also as history.

A critic also serves as a guide. Through his appraisal
of the merits of music and performances he helps you to
clarify your own opinions, if you, too, have heard them.
If you agree with his verdict, whatever it may be, you
gain confidence in your own judgment, and are likely to
find reasons that you may not have thought of why you
arrived at your particular conclusions. If you disagree
with him, at least you are compelled to justify your disagreement, if only to yourself, to analyze the reactions
that caused you to form your opinion. All this stimulates
and develops your own critical faculties. Or, if you have
not heard the particular composition or performance
about which the critic is writing, you get from him, if he
is a good one, a clear impression of how the composition
sounded, how the singer sang, or how the instrumentalist
played. He helps you to decide for yourself whether, if this
particular music or musician happens to come your way
again, it, or he, is worth a hearing.

Another function, and a very important one, in my
opinion, is that of arousing and sustaining his reader's
interest in music. A good critic is always an enthusiast.
He never loses his capacity for being thrilled by a new
piece of great music, or for throwing his hat in the air
over a great performance. Now this sounds like a truism,
since obviously a man whose lifework is hearing and
writing about music ought to be assumed to be interested
in it. As a matter of fact, holding on to his capacity for
enthusiasm is by no means one of the easiest parts of a
critic's job. Speaking from my own experience, I must

confess that there are times when it is very hard for a critic not to hate music. A few weeks of dull or downright bad performances and uninspired programs can so get on his nerves that there comes a night when the last thing in the world that he wants to do is to go out and hear a concert. But the state of being fed up is a luxury that he cannot afford. He must, at whatever cost, always remember that he is serving a great art, must always keep his readers conscious of that fact, must always, so to speak, sell them music. In this respect, at least, the critic who is a brilliant writer has an enormous advantage over his possibly sounder but less-gifted colleagues. The late James Gibbons Huneker is a good example of a critic whom it was always a joy to read, regardless of his subject matter or his conclusions. Shaw is another. His world-wide success as an essayist, dramatic critic, and playwright, has caused us to forget that he once served a term as music critic of the London *Star*. His book, *London Music in 1888-89,* is a reminder that he was one of the most brilliant and stimulating ones that ever wrote.

But the music critic's fundamental function, the one that is his primary excuse for existence, is that of maintaining standards, of keeping always in his mind certain ideals of composition and interpretation, and of judging what he hears in the light of those ideals. That is why experience is such an important part of his equipment. The more singers and instrumentalists, the more orchestras and string quartets, he has heard in the past, the better is he able to appraise new ones. The more old music he has heard, the more likely is he to keep his head in the presence of new music. His duty is to appraise the present, not in the light of what is, not even in the light of

306

what has been, but in the light of what might be. And that vision of what might be he must acquire, and must remain faithful to, always. Your first symphony concert was probably, to you, a magic and unforgettable experience. If the review that you read of it failed to share your enthusiasm, don't curse the critic. He wasn't trying to be a spoilsport and a killjoy. He wasn't necessarily so blasé that he was incapable of any enthusiasm. He was merely telling you, indirectly, that this was not his first, but his five-hundredth symphony concert; and that wonderful as this one may have sounded to you, there were other, more wonderful ones, in store for you.

I mentioned previously some of the disadvantages under which the American newspaper music critic works. Now let me take the other side for a moment, and discuss a few of the handicaps under which his readers and his victims labor. Granted that there is need for music critics, do they invariably live up to the standards of their profession? Speaking as a former practitioner, I must confess that they do not.

Consider, for example, the time element, the necessity for haste in writing his reviews. That necessity is unfair, not only to the critic, but to his readers, and the people whom he is criticizing. A critic, after all, is a human being, and as such, his immediate reaction to a very striking performance or an impressive piece of new music is likely to be an emotional, rather than a highly intellectual one. If he is conservative by nature, he may react violently against some feature of the event that conflicts with his preconceived notions of proper procedure. The composer may introduce some radical innovation in form, the opera or concert singer or instrumentalist may choose to ignore tradition in some scene or passage. His first, human, emotional reaction, is likely to be indignation. If he had time to think it over, he might decide that the innovation was justified, or even admirable. But he doesn't have time to think it over. What you read is what he thought about the performance less than two hours after it was over. Similarly, if he leans to the radical side, some new thing may arouse his enthusiastic approval which, if he could think about it for twenty-four hours, wouldn't seem so wonderful after all. In neither case is the criticism you read likely to represent the critic's ripened and reasoned opinion.

Now there is no defensible necessity for this haste at all. There is no earthly reason why the review of a concert or opera performance should not appear two, or even three or four, days after the event. When a play opens on a Monday night, it is going to be on exhibition also on Tuesday night—and, so the producer hopes, for many nights thereafter. So there is a very good reason why the drama critic's review should appear on Tuesday morning, so as to give prospective theatergoers some idea of what to expect. But concerts, recitals, and operas, as a rule, don't play repeat performances. A music review generally concerns an event that is over and done with, that has no timely news value whatsoever. But a stupid convention among newspapers decrees that musical criticism is a branch of reporting. The music critic must attend the important-sounding event, the event that has news value, and must not only appraise it, but must report that it happened; and that report must appear on the following morning or afternoon.

As I say, there is no sense in this procedure, and no necessity for it. The problem could be solved overnight, if the newspapers would take the trouble, by having a reporter cover the actual news features of the event, and letting the critic write his review at his leisure. As a matter of fact, that is the way it is done in many places abroad. Ernest Newman, for example, writes a weekly page of miscellaneous critical discussions for the London *Sunday Times*. He has no nightly deadline to meet, he is free to ignore events whose musical importance, in his opinion, is not equal to their news value, and he has time to make up his mind, and structure what he writes. The result is a page that has made Ernest Newman one of the greatest and most widely read music critics in the world.

This reviewing against time is also a great hardship for the performer, particularly for the young one. Deadlines being what they are, it is virtually impossible for an urban music critic to remain at a concert, a recital, or an opera performance later than ten P.M. On some papers the deadline is so early that the critic must leave at nine-thirty. This means that the critic never hears the last act of an opera, the last number on an orchestral program, or the last one or two groups of a recital. Now there are such things as artists who are slow in warming up. Only last spring, at the Metropolitan, I heard a world-famous artist sing excruciatingly in the first act, and like an angel in the last act. I don't remember what the reviews were, but I do know that the critics were not there by the time she began to do herself justice. I have been to many a debut recital—since I stopped being a critic—where the terrified beginner made a miserable showing in his or her opening groups and showed brilliant capabilities in the last groups. Yet, thanks to the system, the unfortunate debutant is condemned to be judged solely by what he manages to accomplish before ten o'clock. Incidentally, this system has had a very unfortunate effect upon concert and recital programs. Conductors and recitalists tend to arrange their numbers, not in the order that will make a well-balanced and effective program, but in the order that will get the interesting things out of the way before the critics go out into the night.

One other way in which I think—if not the actual critics, then their managing editors, are at fault, is that they give far too much leeway to the occasional and the assistant critics, who are allowed to utter their opinions with the same freedom, and frequently at the same length, as is the senior critic. The motive for this is a praiseworthy determination not to interfere with an honestly expressed opinion; but the result is dreadfully unfair. It is pretty safe to say that a critic who has been listening for ten years has a broader outlook and better-founded judgment than a critic who has been listening for six months. Logically, therefore, the younger and less experienced critic should be allowed to sharpen his teeth, so to speak, on people who are big enough to survive his mistakes in judgment. If young Mr. A, a year out of the conservatory, and full of enthusiasm, prejudice, and intolerance, writes that Heifetz played abominably last night, that Flagstad was miscast, that Rachmaninoff struck four wrong notes, and that Tchaikovsky's Fifth Symphony is old stuff—there's no harm done. His victims will live. But that, of course, is not what happens. Mr. B, his chief, is assigned to the big shots, while young A reviews the debutants—and in the course of doing so, in my belief, manages every once in a while to retard a promising career by several years, merely because he heard only the faults, and lacked the experience to see the promise.

If his readers would, or could, discount his inexperience, no harm would be done. But they do not. In the first place, very few of them know anything about him, personally, know whether he is old or young, a veteran or a rookie. Even if they did know, they would react much the same. Few of us realize the appallingly persuasive power of the printed word. There is no misstatement so glaring, no expression of opinion so idiotic, that it will not be accepted as gospel truth by persons who "saw it in the paper." You who are reading this chapter accept its statements much less critically than if you were reading the typewritten manuscript, and infinitely less so than if I were speaking them. I have found myself taking seriously the *printed* opinions of a critic whom, in real life, I would not trust to tell me the time of day.

And so, when you are selecting some given critic to act as your guide in things musical, try to find out something about him. Look for his prejudices, for one thing, whether they coincide or differ with yours. Everybody's bound to have prejudices, more or less, and a good critic generally knows and admits his own. But even if he doesn't, his usefulness as a critic is not destroyed so long as you are aware of his prejudices, and learn to discount them. Also, find out how old he is, and how long he has been a critic. Up to a certain point, an older critic is a better and a safer guide than a younger one, simply because he has heard more. Also because, as he grows older, he is likely to discover that there is a good deal of gray in a world which he used to think was only black and white.

I say, up to a certain point. If your favorite critic is past fifty, don't take his word too implicitly when he begins to compare the great performers of the past with those of the present—to the disadvantage of the latter. He may be forgetting the powerful effect of an early impression upon an inexperienced mind. I have caught myself doing that, found myself saying, "Oh, yes, Madame B is very nice in that role. Ah, but you should have heard Madame A! You wouldn't remember her, but *there* was a singer! What she did with that role! There'll never be anybody like her." And then, after I've said that, sometimes I have to stop and admit that what I am really saying is: "Madame A was my first opera singer, and I was eighteen."

Mark Twain and I

"ANOTHER time we went to Mannheim and attended a shivaree—otherwise an opera—the one called *Lohengrin*. The banging and slamming and booming and crashing were something beyond belief. The racking and pitiless pain of it remains stored up in my memory alongside the memory of the time I had my teeth fixed. . . . The recollection of that long, dragging, relentless season of suffering is indestructible. To have to endure it in silence, and sitting still, made it all the harder. I was in a railed compartment with eight or ten strangers, of two sexes, and this compelled repression, yet at times the pain was so exquisite that I could hardly keep the tears back. At those times, as the howlings and wailings and shriekings of the singers, and the ragings and roarings and explosions of the vast orchestra rose higher and higher, and wilder and wilder, and fiercer and fiercer, I could have cried if I had been alone. Those strangers would not have been surprised to see a man do such a thing who was being gradually skinned, but they would have marvelled at it here, and made remarks about it no doubt; whereas there was nothing in the present case which was an advantage over being skinned. I do not wish to suggest that the rest of the people were like me, for indeed they were not. Whether it was that they naturally liked that noise, or whether it was that they had learned to like it by getting used to it, I did not at that time know; but they did like it—this was plain enough."

Thus Mark Twain, in *A Tramp Abroad*. He disliked not only the music, but the form of the work. "There was not much really done," he remarks; "it was always talked about; and always violently. Everybody had a narrative and a grievance, and none were reasonable about it, but all in an offensive and ungovernable state. It was every rioter for himself, and no blending; . . . and when this had continued for some time, and one was hoping they might come to an understanding and modify the noise, a great chorus composed entirely of maniacs would suddenly break forth, and then during two minutes, and sometimes three, I lived over again all that I had suffered the time the orphan asylum burned down."

He did like the "Wedding March." He called it "one brief little season of heaven and heaven's sweet ecstasy and peace during all this long and diligent and acrimonious reproduction of the other place. . . . To my untutored ear the Wedding Chorus was music—almost divine music."

All this, mind you, about *Lohengrin;* poor old *Lohengrin,* which today is rather snubbed by the higher circles of music lovers because it's so old-fashioned and tuneful! What he would have thought of *The Ring,* or *Tristan,* or *Die Meistersinger*—particularly the street brawl at the close of the second act—I cannot even imagine.

I quote Mark Twain at this length because his attitude and reactions were those, not of the average, but of a literate, traveled, and exceptionally intelligent American of sixty years ago. Most of his fellow countrymen knew absolutely nothing about operatic and symphonic music—

in fact, had never heard a symphony orchestra. In the sixties and seventies, outside of New York, Boston, Cincinnati, and St. Louis, symphony orchestras were virtually unknown. In fact, up to 1890, the only orchestras in the United States that were organized on a definitely permanent basis were the Philharmonic and the Boston Symphony. There were, of course, others—the Thomas Orchestra, the New York Symphony, The Philadelphia, for example; but they led a season-to-season existence. It is obvious that Mark Twain, in 1878, had never heard a note of the *Lohengrin* music, except for the "Wedding March" —and it is fairly easy to guess where he had heard that.

We have come a long way since those days—just how long a way I realized afresh when I received a letter, not long ago, from a correspondent who felt aggrieved because he could find only about twenty-one hours a week of serious music on his radio set. It suddenly struck me how extraordinarily music-conscious this country must have become when an average American actually complains that he can hear serious music, sent to him at no expense beyond the cost of a radio set, into his own living room, for only three hours a day! And that set me to thinking back to what music meant to the average American family in my own childhood and youth. I should like to remind you of those times. Forgive me if I take the only way I can take of doing so—by being somewhat autobiographical. My excuse is that what I remember is probably what many of you will remember also, when I remind you of it.

Do you remember, for example, the parlor organ of the eighties and nineties? We had one. Just when it was bought I don't know, exactly, but I do know that one of my early recollections is of hearing my father singing and playing Sir Joseph Porter's entrance song from *Pinafore*. Sometimes he and my mother would sing duets. Just what those duets were, I don't recollect, but I have a suspicion that they were not by the classic masters. Owning that organ made us a "musical" family, as things musical went, in those days. In the average family there was no musical instrument of any sort. Some, like us, had parlor organs, some had square pianos that were cherished as heirlooms —which was lucky, because they were good for little else; a handful of persons in a given community might own upright pianos, invariably ornamented in the prevailing style of the day, which gave them the general appearance of having been made by a confectioner out of black whipped cream, and invariably tuned, whether they needed it or not, about once every fourteen months. The very rich were rumored to own grand pianos, which I knew about only by hearsay. My father was a school teacher, and my mother had been one, so that they moved in a circle that was at least mildly intellectual. Some people must have gone to concerts and the opera in those days, because those things existed; but I have an idea that most of them must have been comparatively new arrivals of Italian and German birth. On the whole, music must have played a very unimportant part in the life of the typical American. Outside my own family, I have no recollection of ever hearing music even mentioned in my childhood. And this was New York of the nineties, then, as now, one of the great cultural centers of America.

Of my days in public school, what memories I have, connected with music, are few and very vague. I do remember that one of the teachers used to play marches for assembly (I can still see the cover of the album she played

316

from; it was called *Musical Gem*); and I have an idea that we sang, in assembly, in unison. I have an impression, too, that we were given some sort of instruction in reading from notes, and that this was a very disagreeable experience. Whatever instruction we did get was given by our regular class teacher, without regard for her musical gifts or inclinations. There were no music specialists, no music supervisors; school bands and orchestras and choruses were not even dreamed of. I do remember that at the age of seven I read a biography of Mozart and decided to become a composer. This idea was not encouraged, and was later abandoned by me in favor of becoming a member of the fire department.

At the age of ten I was handed over to Miss Tacy Knight Marshall to be given piano lessons—chiefly, I imagine, because my parents were sick of hearing me try to play the piano by ear (we had achieved the social distinction of an upright piano by that time). Only one other boy in my set was "taking piano," as it was termed, and our other comrades were inclined to regard us with suspicion, as being a bit freakish and slightly effeminate. Even so, I'm afraid that our passion for music did not glow with a pure flame. As I recall, our chief interest in piano playing lay in which of us could learn and play the longest piece. I triumphed for a while with the "War March of the Priests" from Mendelssohn's *Athalie,* but he finally won out with Leybach's Fifth Nocturne, which was sixteen bars longer.

At about that time I had the luck to be sent to the Ethical Culture School, which was about twenty years ahead of its time in regard to music, art, and general teaching methods. There I did get some regular instruction in music as part of the general school curriculum. We were placed under a teacher who taught nothing *but* music, and from her I learned to write music down and to read vocal music at sight. The school authorities made a practice, too, of inviting a good pianist, or violinist, or singer to perform for us children once a week at assembly. It was there, I remember, that I first heard Schubert's *Marche militaire*—not a masterpiece, perhaps, but a milestone for me.

Today all this sounds like a very modest course in musical appreciation for a twelve-year-old boy. Thousands of schools do as much now, and more, as matter of course. But in those days, in New York, less than forty years ago, the idea of including anything like a serious study of music as part of a liberal education would have been laughed at by the average American educator. I think the most striking illustration of the change in point of view toward music, in educational circles, is to be found in my alma mater, New York University, as it was when I went there, and as it is today.

At the time I entered college, in the early nineteen-hundreds, only a handful of our major colleges and universities had schools of music. Generally speaking, if you wanted a classical or scientific education, you went to college. If you wanted to become a professional musician you skipped college, and attended a conservatory. But if you wanted a college education that included some understanding and appreciation of music, not in a professional, but a cultural sense—you would have a hard time acquiring it. No musical instruction of any kind was included in my college curriculum—nor, by the way, any appreciation of painting or sculpture. A cultured man, thirty-five years ago, was one who had been given courses in English and possibly French literature, history, one or two foreign languages, of which one was likely to be Latin, a little philosophy, a little higher mathematics, a little science—and that was all. No contact with *contemporary* English or American literature, no contact with the graphic or plastic arts, no contact with music. What music we boys made was strictly an extramural activity, to be given no academic recognition and under no circumstances to be allowed to interfere with our prescribed studies. Let me remind you that in this respect my college was not unique. On the contrary, it was a typical American university of the highest academic standing.

Our three musical outlets, as undergraduates, were the glee, banjo, and mandolin clubs. Membership in these organizations was eagerly sought by everybody who was not actually tone-deaf—and I am not so sure of that last statement, either, as I look back. This eagerness, I hasten to explain, involved no passion for music. Everybody wanted to belong to the musical clubs because twice during the term, at Christmas and at Easter, these organizations were allowed to go on a week's concert tour. That trip was a great inducement.

Early in the fall we held tryouts for these coveted memberships. The glee club had a long-suffering professional conductor named Frank P. Smith, while the instrumental clubs were under another professional, Harry Six. To qualify for membership in the mandolin club you had, first, to own a mandolin; second, to be able to learn, either by note or by ear, a maximum of four pieces in two months, and to play them not too outrageously out of tune. Qualifications for membership in the banjo club were about the same, with the exception that as that instrument was considered more exotic and more difficult to play, the rules were not quite so severe. If you could learn *two* pieces you could get on the banjo club. Even so, there were difficulties. Banjos cost a good deal more than mandolins, and it was sometimes hard to enlist enough members to make a respectable showing on a platform. At this late date it is probably safe for me to confess that in some of our concerts the ranks of the banjo club were reinforced by four or five members of the glee club, playing on borrowed banjos that had no strings.

To qualify as a member of the glee club you had to be able to carry a tune. If you could sing the top G on the treble clef you were a first tenor; if you could sing the bottom G in the bass clef, you were a second bass. If your vocal limit was anywhere between the two, you were either a second tenor or a first bass, depending on which were needed most. It was hoped that you could read notes; but that hope was a pretty forlorn one, and was generally given up about the second day of the tryouts. The personnel of the clubs having been chosen, we started rehearsals for the one program that we would sing everywhere during the season. As that program was fairly typical of college glee-club programs everywhere, about 1904 or 1905, I might refresh your memories by outlining it briefly.

It began, invariably, with Bullard's *Winter Song,* sung with awful earnestness by the glee club. Mr. Smith did not conduct. There was no conductor at the concert. The undergraduate, nominal leader of the club stood at one end of the double row of singers and started them off with a nod of his head. After that it was every man for himself. We always hoped that the opening number would not be encored, because we had no encore prepared. It was seldom encored. Following that, the banjo club would assemble and play a march, which was always on the "patrol" order—that is, it began very softly, grew very loud in the middle, and ended very softly. This always created a terrific sensation. After loud applause the club would play it all over again.

Then another number by the glee club—I forget just what. Something about the crusaders, I think. Then a baritone solo. Reinald Werrenrath, later a famous baritone, was on the club in those years, so his baritone solo was about the only decent thing on the program. He generally sang *Danny Deever,* with *Punchinello* for an encore. Next, the *Symphia* waltzes, by the mandolin club; then a banjo solo by Harry Six, who was listed as an undergraduate over a period of twelve years, and who always stopped the show. Then a sentimental number, *She is Sleeping by the Silv'ry Rio Grande,* by the glee club. Next, a specialty by myself, consisting of a melodrama, with myself playing all the parts. I stole it from a vaudeville act that I had seen on Fourteenth Street. I still wake up in the night, thinking about it. Then, something else by the glee club, generally comic—a young man sitting on a sofa with a young woman, and stealing a kiss—something sidesplitting like that. Last of all, "Here's to the land I love," from *The Prince of Pilsen,* rendered with magnificent *élan* by the combined glee, banjo, and mandolin clubs. Then a dash for the train, and so back to the humdrum of academic life.

As I say, we went on tours. Our principal patrons were Y.M.C.A.'s desperate for entertainment, girls' boarding schools desperate for the sight of a boy, an occasional long-suffering woman's club, and the Lakewood (N. J.) Hotel. It has since burned down, I hear—a possibly drastic, but definitely effective method of keeping us from coming back. I might add that we seldom played return engagements.

Now compare those primitive goings-on with the personnel and achievements of the glee clubs, not only of my own alma mater, but of colleges and universities all over the country today. These organizations are almost invariably under expert professional leadership, their members are given academic credits for their musical work, their vocal standards are high, and they present programs drawn from the finest works in the world's choral repertoire. Only a year or so ago my seventeen-year-old nephew, a member of the N.Y.U. Glee Club, sat me down one Sunday afternoon and gave me a severe lecture on the music of Palestrina. When I was his age, and singing on that same glee club, all that I knew of Palestrina was that the name suggested something vaguely to do with the Holy Land.

The glee club is only one phase of the part that music plays in present-day education. The college bands and orchestras are still another story. All of which is why I remain unmoved when someone complains that he has only twenty-one hours a week of good music at his elbow. If you are over forty, think of what your son or daughter is getting today, as a matter of course, in the way of musical contacts and experience, in school, in college, at home, and on the air; and think back to what you got. If you are under forty, be grateful that you were born in your generation, and not in ours.

Index

INDEX

INDEX

INDEX

INDEX

327

INDEX

Kreisler, Fritz, 106, 107-108, 192

"La donna è mobile," Rigoletto (Verdi), 276

Lambert, Constant, 9, 122

Landis, Kenesaw Mountain, 153

Lauf der Welt (Grieg), 180

Leave It To Me, 231

Le Baron, William, 70

Lecocq, Alexandre, 73

Leipzig Conservatory of Music, 34

"Leonora" Overture, Third, 134

Leybach, Ignace, 317

Liadoff, Anatol, 278-279, 280

Lichnowsky, Prince Karl, 118

Liebesverbot, Das (Wagner), 27

Lied der Braut (Schumann), 93

Liszt, Franz, 29, 30, 31, 34, 94, 236, 241, 246, 250, 262

Little Duck in the Meadow, The, 94

Little Foxes, The (Hellman), 60

Little Johnny Jones (Herbert), 69

Little Pleasure Trip on the Train, A (Rossini), 80

Lohengrin (Wagner), 21, 29, 30, 31, 254, 313-314, 315; "Wedding March," 91, 314, 315; King's Prayer, 252, 254

London Music in 1888-89 (Shaw), 304-305, 306

London Philharmonic Orchestra, 30

Louise (Charpentier), 57

Louis Philippe, King of France, 19

Louvre Museum, 42

Lucia di Lammermoor (Donizetti), 56; Mad Scene, 56

Ludwig II, King of Bavaria, 32, 226

Lully, Jean-Baptiste, 183

Lusby, Professor, 167

Macbeth (Shakespeare), 60, 64, 96

Macdonald, Fraser, 102-108

MacDowell, Edward, 93, 262

MacEwen, David, 259

Madame Butterfly (Puccini), 57, 93, 252

Malbrouck s'en va-t-en guerre, 50

Man and Superman (Shaw), 279

"M'appari," Marta (Flotow), 185

Marche militaire (Schubert), 318

March of Kings, The, 95

"March of the Toys," *Babes in Toyland* (Herbert), 67

Margin of Hesitation, The (Colby), 258

Marseillaise, La (Rouget de Lisle), 229, 230

Marshall, Tacy Knight, 317

Marta (Flotow), 185; *"M'appari,"* 185

Marx, Karl, 231

Marx Brothers, 222

Mary II, Queen of England, 18

"Mascot of the Troop, The," *Mlle Modiste* (Herbert), 70

Masked Ball, A (Verdi), 222-223

Massenet, Jules, 95

McCarthy, Charlie, 148

McCormack, John, 91, 288

McMein, Neysa, 215

Measure for Measure (Shakespeare), 27

Meck, Nadejda von, 119

Meistersinger, Die (Wagner), 21, 29, 31, 91, 93, 290, 292, 314; Dance of the Apprentices, 31; Entrance of the Masters, 31; Homage to Sachs, 31; Prelude to Act III, 31; Prize Song, 93, 291-292

Mendelssohn-Bartholdy, Felix, 33-34, 91, 214, 222, 227, 251, 262, 317

Meremblum, Peter, 216

Metropolitan Opera House, 15, 17, 58, 59, 78, 309

Meyerbeer, Giacomo, 27, 78, 81, 222, 245

Michelangelo Buonarroti, 38, 40, 236, 238

328

INDEX

INDEX

330

INDEX

331

INDEX

INDEX

ABOUT THE AUTHOR

DEEMS TAYLOR *was born in New York City in 1885. After receiving his A.B. degree from New York University he studied music and held several editorial positions. In· 1916 he became assistant Sunday editor of the New York* Tribune, *leaving shortly afterward to represent that paper in France. From 1917 to 1919 he was associate editor of* Collier's Weekly, *and from 1921 to 1925 music critic on the New York* World. *He was editor of* Musical America *from 1927 to 1929, and music critic on the New York* American *from 1931 to 1932. More recently he has acted as commentator for the New York Philharmonic Symphony Orchestra's Sunday afternoon broadcasts. In 1937, he wrote the best-selling* Of Men and Music.

In addition to writing about music, Deems Taylor also composes it. In 1910 he wrote The Echo, *a musical comedy, and in 1912 his* Siren Song *won the orchestral prize awarded by the National Federation of Music Clubs. His most famous compositions since then include* Through the Looking Glass, *an orchestral suite that is in the repertoire of virtually every major symphonic organization in America and Europe,* The King's Henchman, *with a book by Edna St. Vincent Millay, and* Peter Ibbetson, *both of which were commissioned and performed by the Metropolitan Opera Association. A third opera,* Ramuntcho, *based on Pierre Loti's novel, is now completed and awaiting production.*